Books by Amelia Autin

Harlequin Romantic Suspense

Man on a Mission

Cody Walker's Woman
McKinnon's Royal Mission
King's Ransom
Alec's Royal Assignment
Liam's Witness Protection
A Father's Desperate Rescue
Killer Countdown
The Bodyguard's Bride-to-Be
Rescued by the Billionaire CEO

The Coltons of Texas

Her Colton P.I.

Silhouette Intimate Moments

Gideon's Bride
Reilly's Return

Visit the Author Profile page at Harlequin.com.

For Susan Naomi Horton, who as Naomi Horton wrote *In Safekeeping*, the very first romantic suspense book I ever read...and still on my keeper shelf after 25+ years. Thank you, Susan, for opening up new worlds for me as a reader and an author. And for Vincent...always.

The memory of her own abduction swamped her…especially those moments of near-despair on the bed in that horrible apartment, and she sank to her knees, hugging herself for warmth.

"Oh, God," she whispered to herself. "Oh, God."

Jason had his back to her, but when she glanced up, she could see he was talking into his cell phone. Then he turned around, saw her and disconnected almost immediately. He was at her side in an instant.

"Alana?" She knew he meant *Are you hurt?* by the way his face contracted with concern, the way his hands touched her so gently yet with implacable purpose.

"I'm fine," she managed, trying desperately to catch her breath.

He drew her to her feet and pressed her head against his chest, then his arms closed around her. "It's okay," he soothed as if he realized exactly what she needed to hear. "Just breathe. That's right. Just breathe."

His body heat transferred itself to her, dispelling the chill. But it was his embrace that truly gave her what she needed. *Safe*, her frantic mind reassured her, just as it had during her dramatic rescue three weeks earlier. Jason's rescue. *You're safe.*

* * *

Be sure to check out the previous volumes in the Man on a Mission miniseries!
Man on a Mission: These heroes, working at home and overseas, will do anything for justice, honor…and love

* * *

If you're on Twitter, tell us what you think of Harlequin Romantic Suspense! #harlequinromsuspense

Dear Reader,

When I began writing *A Father's Desperate Rescue*, part of my Man on a Mission miniseries, I had no idea my heroine's older brother, Jason Moore, even existed. I was halfway through that book before he made his first appearance, along with his highly secret and totally illegal covert-operations organization, Right Makes Might (RMM).

Once Jason took the stage, however, it was one of those "aha" moments for me, and I fell in love with him (as I do with all my future heroes).

But while I knew my *hero*—a man shaped by two cultures and one life-altering tragedy, a true knight in shining armor (in the heroine's own words, *sans peur et sans reproche*)—I had no idea who my heroine might be. This is a common problem—my heroes always appear first.

Then suddenly *she* appeared—Alana Richardson, cousin to the heroine of *King's Ransom*. Alana has traveled halfway around the world to escape the privileged life she was born to lead...and runs headlong into trouble. Who else but Jason can rescue her...from her abductors *and* her uneventful past? And who else but Alana can accept that the man she loves could die or end his days in prison... all in the name of protecting the innocent?

I hope you enjoy reading *Rescued by the Billionaire CEO* as much as I enjoyed writing it. And I hope you agree Jason and Alana are a perfect match.

I love hearing from my readers. Please email me at AmeliaAutin@aol.com and let me know what you think.

Amelia Autin

RESCUED BY THE BILLIONAIRE CEO

Amelia Autin

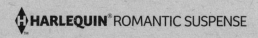

HHARLEQUIN® ROMANTIC SUSPENSE

Recycling programs
for this product may
not exist in your area.

ISBN-13: 978-1-335-21894-0

Rescued by the Billionaire CEO

Copyright © 2017 by Amelia Autin Lam

Printed in U.S.A.

Chapter 1

Gagged and blindfolded, her hands bound cruelly behind her back, Alana Richardson huddled on the cot in the tiny bedroom where her kidnappers had left her, trying desperately not to cry. It wouldn't do any good anyway, and would only make her feel worse, especially since she wouldn't be able to blow her nose once she got to the blubbering stage.

Since crying was out, that meant she couldn't let herself fall into despair. Which meant she couldn't allow even a trace of self-pity to linger in her mind, either...even though her head throbbed where she'd been struck, she felt more than a little queasy from whatever it was they'd made her breathe in—chloroform, she'd bet—and her fingers were going numb from futilely trying to wriggle free from her bonds.

Fierce anger shook her, and a determination that she wasn't going to give up. She wasn't going to be a meek victim. She concentrated on remembering as much as she

could about every minute detail related to her abduction...
and her abductors. Committing what little she knew of them
to memory, including those few moments at the beginning
when she'd fought them. The men had been masked, but
still...she'd drawn blood. She'd hurt one of them. Marked
him.

DNA, she thought, her mind racing. *Blood and skin
under my fingernails?*

She needed to remember that, along with everything
else. So if—*when*—she escaped, she might be able to assist in bringing the men to justice. It was a long shot, but
it was better than dwelling on the negative. It was better
than imagining the worst...which she could all too easily
imagine if she let herself.

Alana also had no idea what the men intended to do with
her, although she could hazard a guess. She hadn't been
raped, though. Not yet. She would know, even though she'd
been unconscious for some unknown amount of time. But
she'd come to as she was being carried here...wherever
here was. She'd been swathed in something before they'd
removed her from the van. A blanket? A rug? Something
that had made breathing difficult. But then her captors had
dumped her on this cot and unwrapped her.

She hadn't had an opportunity to make a run for it,
though, because almost immediately rough hands had
grabbed her, and she'd been gagged so she couldn't scream
for help, tied up so she couldn't escape, and blindfolded.
She wondered about the blindfold. All three men had been
masked, so it wasn't to conceal their identities. Could there
be something here they didn't want seen? Or just that they
didn't want her to know where she was?

But speculating about motives was fruitless at this stage,
and a waste of time. Just as there was absolutely no point
in second-guessing her decision to travel halfway around

the world to Hong Kong for a job her parents had advised against taking…although she couldn't quite help it.

"Richardsons don't have to work for a living, darling." How many times had her mother said that to her? She'd said it again last month as Alana was packing, adding, "But if you insist on working, what was wrong with your job at your father's company? At least you had a *title* there. It's ridiculous for you to work at such a menial job…for an *actor*, of all people. I don't care if he *is* a good friend of Juliana's."

And her father had chimed in. "Yes, yes, I know your cousin Juliana vouches for him. But remember, she was an actress…just like her mother." The supercilious way he'd said *just like her mother* had rubbed Alana the wrong way. Her aunt had been a renowned Shakespearean actress, and she hated her father talking about Juliana's mother that way. Implying she hadn't been good enough to marry into the Richardson family.

Then he'd added, "At least your cousin had the good sense to quit acting when she married the King of Zakhar." As if Juliana hadn't risen to the top of her profession by dedication, talent and incredibly hard work. As if she'd just been waiting for her Prince Charming to come along and take her away from all of that. As if Juliana's marriage to one of the world's wealthiest and most powerful men was the only thing she'd managed to accomplish that was worth anything in her father's eyes—completely ignoring all the professional accolades Juliana had won, including two Academy Awards and a handful of Golden Globes.

"And why Hong Kong of all places?" her mother had thrown in. "With all *those* people."

Alana had struggled with herself, then said as levelly as she could, "If you mean the Chinese, Mom, it's their country."

"Well I didn't mean *that*," her mother had huffed...but Alana had known she really had. Both her parents, in fact.

She wondered about that now, her mind veering off on a tangent. Her parents had tried to inculcate their values, their beliefs, in her. But she wasn't—*couldn't be*—like them. Maybe her uncle Julian had something to do with it, since she'd spent so much time with him after he retired. Maybe his influence had made the difference in shaping the woman she was. Juliana's father was a Richardson, too, had been raised to believe Richardsons were a cut above, just like Alana's own father. But maybe serving as a foreign ambassador for all those years had taught her uncle things about the world and its people her father had never learned.

Or maybe she should stop making excuses for why her parents were insular, narrow-minded and...and prejudiced. Maybe she should just accept it. Just as she had to accept she could fight the rope cutting cruelly into her wrists until they were bruised and bloody...but she wasn't going to escape.

Jason Moore double-checked the harness strapped around him, making sure it was securely fastened. He lightly buckled the second one around his waist to keep his hands free and glanced at the two men opposite. Like him, they were dressed in black from head to toe, including paper-thin black latex gloves and soft leather boots. Their faces were smeared with camouflage face paint, just as his was, so as not to stand out in the dark night. And, of course, to disguise their identities. Right Makes Might didn't want any witnesses able to describe them, even when they weren't breaking the law.

He tapped his earpiece. *"Yat, yee, saam,"* he said, speaking Cantonese, and getting affirmation he could be clearly heard through their earpieces by the thumbs-up signal from his men on the roof. Then he switched to English. "Testing, one, two, three."

"Roger that," said a voice in his ear from one of the men on the ground.

Jason flashed a smile at the men standing guard over the equipment the three of them had just set up. Slid into place his prohibitively expensive night-vision goggles that had started life as equipment for a US Navy SEAL team. Nodded once. Then stepped backward off the roof of this high-rise apartment building in a seedy neighborhood.

The passive arrestor system on the zip line kicked in immediately. So instead of plummeting to his death, Jason slid slowly down the side of the building. He mentally suppressed the totally-to-be-expected unreasoning fear of falling that sent a dart of adrenaline coursing through his bloodstream. Then he used his feet to lever himself away from the building so he didn't scrape against the concrete, counting floors as he went. Right before he reached his destination, he depressed a button on the radio signal control mechanism strapped to his wrist, and he came to a complete halt.

"Three feet to the left," Jason said quietly. Within seconds, the zip line moved until he could grasp the metal railing around the tiny balcony that was his destination, and lightly vault over it. His feet made no sound as they landed, because his soft-soled boots had been designed for that purpose. And besides, he'd trained for this until he could practically do it in his sleep.

Jason smiled grimly as he grasped the handle on the poorly fitted sliding glass door, and with a sharp jerk popped it right out of its tracks. He and his men had already discussed how lucky they were their victim was imprisoned in this older apartment building, which had been constructed back in the sixties. Newer high-rises had been built to stricter construction codes, but not older buildings like this one. They were a lot easier to break in to.

He silently lifted the door to one side. "Slack," he uttered in a monotone, and after a few seconds the tension sagged on the wire to which he was connected. He could have unbuckled the harness before entering the room, but then he would waste precious seconds getting back into it. Seconds he might not have on the back end.

The room was shrouded in darkness, but with his night-vision goggles he could clearly see the slight form huddled on a cot in the corner, a few feet away. He headed straight for it.

Alana hadn't thought she could possibly sleep, but she must have. Because she woke to a gloved hand over her gagged mouth and a deep male voice with an upper-class British accent whispering in her ear. "Shh. Not a sound, Miss Richardson. I'll get you out of here, but you must do exactly what I say without question. Nod your head if you can do that."

Alana nodded. She didn't know who this was, but she immediately knew he was here to rescue her. His deep voice held even more reassurance than the words themselves, so whatever he told her to do, she would do. Without question.

He moved slightly, and there was an odd sound she couldn't place—like metal rubbing against leather. Then the gag melted away. The blindfold followed, and now she could see the flash of a knife in the darkness before the binding around her wrists was carefully cut loose. She bit her lip to hold back the moan that wanted to escape when her arms were finally free and she tried to move them. Tears sprang to her eyes as agonizing pain shot through her muscles, but she was proud she managed not to make a sound.

The knife flashed again as he sheathed it. Almost immediately strong hands were massaging her arms, fingers digging into her muscles until she squeezed her eyes shut against the pain. Tears seeped onto her cheeks, but the sob that might have escaped her lips under normal circumstances…didn't. Then her rescuer was lifting her effortlessly and carrying her to what she now saw was the doorless opening onto a balcony.

He stood her on her feet and quickly unbuckled something from his waist, which he then proceeded to fit around her—a harness of some kind, she realized. A harness that was attached to a slack wire. A slack wire that grew suddenly taut when he said, "Ready."

Alana could see her rescuer in the faint moonlight. A lithe figure dressed all in black, with some kind of camouflage paint on his face, as well. And high-tech goggles that somehow made him look superhuman. He towered over her, which wasn't a surprise—she wasn't much taller than her famous cousin Juliana, who stood only as high as her husband's heart. Alana didn't know what made her think of that out of the blue, but then the thought was wiped from her mind when he lifted her up onto the balcony railing and balanced her there. "Hang on."

She didn't have time to be afraid before he was on the outside of the railing, maneuvering himself and her as if they weren't perched precariously high above the street below. "Legs around my hips," he ordered, and when she did so, he pressed something on his wrist before wrapping his arms around her in a bear hug. "Hold on tight." Then he pushed away from the balcony.

They swung in the air for a dizzying moment, and Alana could only pray she wouldn't be sick. But she wasn't afraid. She didn't know why, but the strength in the arms that held her so securely made her trust her rescuer implicitly. She felt as safe with him dangling from a wire as she would have been with both feet on the ground.

The cable pulled taut and they descended with a hissing sound of metal on metal. "You okay?" he asked, his lips pressed against her ear, and all Alana could do was nod. Endless seconds later they touched down on solid earth. He didn't let her go for a moment, and she stared at his face, memorizing what she could see of it. Wishing with all her heart she could see his eyes behind the concealing goggles. Wishing she dared ask him any of the half-dozen questions that suddenly teemed in her brain.

Until she realized her legs were still clasped around his hips. Until she realized just how *intimate* that was…which his body made known to her in no uncertain terms.

Alana hoped the faint moonlight meant he couldn't see the blush she could feel creeping into her cheeks as she unwrapped her legs and he lowered her to the ground. "Sorry," she said. "I wasn't…" *Thinking*, she'd intended to say, but her words trailed off.

Then she was free. And a tiny part of her acknowledged she hadn't wanted to be. She'd wanted to stay in his embrace. Wanted to explore the unmistakable evidence that he was attracted to her as much as she was attracted to him. Which was *crazy*. Because she'd never…

Two men converged on them, but the staccato patter of Cantonese that flew between her rescuer and one of the men made their conversation unintelligible to Alana. Male hands quickly and impersonally assisted her in unclipping the harness from the cable and unbuckling it. Then they were bundling her into a dark van, tugging a seat belt into place and strapping her in. Doors slammed before she could protest, and the van's engine roared to life. She had one last vision of her rescuer stripping off his own harness then heading back toward the building they'd just escaped from, as the van sped away.

"Wait," she choked out to the driver and the man in the left front passenger seat. "What about—"

"The operation's not finished, Miss Richardson," the man who wasn't driving said in clipped British tones. "There's still the little matter of the men who kidnapped you to take care of. But our job is to get you to safety."

"Rendezvous" was all Jason had to say. He knew his men on the roof would meet him on the twenty-second floor with the other equipment RMM had brought along, including lock picks, stun grenades, tear gas and guns. Normally-illegal-in-Hong-Kong guns for which RMM had paid handsomely under the table to obtain special licenses.

But when they arrived at apartment 2211, the door was already standing wide open. They entered cautiously, guns drawn, but it was quickly evident it was empty. Jason cursed under his breath. Someone must have gone to check on their victim and realized she'd been rescued. Then the kidnappers had hightailed it out of there.

There was still a chance the police might recover decent evidence. But before he could give the order, one of his men said, "I'll call in a tip to the police, Jason. Worth a shot anyway. At the very least, Miss Richardson's fingerprints should be here somewhere, even if the kidnappers wore gloves the entire time. Her purse is here, too. That will prove she was here. And the bindings in the bedroom will be proof she was being held against her will."

As the van wound its way up the mountain road, Alana shook off her semi-stupor and rattled off a string of questions without waiting for answers. "Who are you? How did you know where I was? Do you have any idea why I was—"

The man who'd spoken before answered her last question first. "Prostitution, Miss Richardson, plain and simple. We've been after this triad gang for a couple of months. More than two dozen women have been abducted in nearly the same fashion—snatched right off the streets in broad daylight. We don't know who…not for sure, although we have our suspicions. And the women are being transported to Macau, but we don't know exactly how…not yet. But we do know why. You're young, pretty and you were on your own in an area that made you an easy tar—"

He broke off as the van halted suddenly at a gate that was familiar to Alana. The driver rolled down his window. "We have her safe," he told the person who answered when he buzzed. Then the gate swung open, admitting the van, which drove smoothly through.

Light spilled out of the open front door of the DeWinters' home, which was Alana's home in Hong Kong, too. "We have the room," Dirk DeWinter had told her when she'd arrived to interview for the job as his executive assistant last month. "It'll be more convenient for all of us, but especially you. Don't worry—your free time is yours, and you can come and go as you please."

His wife, the beautiful Mei-li, who had a decidedly British accent, had chimed in with an understanding smile, "We know you want to be independent, Alana. We understand that's a big part of why you're here. But this will give you a safe place to live until you find your feet in Hong Kong. We can reassess in six months or so."

Alana hadn't needed her beloved cousin Juliana's sterling reference for her dear friend and former co-star Dirk DeWinter in her decision to take the job *and* to live in. All she'd needed was to see the way her prospective employer had looked at his wife, as if she was his world. The same way her cousin's husband looked at her. She'd sighed a little to herself at the time, she remembered now. Envious. Because that was the way she wished to be loved someday. *Not* the bloodless relationship her parents had. Something passionate. Something *heated*.

All at once she thought of the man who'd rescued her, and what she'd felt in his arms. Safe…but wanted. Safe…but desired. Triggering a corresponding desire that had taken her by complete surprise, especially under the circumstances.

She dragged her thoughts away from the memory with an effort. *You'll probably never see him again*, she chastised herself, unbuckling her seat belt and scrambling out of the van as her employers anxiously approached.

"Alana!" Mei-li reached her first and embraced her. "I'm so glad you're all right."

Then Dirk was there. He didn't say anything, just enveloped her in a bear hug that conveyed how worried he'd been, too, and how thankful he was she'd been rescued safe and sound. She knew it had to have brought back nightmares for him—his twin daughters had been kidnapped and held for ransom just over a year ago. That story, and the dramatic rescue, had been splashed across the front pages of newspapers, tabloids and gossip magazines, as well as the internet.

"I'm so sorry," she breathed. "I'm so sorry you had to go through this again. But I wasn't careless. Honest. Those men came out of nowhere with hundreds of people around, and—"

Dirk held her away from him at arm's length, a frown marring his handsome features. "Don't apologize. This wasn't your fault. I should have warned you. And I should have made sure you knew about the—"

Mei-li put her hand on her husband's arm, cutting off the flow of words. "Dirk," she murmured. Just his name, but there appeared to be some sort of unspoken communication between them because his self-recriminations ceased. Then Mei-li smiled her gentle smile. "You're safe. That's all that matters. RMM came through for us…again."

"RMM?" Alana couldn't help but ask. Then she realized she'd never thanked the men who'd brought her here. She hadn't thanked her rescuer, either, but at least she could ask these men to convey her heartfelt gratitude to him. She turned, but the van was already pulling away. "Wait!"

She took two steps forward as if she was going to chase after it, but Mei-li was suddenly there, stopping her. "They don't look for thanks," she explained softly.

"What do you mean?"

"RMM. They do what they have to do to rescue the innocent, even if it means breaking the law. But they don't look for thanks. That's not why they do it."

"I don't understand."

Dirk came up on her other side. "RMM stands for Right Makes Might. It's from a quotation by Abraham Lincoln." His smile held admiration and something more. Deep gratitude, the kind Alana was feeling right now. "It's not common knowledge, but they were instrumental in rescuing my daughters when they were kidnapped."

Chapter 2

Jason walked through the door of his penthouse condo three hours later. He and his men had quickly scoured the tiny apartment where Alana had been held, noting everything and taking copious pictures, but touching nothing that would contaminate the crime scene. Then they'd melted into the darkness when the police sirens could be heard in the distance.

He dropped his keys and iPhone in a large Ming bowl on the credenza by the front door, then headed for the bathroom, stripping off his clothes as he went. He was naked by the time he arrived, and he bundled his clothes into the laundry hamper. Then he grabbed the jar of cold cream from the bathroom counter and proceeded to smear some across the camouflaging face paint. He wiped most of the paint off with a handful of tissues, then stepped into the shower and let soap, hot water and vigorous scrubbing do the rest.

Clean, he pulled on boxer shorts and padded into the kitchen, where he snagged a cold bottle of water from the refrigerator and downed half of it in two gulps. Then he headed for his office, detouring on the way to pick up his smartphone in the vestibule. He took a moment to run one hand over the foot-high statue of Bruce Lee also on the credenza, a replica of the life-size one on the Avenue of Stars in Tsim Sha Tsui.

The statue had cost him an arm and a leg, but like the gold medallion he wore it was a constant reminder, and worth every penny. Bruce Lee was revered in Hong Kong—and in much of the rest of the world, for that matter—both as a proponent of martial arts and as a man whose films always depicted him standing up for what was right, not what was expedient. A man who protected the innocent. Bruce had died before Jason was born, but his legacy would live forever. A legacy Jason tried in his own way to emulate.

He settled into his leather and ebony office chair, flicked on his laptop, then keyed in the complicated encryption password. Tonight was going to be one of those nights... as usual. Sleep, which his adrenaline-sapped body craved, would be elusive. Rescues always wired him to the point where going to bed was useless, so he wouldn't bother. Besides, he still had work to do.

While he waited patiently for the laptop to power up, he leaned back in the chair with a creak of leather, rehashing tonight's rescue in his mind.

So many things could have gone wrong. Not the least of which was, he and his men could have picked the wrong apartment. GPS was good, but it wasn't perfect. The coordinates they had in their possession had indicated that building and a most likely floor, but not which apartment. That had required a little old-fashioned deductive reasoning...and prayer. If they'd guessed wrong, screams from some surprised apartment dweller when Jason broke in would probably have alerted the triads that something was up, possibly even that a rescue was being attempted. And what that would have meant for Alana Richardson didn't bear thinking about.

Alana Richardson. A tiny slip of a thing, really. Not even as tall as his sister, Mei-li, who wasn't all that tall, either. But that wasn't really relevant. No, what really mattered was how she'd handled herself during the rescue. Despite being bound, gagged and blindfolded, she'd been instantly alert when he'd awakened her. And she hadn't questioned his orders. Hadn't insisted on any kind of explanation. She'd just done what he'd told her to do…instantaneously.

He laughed softly. It wasn't blind obedience he'd been hoping for; it was a woman smart enough to instantly grasp that explanations could wait for a more opportune time. Who could make split-second decisions the way he did, and follow through on them. And Alana Richardson fit that description the way she'd fit into his arms. Perfectly.

He sat up abruptly, muttering, "Hold on a minute." Where the hell had *that* thought come from?

You shouldn't even be thinking about how good she felt in your arms, he chastised himself. *And you damn well shouldn't have been aroused when she wrapped her legs around you and held on tight.*

It did absolutely no good telling himself what he *should* have done…because it was too late for that. He *had* been aroused. Painfully aroused. And now that his mind had gone down that path, it was impossible not to remember slight breasts pressed firmly up against his chest. Impossible not to remember thighs clinging to his hips with unexpected strength. Impossible not to imagine those same thighs holding on tight as he rode her soft and slow and—

His smartphone dinged for an incoming text, an interruption he both blessed and cursed. He swiped a finger over the touchpad and saw it was from his sister.

Thnx, he read. Knew I could count on you. Call me?

He frowned. It was way past midnight, and his sister should be sleeping. *But she knows you well enough*, he reminded himself. *She knows* you're *not sleeping*.

He pressed speed dial, and when the phone was answered, surprised himself when the first words out of his mouth were, "How is she?"

"Recovering," Mei-li said. "The police were here. Dirk insisted we file a police report immediately, even though Alana had already been through a lot for one day. And it's a good thing we did report it, because *someone* tipped off the police there was an abduction and rescue." The emphasis on *someone* conveyed his sister knew exactly who that was, even though she wasn't saying. "But the police are gone now. Finally. They took scrapings from beneath Alana's fingernails for DNA analysis—apparently she scratched one of the men, and it looks as if she drew blood."

He heard the unspoken approval in her voice. "They wanted Alana to go down to the police station to look through some mug shots," she continued. "But she told them she really didn't see her abductors' faces. All three men were wearing full head masks. Black. Balaclavas, I'd bet, by her description."

She paused for a moment, but Jason didn't say anything. "After the police left, Dirk and I took her to hospital, over her vehement objections."

"And?"

"And she's fine, just as she insisted. A little nausea, but that's a normal aftereffect of the chloroform they used on her. And she's still feeling a little shaky from the blow she took."

"What?"

"She fought them, remember? She said she tried to hold her breath when they placed the cloth over her face, but then one of the men struck her with something and that's when she lost consciousness."

Jason's admiration for Alana rose, and her perfect response during the rescue tonight took on even more luster. If she was still shaky after all this time, that meant she had to have been still suffering from her head injury when he'd woken her and carried her out of the apartment. But she hadn't said a word. Hadn't complained.

"They took X-rays, just as a precaution, but no fractures. No subdural hematoma, either. And based on her responses to the doctor's questions, he wasn't worried about a concussion. He prescribed rest and lots of it."

"Which she's getting now?"

"Yes. For all her protestations that she was fine, Alana fell asleep in the car on the way home. Dirk had to carry her to her bedroom. I don't think she even knows I tucked her in, so I'll make an educated guess and say she's still sound asleep."

"Why aren't you?"

"I could ask you the same question."

"You know I can't."

"Same for me." Her voice, normally so light and musical, took on a slight strain. "I can never forget—"

"Sean," he finished for her. His tone roughened. "Neither can I."

"I know." Mei-li sighed in his ear. "What did the triads say when you interrogated them?"

"Nothing. They must have gone to check on Miss Richardson shortly after I got her out of there, because by the time my team and I were able to storm the apartment, those men were long gone."

"Damn!" That wasn't quite the word Jason had used at the time, but his sister didn't curse often. A *damn* from her was equivalent to cursing a blue streak. "At least Alana's safe. Which means this one goes in the win column anyway."

They were silent for a few moments, both remembering a day more than twelve years ago and an abduction that had gone heartbreakingly wrong.

"Thank God you had the GPS coordinates of where she was being held," Jason said, finally breaking the painful silence. "We couldn't have rescued her without that."

"Yes, thank God, but also thank Dirk…and you," Mei-li said, and Jason knew she was referring to the high-tech electronic transmitter. Beacon, actually, but it only transmitted if it was manually set off or activated remotely from the parent server. Highly secret equipment not yet available to the general public, the prototype of which Jason had designed and had his company produce at his brother-in-law's request. Alana had carried one on her keychain, although she hadn't known it.

"Don't forget to give yourself credit for quick thinking while you're handing out praise," he said drily. "I'm not sure what that triad gang was waiting for—the cover of darkness, probably. But if you hadn't mobilized RMM right away…"

"All I did was—"

"—text Miss Richardson when she didn't come home for dinner the way she said she would. And when you got no response, you called her cell phone. And when she didn't answer, you activated the beacon."

"Well, it made no sense to me," Mei-li explained. "I knew she was going to Mong Kok, but when I activated the transmitter and mapped the location, I knew something bad was going down. She had no business being in that neighborhood—both Dirk and I had warned her where not to go by herself. And there was no ransom demand. If it wasn't a kidnapping, I knew it was outside my area of expertise. So I called you." Then she asked, "How did you know which apartment she was being held in?"

"Clutter...that wasn't there."

"An empty balcony," his sister said softly. "Of course." Admiration was evident in her voice, and he knew she'd made the connection without him having to spell it out. Space was at such a premium in Hong Kong, the vast majority of balconies weren't used to take the air, but to store things that wouldn't fit in Hong Kong's tiny apartments. In addition to that, almost no one dried their clothes in a dryer, even if they had a washing machine in their unit. Even the residents of high-end apartments and condos hung their clothes to dry on their balconies. When you were looking for the slightest aberration, an empty balcony stood out like a red flag for RMM.

"So what did Miss Richardson tell the police?"

His sister laughed unexpectedly. "Based on her description, you're about ten feet tall, have the strength of a gorilla and can scale walls like a superhero from a comic book."

He chuckled. "I guess I'm safe, then. The police won't be searching for *me*, even though I didn't break the law. Much." But he couldn't help the little thrill of ego-stoking male pride that shot through him at the description. So Alana saw him as a superhero, did she? He liked that idea. No, he *loved* that idea. Because while the opinions of those he rescued had never been important to him before, Alana's opinion of him mattered. A lot.

The High Tiger of the Eight Tigers triad organization—although it had far more than eight members—sat in a hastily called conference with the seven other leaders of the triad. Each of the seven was an enforcer, overseeing a cadre of men. Each cadre was responsible for a different aspect of the criminal endeavors that constituted the backbone of the Eight Tigers: drugs, gun-running, prostitution, kidnapping, extortion, money laundering and pornography. And they all answered to the High Tiger—chairman of the board, as it were.

The Eight Tigers was a radical departure from most Hong Kong triads. Except when it came to women, it was an equal opportunity employer—if they cared about such things, which they didn't. All they cared about was whether a man had it in him to carry out the dicta of the ruling tribunal…and could keep his mouth shut in the unfortunate event he was arrested. Of the eight men seated around the conference table, three were Chinese, two were British, two were American and one was Australian. And they'd had a secret stranglehold on crime in Hong Kong and Macau for years.

The High Tiger turned to the enforcer in charge of prostitution and demanded, "How did it happen?"

The man on the hot seat nervously cleared his throat. "Unclear."

"What do the men say?"

"All they know is she was gone when they went to move her to the boat. Then they got the hell out of there."

The High Tiger's voice was soft, yet his tone was threatening, when he asked, "Are you aware this was an RMM rescue?"

The other man blanched. Every man at the table knew of RMM. Knew it was more to be feared than the Hong Kong Police Force or the Public Security Police Force of Macau for three reasons: it was a highly secret organization, more secret than their own; its members were impervious to bribes, unlike many on the police forces in the jurisdictions in which the Eight Tigers operated; and it was bankrolled by a man who seemed to have an unending supply of money...even greater than theirs.

"No, I...I was not aware," the man finally admitted.

The High Tiger then asked the question that held the most importance to the men assembled there. "What trail might lead RMM...or authorities...to us?"

"Nothing." The man being questioned glanced around the table, reassuring the assemblage. "Nothing at all."

Alana woke at her normal time. Dirk had told her as they'd left the hospital last night to take it easy, to sleep in and recuperate from her ordeal, but she wasn't going to act like an invalid. Okay, her arm and shoulder muscles were stiff and sore from being bound. And yes, her wrists were raw and chafed from the rope she'd tried to wriggle out of. And...

She tentatively touched the back of her head where she'd been hit. *Ouch!* she thought. It was still tender to the touch. There was a little swelling, too, but her nausea was gone and she felt fine. Energized to jump right back into her job. She didn't want to lie in bed and remember her close brush with all the bad things that *could* have happened to her—including rape and death. She needed the distraction of work to take her mind off what had nearly occurred.

She dressed quickly and was brushing her teeth when a good memory surfaced...her miraculous rescue. That was immediately followed by memories of the man who'd rescued her. The way he'd held her so securely she hadn't been afraid, even dangling from a harness hooked to a cable, with terra firma far below. The incredible hardness of his body plastered against hers. Not to mention the arousal that had intrigued her to the point where she'd almost said something about it.

She wished she knew who he was. Wished she at least had a first name she could use when she thought of him, instead of the slightly blasphemous "savior" that came to mind.

Okay, so maybe she'd exaggerated his physical characteristics when she'd described him to the police last night. And he probably couldn't walk on water, either, although she had a feeling he would try if it was necessary to save someone. He would have done whatever was necessary to save *her*, even though he didn't know her. She couldn't have said how she knew, but she was absolutely certain that from the minute he'd entered the room where she was imprisoned, he wouldn't have left without her. Even if her abductors had surprised them, he would have done whatever was necessary to effect their escape. And that was such an incredibly glorious, albeit humbling, feeling, knowing there were still heroes in the world willing to risk their lives for others.

But darn it, she needed a name!

Then she remembered what Mei-li had told her last night, that he worked for an organization called RMM. If Dirk's wife knew that much, she just might know *him*. It was worth a shot anyway.

On that thought she made her way downstairs to the kitchen.

Hannah, the DeWinters' housekeeper, was at the stove, but she turned the fire off and bustled over to Alana when she entered the room, enveloping her in an encouraging hug. "I'm so glad you're safe!"

"Thanks, Hannah." She stepped back and looked around. "Where is everyone?"

"The twins are still sleeping, and so is their nanny. Mr.

DeWinter had an early call on the set. He said to tell you there's some fan mail to go through in his office…but only if you feel up to it. Mrs. DeWinter also went out early. She said she might be back for lunch, but she'd let me know."

"Darn it!" Alana said out loud. "I was hoping to catch her before she left."

Hannah resumed her cooking. Oatmeal, Alana saw, which both she and the DeWinters' daughters loved. "Was it something urgent? You could always call or text her."

"Important to me. But not urgent enough to interrupt whatever she's doing. If she went out this early, she must be working on a case. I'll see her at lunch or dinner."

Hannah took down a bowl from one of the cabinets and served Alana from the pot on the stove. "Here you go, Miss Richardson. Put yourself on the outside of this."

Alana smiled and accepted the bowl. She'd only been living with the DeWinters for a month, but she adored Hannah almost as much as the twins did. Not just for her quaint expressions and her insistence on addressing Alana with old-fashioned formality, but for the heart of gold that was obvious within minutes of meeting her.

She sprinkled a spoonful of brown sugar on her oatmeal and stirred, then seated herself at the kitchen table with a despondent sigh. She'd tried to love her own mother; she really had. But except for the residual attachment left over from her childhood, it wasn't possible. How could she love a woman whose outlook on life was totally alien to her? Who judged people by their social status…and more?

She couldn't help wishing her mother was more like Hannah. For that matter, she couldn't help wishing her father was different, too. Not like Hannah so much, but like her uncle Julian. She'd never envied Juliana anything except the close relationship she had with her father, a father she could be proud of. If only Uncle Julian had been *her* father, too, instead of—

Don't go there, she warned herself. *No pity parties. That never does any good. Think of all the people in the world who would change places with you*, she reminded herself as she ate her porridge, enumerating all the positives in her life. *Your parents never abused you. You never went hungry. You always had a roof over your head and decent clothes to wear.*

But…those weren't the only things that mattered when raising a child.

The fact that her parents were the way they were wasn't something she could change, either, although she'd tried. Repeatedly. But she'd never made a dent in their prejudices. Wasn't that one of the reasons she'd run across the world to escape? So she could live her life free from the entitled, *superior* mentality they'd tried to impose on her?

They would never understand that Alana didn't see the world the way they did, no matter what she said. So all she could do was distance herself from them, even if it meant taking a job they saw as beneath her.

Living with Dirk and Mei-li had been an eye-opener. Watching them together. So loving. So supportive. So accepting of their differences. No, not just accepting, *rejoicing* in their differences.

Then seeing how Dirk's daughters looked upon Mei-li as their mother without question, even though both Mei-li and Dirk made sure the twins knew how much their birth mother had loved them and sacrificed for them before they were born.

Alana knew one thing for sure now. The way she'd been raised *wasn't* the way she'd raise her own children…if she was fortunate enough to have any.

And just like that her memory winged to last night and

the man who'd rescued her. A man who, as Mei-li had put it, did what he had to do to rescue the innocent, without looking for thanks.

She hadn't really put a lot of thought into it before, because she was only twenty-six and her biological clock hadn't yet sounded the warning alarm. But she *was* deeply attached to the children she knew—Juliana's little boy, Raoul, and Dirk's daughters, Linden and Laurel. And she'd always known that when she found the right man she wanted children. Children, plural. Two, maybe three. *Not* the lonely only child she'd been.

No, she hadn't given it a lot of thought before. But she was thinking of it now. She was definitely thinking of it now…because *that* was the kind of man she wanted as the father of her children.

And she didn't even know his name or what he did for a living.

Chapter 3

"Dirk was right," Alana muttered to herself. Her boss's fan mail—the real kind, not email—went to a PO box address, and the accumulation was delivered bright and early every Monday morning. Dirk had a social media presence she maintained for him, too—website, Twitter, Facebook. He couldn't possibly have managed it all on his own, which was why Juliana had recommended Dirk to Alana and Alana to Dirk.

And she loved her job. Unlike the glorified but meaningless position she'd had working for her father's company ever since she graduated from college, she never felt superfluous. She never felt as if no one would miss her if she didn't show up. Dirk needed her to keep him organized, to keep his fan base happy.

Not that Dirk didn't take an interest. He did. He set the tone, gave her the parameters to work from to maintain his public persona. He also read the more interesting posts, tweets and emails she filtered for him. And he reviewed anything that went out under his name, of course. But only once had he firmly put his foot down on Alana's suggested response, one that would have capitalized on a touching photo of Dirk with his family that had just recently been published, a picture that had been taken without his knowledge or consent. After which she'd gotten the message—his wife and children were *never* to be used.

That didn't mean photos of the DeWinters didn't circulate. The paparazzi stalked Dirk relentlessly, and Mei-li was incredibly photogenic. But Dirk tried to minimize public access to his twin daughters, including a state-of-the-art security system surrounding his estate on Victoria Peak here on Hong Kong Island, and bodyguards who fiercely protected his little girls whenever they went out anywhere. Nevertheless, pictures surfaced occasionally. That was one of Alana's more esoteric duties, too. To track the photos and figure out how, when and where they were taken, so Dirk could do his best to prevent others from being snapped in the future.

Even though Juliana had lived her entire adult life in the public eye, attention that had become even more rabid when she married the King of Zakhar, Alana had never understood just how little privacy celebrities had these days until she'd gone to work for Dirk. Until she'd experienced firsthand what almost amounted to harassment when a photographer had lain in wait and snapped pictures of Alana, the twins and their nanny outside the ladies' room of the restaurant Dirk had taken them to her first week on the job. And she'd quickly realized the steep price Dirk and his family paid—would always pay—for his superstardom.

The morning passed in a busy blur. When she'd first started her new job she'd been overwhelmed by the barrage of incoming data. But she had a system now, so she quickly dealt with the backlog of fan communication, divvying them up into her little "buckets." Adoring. Begging. Threatening. And the category that always made her laugh at how creative people could be: investment "opportunities." Not a single one was anything other than a scam, but she'd shown a couple of them to Dirk to make him laugh, too.

Mostly the scam emails were deleted after reading the first couple of sentences, but not the threats. Dirk would have had Alana just delete them, too, but Mei-li had shaken her head, saying in her soft voice, "Don't respond, but don't delete. We need to keep a record, just in case..." And when the eyes of the two women had met, Alana had understood without another word being spoken.

Mei-li was a highly regarded private investigator and a ransom negotiator, and was unwaveringly protective of her beloved husband. She read every threatening communication, ranking them on a scale of one to five, with one being "no threat," three being "credible threat," and five being "imminent threat." The "imminent threat" communications were turned over to the Hong Kong Police for investigation.

The begging requests were more problematic, because Dirk, Alana had soon learned, had a tender heart. Which meant another of Alana's duties revolved around investigating the legitimacy of whatever the senders were asking Dirk to do. And on three separate occasions in the past month Dirk had quietly and without fanfare fulfilled a request—including sending money to the parents of a child with a severe form of spina bifida whose dying wish was to visit the Eiffel Tower, and a personal visit to the bedside of a longtime fan dying from cancer.

But the vast majority of the emails, tweets and posts were of the adoring variety. And Alana had a stock response she sent out on Dirk's behalf, thanking the sender and promoting his latest movie, including links to positive reviews.

She'd just replied to the last email when Mei-li walked into the office. "Hannah said you needed to talk with me?"

It took Alana a moment to come out of the zone she'd been in. "Oh," she said. "I wanted to ask you…" Her cheeks felt suddenly warm. "The man who rescued me last night. Do you know who he is?" When Mei-li didn't immediately respond, Alana rushed to add, "You said he and the other men are with a group called RMM. I know you said they don't look for thanks, but I…" She faltered. "I just wondered."

An enigmatic expression crossed Mei-li's face. "I know, but I can't tell you." She sat down in the chair in front of Alana's desk. "I contacted RMM because they're my last resort. But they operate in the shadows. And some of the things they do are illegal. Not *bad*, just illegal. So…"

Alana nodded. She wasn't naive…not in that way anyway. She knew the difference. "Last night the driver and the man riding shotgun said I was abducted by members of a triad gang. That other women had disappeared in the same way, and they—RMM, I guess is what he meant—they've been after this gang for a couple of months. But…" She trailed off as another thought occurred to her, and she frowned. "How did they know where I was? I mean, I'm incredibly grateful someone figured it out and RMM rescued me, but…"

Mei-li's lips quirked into a tiny smile. "Modern technology is wonderful…most of the time. You know those little lockets the twins wear, the ones with a picture of their mother?"

She wasn't sure where the other woman was going with this. "Of course."

"You probably thought they were a tad young for jewelry."

"Well...yes," she admitted. "But I just figured Dirk wanted the girls to know their mother loves them, even though she died when they were born."

"You're right, of course, but it's more symbolic than you know. In Dirk's mind Bree is protecting them from harm... but so is he. Those lockets contain tiny transmitters. Little beacons that can be remotely activated. The girls have worn them ever since they were rescued from their kidnappers. We were fortunate last time that they were sending Dirk pictures of his daughters that had been geotagged, but we can't rely on that happening again."

When Alana raised her brows in a question, Mei-li explained, "Geotagging just means the pictures have GPS coordinates embedded in them. Most people don't realize this is enabled in their smartphones, and neither did the twins' kidnappers. But that was a fluke. Dirk wanted to be sure we could track the girls if they're kidnapped again, and the locket beacons were the best thing he and—that is, the best thing he could come up with."

Alana wondered why Mei-li had hesitated, then said, "Okay, I get that. But..."

"But how did we know where you were?"

"Yes."

"You carry the same beacon transmitter as the twins. Just as I do."

Alana gawked at her. "What?"

Mei-li made a face. "I told Dirk he should tell you, but..."

"But what?"

"He didn't tell you because he was afraid you'd think he was intruding on your privacy after he promised you he wouldn't. And to be honest, he really didn't think we'd need to activate it, so you'd never have to know."

"Why didn't he ask me? I'm not stupid. I wouldn't have refused to carry something that would protect me."

"I know, I know. But he didn't know you when you first came to work for him, and he couldn't take that chance. He's hyper-concerned for the safety of everyone around him, not just his daughters. Not just me. And given what he suffered when Linden and Laurel were kidnapped, I can't really blame him. I hope he never has to go through that again with anyone."

"How...?"

Mei-li's tiny smile returned. "Didn't you ever wonder about the key fob on the key ring we gave you when you moved in last month? The one that looks like something you'd use to electronically open a car door...even though you don't have a car here in Hong Kong?"

Alana opened her mouth, then closed it. She stared at the other woman for a moment before admitting, "I thought it *was* a key fob for one of the cars in the garage. Not that I would even *think* about driving here as a general rule, not where everyone drives on the opposite side of the street. But in an emergency..."

"They *do* operate as a car door key fob. But they also contain a transmitter beacon, which can be remotely as well as manually activated. They're deliberately designed to look like something innocuous, so no one would suspect their true purpose. Even if the men who abducted you went through your purse, it's highly unlikely they'd have been suspicious of that key fob."

Alana struggled with conflicting emotions for a moment. On the one hand, Dirk should have told her. But on the other, she couldn't be anything but grateful she *had* carried the beacon that had led to her rescue. And if she was honest with herself, even if she'd known about it, she'd been incapacitated too quickly. There was no way she would have had a chance to activate it manually, so the remote activation was actually a blessing.

But that didn't mean she wouldn't give Dirk a piece of her mind about keeping her in the dark.

Jason, known as J.C. by his board of directors and employees alike as a way of keeping his private life separate from his public persona, had muted his smartphone as he always did during board meetings, but he felt the vibration for an incoming text. He ignored it as his smiling board of directors filed out of the conference room, several of them stopping to shake his hand.

Another profitable quarter had gone into the record books for Wing Wah Enterprises, the electronics company his maternal grandfather had founded seventy years ago. The company was publicly traded, but his 51 percent stake meant that even without his mother's and sister's shares—whose proxies he held—he had a controlling interest. *With* their proxies, he was unassailably in command.

That didn't mean he wasn't answerable to the shareholders. He was. And he'd given them a more-than-respectable return on their investment every quarter since he'd taken the helm at the tender age of twenty-five upon the death of his grandfather, almost ten years ago. But running the company was just a job to him. One he was incredibly good at. One that supplemented the fortune he relied upon in his other life. But just a job. It wasn't his life's work.

That was RMM. Right Makes Might. "'Let us have faith that right makes might,'" he murmured to himself in the now-empty conference room, "'and in that faith let us, to the end, dare to do our duty as we understand it.'" His fingers subconsciously touched the gold medallion he wore beneath his dress shirt, an ever-present reminder of both RMM and the reason behind it.

Then he remembered the incoming text he'd received earlier. Fewer than a dozen people had his personal cell phone number, so it had to be important. When he pulled out his phone he saw the text was from Mei-li.

Alana was asking about you, he read. Should I tell her... anything?

He cursed under his breath, but lightly. Then he shook his head with rueful humor. Damn, but his sister knew him too well. How the hell had she picked up on his totally un-anticipated attraction to Alana? And what was she expecting him to do about it?

He was torn. On the one hand, he wanted to see Alana again. *Not* as the man who'd rescued her—no way would he use that to his advantage. But he wanted to meet her in a social setting. Wanted to prove to himself that what he was feeling would quickly dissipate without the adrenaline rush engendered by their dangerous first encounter.

On the other hand, could he risk having Alana figure out who he was? He could count on the fingers of both hands the people who knew that J.C. Moore, CEO extraordinaire, and Jason Moore, the founder and driving force behind the highly secret RMM, were one and the same man.

He could go to jail for some of the things he and RMM had done. He'd accepted that risk long ago with a philosophical shrug. But he hadn't been careless about the danger. Only three people who weren't associated with RMM knew how far the organization was willing to go. And of those three, one was related to him by blood, one owed him his daughters' lives and one...one had been the third Musketeer with Sean and him ever since they were toddlers together.

His sister and her husband knew enough of his clandestine activities that they could be a threat. But Mei-li would burn at the stake for him. And DeWinter? Expose the man who'd been instrumental in rescuing his beloved twin daughters last year? "Not bloody likely," Jason told himself, laughing under his breath.

And the third person? They'd wept together at Sean's grave. He wasn't a member of RMM only because his job prevented him from taking the oath...but that didn't mean he wasn't *bound* by the oath the same way Jason was. That didn't mean he wasn't inextricably bound to the founding principles of RMM, either. Which meant Jason had nothing to fear where he was concerned.

That brought him right back around to the question he'd asked himself in the first place. *So what are you going to do about Alana?*

Making a decision, he hit speed dial to call his sister. "I thought that would pique your interest," she said when she answered the phone.

"Stop reading my mind."

She laughed softly. "So why don't you just come for dinner?"

"What if she figures out who I am?"

"You saved her life and she knows it. You think she'd do anything to put you at risk?"

"When you put it that way...no, I don't. But—"

"But you don't want her to be attracted to you because you saved her life."

"Damn you," he said without heat. "I knew you were perceptive. Intuitive. But it's as if you're a witch now."

"I'll take that as a 'yes, Mei-li, I'd love to come for dinner tomorrow night.'"

"Not tomorrow night. I have to fly to Bangkok on business. Then London. But I'll be back on Friday. What about that Friday night?"

"Done," she said promptly. "I'll ask Hannah to prepare your favorite curried chicken."

He made a teasing comment in Cantonese about the way to a man's heart, but Mei-li didn't rise to the bait. He was just about to disconnect when she said, "You never answered my question. Should I tell Alana anything?"

"That would be a big n-o."

His sister laughed softly. Meaningfully. And Jason knew she'd correctly interpreted exactly what it meant.

The following Friday Jason drove his fire-engine-red Jaguar F-TYPE SVR Coupe up Mount Austin Road, effortlessly shifting gears as he darted between traffic. He was running late and had already texted his sister before he left—there'd been a customs holdup with his private jet at the airport. Nothing serious, just annoying and time-consuming. Then he'd stopped at a florist on the way, one he often used. He'd called ahead and placed his order, so his floral apology for being late was ready and waiting for him when he arrived. But it still ate up more precious minutes.

If any car could make up for lost time, though, it was his beloved Jag. He'd driven Jaguars since his first car at eighteen, a birthday present from his maternal grandfather over the protests of his parents. Unlike his private jet, which was a necessity for his business, and unlike his penthouse condo in an exclusive area of the island, which had been a gift from his grandfather when he graduated from Oxford with highest honors thirteen years ago, the Jag was his only self-indulgence. His only concession to an inheritance that sometimes seemed more of a curse than a blessing.

It had bothered him greatly when his grandfather's will had been read, and he'd learned that not only had his old-school Chinese grandfather passed over his only child— the daughter who he'd never truly forgiven for marrying a foreigner against his wishes—he also hadn't divided his vast wealth equally between his two grandchildren. Minor shares in the company had been bequeathed to Jason's mother and sister, along with some personal effects, but the bulk of the estate had been left to Jason…the only male heir.

That's not right, he'd furiously stated to his grandfather's solicitor in the office where the will was being read.

He'd immediately offered to sign everything over to his mother, who'd only smiled and shook her head. *I knew what I was doing when I married your father*, she'd said in her gentle voice, turning her breathtaking smile on her husband, famed producer/director Sir Joshua Moore. *I have no regrets.*

And though Jason had still been angry over his grandfather's actions, it had been impossible not to be moved by the loving, wordless exchange between his parents. He'd grown up seeing their devotion to each other all his life, of course. But in that moment he'd finally understood what it really meant. And for the first time in his life he'd actively prayed to find a woman like his mother. A woman who would sacrifice everything for him.

"Ten years," he whispered now, shifting gears automatically as the traffic ahead of him slowed. "Ten years, and still…"

He'd never found her. Never found the woman who would look at him with that unmistakable expression in her eyes, the one that said the world was well lost if she had him. "Wishing for the moon," he scoffed at himself. And yet…

Mei-li had found a man who looked at her that way. Not once, but twice. First Sean all those years ago, and now DeWinter. But then, his sister never had to worry about being loved for anything other than her wonderful self.

Mei-li had turned him down when he'd offered to split the inheritance evenly between them. Had she somehow seen into the future and divined the price Jason would pay for that wealth…and wanted nothing to do with it?

He took the turn that would lead him to the DeWinter estate and drove nearly half a mile before pulling up in front of the gate, no closer to an answer than he was when he'd started his little soul-searching episode. He rolled down the window and touched the electronic key card that would open the gate against the card reader. His sister had given it to him when the DeWinters had moved up here. He hadn't told her he already had one—he'd designed the estate's security for his sister and brother-in-law, and his company had installed the entire system. And like some software designers, he'd made sure he had "backdoor" access.

He tapped his fingers impatiently against the steering wheel, waiting for the gate to swing open, then drove through. The Jag passed through an electronic beam, and the gate automatically shut behind him.

A minute later Jason pulled up to the main house, but to his surprise there was a police car parked in front of it. Perturbed, he grabbed the flowers off the seat next to him and headed for the front door, which swung open before he could ring the bell. "Sorry I'm late," he told his sister, holding the flowers out in front of him, but hooking a finger over his shoulder at the police car. "What are the po—" He stopped abruptly, because the somber expression on Mei-li's face warned him. "What's wrong?"

"The police are here to question Alana again," she said. "It hasn't hit the news yet, but it will soon. There was another abduction while you were gone. Almost the exact same MO as the way she was snatched. On a crowded street. In broad daylight."

Chapter 4

"I really can't tell you anything more about the men who grabbed me," Alana was saying when Jason approached the family room. "I wish I could." From her voice Jason could tell she was practically in tears. "Especially now that another woman—" She broke off abruptly, then continued. "But they were wearing masks that completely covered their heads and faces except for their eyes. Then I was unconscious when they transported me to...wherever. I already told you they were speaking Cantonese when I could hear them, but they kept me blindfolded the entire time. I have no idea what they look like or where they were holding me, or *anything*."

Both policemen turned when Jason and Mei-li walked into the room, and his sister quickly said, "You know Detective Inspector Lam, of course, of the Organized Crime and Triad Bureau. And this is Sergeant Wo of the same unit. Sergeant, this is my brother, Jason Moore. We were expecting him for dinner." She turned to Alana and added smoothly, with almost no hesitation, "And this is Alana Richardson, Dirk's executive assistant. She was abducted last Sunday and miraculously rescued. I told you about it, remember? The police are here trying to learn what they can."

"Unnecessary to introduce me to either gentleman," Jason said. He shook hands with the two policemen, addressing them formally. "Detective Inspector. Sergeant. Good to see you again, although not under these circumstances." Then he turned to Alana, who had risen to greet him when the policemen did, and took her hand. "Miss Richardson. Glad to make your acquaintance. I was very sorry to hear from Mei-li what you had to go through, but needless to say I'm happy you suffered no permanent injury."

Alana's eyes widened as he spoke, and Jason cursed internally. Although he allowed nothing but polite interest to reflect in his expression, he realized she'd made the connection. She knew who he was. There was no way she recognized his face, so it had to be his voice.

She didn't blurt it out, however, and Jason gave her bonus points for quick thinking and effective dissimulation. "I'm glad to meet you, too, Mr. Moore. Your sister has told me a lot about you. And Linden and Laurel are full of their 'Unca Jason,'" she said. "You're quite a favorite with them."

Jason let himself smile in response. "And they're quite the favorites with me, too." Then he glanced at the policemen. "But don't let me interrupt. You were in the middle of an interrogation, yes?"

"Not an interrogation," the detective inspector was quick to point out, his face impassive. "Miss Richardson is a victim, not a suspect. But we were hoping she could shed some light on the men who abducted her." His dark eyes met Jason's. "Or on her miraculous rescue," he added drily. "We received an anonymous tip the night she was rescued." A muscle twitched in his cheek. "And we did a thorough forensics analysis of the crime scene. DNA results on the man she scratched aren't back yet, so if we knew who rescued her and how she was located, that could yield important information."

When Jason's expression betokened nothing but bland interest, the detective inspector went on. "We have reason to believe Miss Richardson's abduction is related to a string of similar ones, most recently one that occurred yesterday."

"That *is* unfortunate," Jason agreed. Not by the tiniest flicker did he let on he knew anything more than he'd just been told. But his mind was working feverishly. He couldn't reveal he knew exactly where Alana had been held or how she'd been tracked to that apartment. Nor could he reveal how she'd been rescued, not without putting himself and his men in an untenable position. Not without putting RMM itself at risk.

"What ties them all together?" To Jason's surprise, it wasn't his sister asking the question; it was Alana.

The two policemen exchanged glances, then the detective inspector said, "The MO, for one thing—*modus operandi*. We're not at liberty to discuss anything more than that, Miss Richardson. Suffice it to say we have overwhelming evidence they *are* connected."

Which made Jason wonder if the crime scene had yielded any clues. He hadn't followed up on the police investigation the way he usually did, and he wondered about that, as well. Was it because he was trying *not* to be too involved? Because of the attraction he felt toward Alana that he didn't *want* to feel? If so, it was a mistake, because now another woman had been abducted, and RMM needed to add that to its own investigation.

No one spoke for the space of five heartbeats, then the detective inspector said to Mei-li, "We should be going." He turned to Alana. "You have my card, Miss Richardson. If you remember something—*anything*—please don't hesitate to call that number. If I'm not there, you can leave a message with the desk sergeant."

Mei-li walked the policemen out, but Jason stayed where he was. He glanced at Alana, noting she looked much better than the last time he'd seen her, her tear-stained face pale in the moonlight. But one thing hadn't changed at all…he was still attracted to her. And that disconcerted him.

He was even more disconcerted when she said softly, "You look different from how I remember you." He raised a questioning eyebrow as if he had no idea what she was talking about, but she wasn't fooled. "Oh, don't worry," she reassured him. "I have no intention of revealing who you are to anyone, especially the police. Mei-li wouldn't tell me anything about you, not even your first name. Not surprising, now that I know you're her brother. But she *did* say sometimes RMM breaks the law."

"That doesn't bother you?"

"That you broke the law…for the right reasons? That you did whatever you had to do to rescue me?" Her oddly colored eyes—almost amethyst, really—glowed with an inner fire, holding his gaze. "What do you think, Mr. Moore?"

He smiled faintly. "Jason, please. And I think perhaps you're romanticizing what happened."

She shook her head. "I may be idealistic, but I'm not naive. Tell me that if the men who abducted me had come into the room you would have escaped without me. Tell me and I'll believe you." When he remained silent, her voice dropped a notch. "You would have done *anything* to rescue me. Even if it meant killing those men. Even if it meant dying yourself."

He couldn't lie. Not about this. "Yes."

"I knew it. I knew it that night. You have no idea how much that means to me, knowing there are men like you left in this world."

"Don't make me out to be some kind of hero, Miss Richardson," he began.

"Alana, please."

"Alana," he acknowledged. "Don't make me out to be a hero. I—"

"You are. But that's not the only reason why I'm—" She broke off, warm color tingeing her cheeks.

Mei-li walked back into the room at that moment, saying, "Dirk's running late, Jason. Later than you. He said not to wait dinner for him, that he'll—" She stopped short, and he knew his sister had read and correctly interpreted their body language. "I didn't tell her, Jason, I swear."

"I know." He smiled at Mei-li with a touch of ruefulness. "She recognized my voice."

Her concerned expression morphed into a smile. "Yes, that *would* tend to give you away." Then she looked at Alana. "Since you didn't say anything to the police about it when they were here, does that mean you don't intend to? Ever?"

"Don't put her on the spot like that," Jason began, but Alana broke in.

"Never." The implacable way in which the one word was uttered was even more revealing than the word itself. "If your brother hadn't rescued me, I…I'd be in Macau right now. Forced into…" She shook her head slowly, then turned to gaze at Jason, everything she was feeling reflected on her face. The horror at what could have happened to her. Her fervent gratitude over being spared that fate. "Much as I'd like to help the police find the woman who was abducted yesterday, I don't think telling them who rescued me will do any good, so your secret is safe with me."

Jason wanted to make light of his actions, but for some reason he couldn't think of a single thing to say. He didn't want Alana's gratitude. Or did he? Last week his ego had been stoked by the idea that Alana saw him as a superhero. Apparently that hadn't changed. Because the way she was looking at him? He wanted that. The same way he wanted her.

And he knew he was in trouble.

Verbal conversation at dinner was almost nonexistent between Jason and Alana. Mei-li kept the conversation going by addressing questions to both of them, questions they were forced to answer. But in between their gazes locked on each other, and they communicated without words.

Don't look at me that way. You know nothing about me, his eyes said.

I know everything important there is to know, hers replied, then added, *I could say the same to you about me. You know nothing about me.*

His eyes flickered down to her wrists, which still bore the marks of the rope that had bound them—the rope she'd struggled against—then back upward. *You're a fighter. You refused to surrender. And when I showed up you knew not to ask questions right then. That tells me all I need to know.*

Even after Dirk arrived, full of apologies for being late, Jason and Alana continued their silent conversation over the curried chicken.

I'm a criminal...in the eyes of the law.

You answer to a higher law.

Jason had believed that about himself since he'd found his true calling the day Sean had been buried, but he'd never thought he'd find a woman who understood. Was it possible? Could Alana understand? Truly understand?

Long before dinner was over Jason knew he wanted to see Alana again. And not just because he was physically drawn to her, although he wouldn't lie to himself—there *was* a strong physical element to his attraction. But he also craved an opportunity to talk with her one-on-one, to get to know her as a person. And that was new for him. His previous relationships with women hadn't prepared him for this at all.

Your own fault, he chastised himself. *You gravitated toward women who knew the score. Who were expecting exactly what they got from you...and nothing else. And who gave you exactly what you asked of them...and nothing more.*

The thought brought him up short. Had he become so jaded he hadn't *allowed* himself to find the woman he'd been searching for all these years? Had he let his money and his complicated childhood become a barrier...and a self-fulfilling prophecy?

And what did that mean where Alana was concerned? Wouldn't she be better off if he left her the hell alone?

The Eight Tigers only met as a group a few times a year as a general rule. But the enforcer in charge of prostitution had asked for this special meeting, and the High Tiger had acquiesced...once he knew what the other man had to report.

"We are back on target," the man boasted to the assemblage. "A new woman has been added to our premier house in Macau." His eyes took on a lascivious leer. "She is quite a prize—I have sampled her myself."

The High Tiger ignored the expressions of disgust on the faces of three of his fellow Tigers. Prostitution was not to every man's taste, especially when women were abducted and forced into one of the Eight Tigers' illegal brothels. Which was why those men were *not* in charge of the prostitution arm of their criminal organization.

This was business—an extremely profitable one for the Eight Tigers. It generated nearly as much money as heroin, cocaine, ecstasy and the other illegal drugs they dealt in, which he privately deplored but allowed to continue because the market was too profitable to ignore.

So just as he suppressed his personal dislike of that enterprise for the good of all, so, too, would the men who objected to forced prostitution. They might be personally disgusted, but they would say nothing, do nothing. Nothing at all.

It was very late by the time Jason left. Alana said her good-nights to the DeWinters and headed for her bedroom, unable to get Jason out of her mind. Also unable to eradicate the terrible disappointment that he hadn't asked to see her again. She'd given him as much encouragement as she could without being too obvious, and a bubble of excitement had sustained her throughout the evening. Now her bubble had burst, leaving her crushed.

Could she have mistaken the very male intent in his eyes? She didn't think so. She wasn't *that* naive. She'd dated steadily in high school and college, and had already gently turned down three marriage proposals, one of which had caused her a pang because she'd known the man had genuinely cared about her, unlike the other two who'd proposed only because her family's money and prestige made her a "suitable" bride for someone in their social stratum.

But she'd never found a man whose kiss, whose touch, made her want more. Had never even come close. She'd been so concerned she'd even mentioned it to Juliana. Her cousin had reassuringly dismissed those fears, saying, "Don't sweat it, honey. It'll happen, I'm sure. Some women are just a one-man woman. I was. All the men I dated in Hollywood? Zip. Zilch. Zero. But with Andre..." Juliana had laughed softly, suggestively, adding, "When you meet him, you'll know. Trust me."

Jason hadn't kissed her. But he'd touched her a week ago. And just like that, she'd wanted him. As if her body had recognized he was the one she'd been saving herself for...even though she hadn't consciously been doing it for anyone.

But apparently Jason didn't feel the same way, despite what she'd thought were their nonverbal exchanges this evening. Had it all been in her mind? Had she imagined the emotional and physical bond that had seemed to spring to life between them?

Alana brushed her teeth, donned her pj's and slipped into bed, still wondering. Then buried her face against her pillow. "Right, Jules," she muttered, using her pet name for her absent cousin. "When I meet him I'll know. Terrific advice. But what if he doesn't feel the same way? What then?"

Her smartphone chirped in the stillness.

She scrambled out of bed and rushed to answer it. "Hello?"

"Alana?" She caught her breath, because only one man said her name that way. Only one man's voice made her go weak in the knees. She didn't even need him to say "It's Jason Moore" to know who was calling her.

She clutched the phone tightly against her ear. "Hi, Jason." Then couldn't think of another single, solitary thing to say except, "How did you get my cell phone number?"

He laughed softly, and her nipples tightened until they ached. "I'd better not tell you. I don't want you to think I'm stalking you."

She let her breath out in a whoosh, and only then realized she'd been holding it. *Jason called you*, she exulted as she padded back to her bed and slipped beneath the covers. *It wasn't your imagination after all.*

"I didn't wake you, did I?"

"No. I wasn't asleep. I was hoping you'd call." Which wasn't *exactly* true, but true enough.

"I debated with myself for the longest time," he admitted. "My better self said I shouldn't. But here I am, calling you."

"I'm glad," she whispered. Then she focused on what he'd said. "Why would your better self say you shouldn't? Couldn't you tell that I…" She cleared her throat. "What I mean is, I'm a nice person. At least I think I am—most people like me."

His voice deepened. "It's not you, it's me." Then he laughed suddenly. "And isn't that the stereotypical response when you're trying to brush someone off? 'It's not you, it's me'?" The humor fled his tone. "But in this case, it's true. I can think of a hundred reasons why you should avoid me like the plague, and only one reason why you shouldn't."

"And that is…?"

He breathed deeply in her ear. "Because a connection exists between us, whether we want it to or not. Physical *and* emotional."

She didn't even hesitate. "Yes."

"You admit it."

"Yes."

"Then would you spend the day with me tomorrow? It's Saturday. Are you free?"

"Yes, I am, and yes, I will. I'd love to."

There was silence at the other end until he said, "You don't play games, Alana." The approving note in his voice wasn't lost on her.

"No, I don't play games. But I also don't…" She couldn't

quite bring herself to finish that statement, but he finished it for her.

"You don't sleep with a man on the first date."

Warmth inundated her cheeks, and she couldn't tell him that not only did she not sleep with a man on the first date, she also hadn't slept with *any* man. Ever. But she hadn't been tempted before. She hadn't known Jason before. If she had, she wasn't sure she'd still be a virgin at the ripe old age of twenty-six.

Once upon a time that wouldn't have been an issue. But nowadays it made her an anachronism. And everyone assumed—men and women alike—that she had more experience than she actually did. Men in particular thought a woman who was still a virgin at this age either had to have strong religious beliefs about chastity or wasn't into men at all. Neither of which was the case for her. She just hadn't met a man who made her want to sleep with him. Until now.

"You don't have to worry, Alana. Do I want to sleep with you? Absolutely. But would I pressure you when you're not ready? Never."

"I know you wouldn't. It's not you, it's me." As soon as the words left her mouth she laughed, embarrassment combining with dismay. "Oh, no, did I really say that? What I meant was—"

"Part of you wants to…but you're not sure." His deep voice curled through her. "Don't worry. When you're ready, and not a moment sooner. You'll be as safe with me as you want to be."

Which only raised the question in Alana's mind…how safe did she want to be?

Chapter 5

Just over two weeks later Alana and Jason stood on the sidewalk in the Ladies' Market in the Mong Kok district, browsing the gaily colored scarves on display at a stall. "It *looks* like silk to me," she said, stroking one that had swirls of amethyst fading into lavender blue, colors she loved. "But how can I really know?"

"Easy." Jason took the scarf from Alana and rubbed it between his fingers. "Real silk will feel warm when you rub it." He made a sound of dismissal. "This isn't real silk."

"It's beautiful, though," Alana said wistfully.

"Yes, but the price he's asking is unreasonable. You need to bargain." When Alana hesitated, because that wasn't something she felt comfortable doing, Jason turned to the smiling shopkeeper, saying something in rapid Cantonese she figured was an offer. And from the exaggeratedly shocked expression on the shopkeeper's face and a couple of words she recognized, it was a lowball offer.

"How much?" she whispered.

"Shhh. He probably knows more English than he lets on. Let me handle this."

Five minutes of heated bargaining later, Jason drew a banknote from his wallet to pay for the scarf. "Wait," Alana said, tugging at his arm. "I can't let you—"

He ignored her protest, pocketed his change, then dexterously looped the scarf around her neck and tied it in a festive bow. He smiled down at her. "It's less than the cost of our lunch," he said patiently. "You didn't say anything about that."

"That was different." She struggled to explain. "That was a…a date. Like all our other dates. This is a gift."

He brushed back a lock of her hair that had fallen forward and tucked it behind her ear. "The scarf was made for you. It matches your eyes, you know."

"Yes, but…"

"I paid a tenth of the asking price. Not so expensive."

"Yes, but…"

"It gives me pleasure to see you wearing my gift, Alana. Would you deny me that small enjoyment?"

When he put it that way, she could only accept with as much grace as she could muster. "Thank you. It's very sweet of you. I just don't want you to think I expect…that is, I can afford to buy…I mean—"

"I understand. And I'll answer the question you wouldn't ask. I can afford it." His smile was tender. "Did you think I wouldn't notice you picked the least expensive item on the menu at every restaurant I've taken you to these past two weeks?"

Now she was really flustered. "Oh, I…"

It was really quite endearing, Jason thought. But did she honestly not know he could well afford to buy her anything her heart desired? *But you haven't driven the Jag since you began taking her out*, his conscience reminded him. *You didn't want her to know...*

Alana came from money. Mei-li had told him all about it, including how Alana had ended up as Dirk's executive assistant. But there was money...and then there was *money*. Millions versus billions. Just as he didn't want Alana to confuse gratitude over her rescue with the attraction she felt toward him, he didn't want her dazzled by his immense wealth, either. Which was why he'd rented a middle-class car for his dates with her. He didn't mind her knowing he was comfortably well-off. He wasn't going to pretend to a life of poverty. But he wasn't going to flaunt anything, either; wasn't going to announce that he could buy and sell her father's company ten times over.

He took Alana's arm and they continued strolling down the crowded street. They paused every now and then to look at something that caught her eye, but she wouldn't let him buy her anything more even though he offered several times.

Jason was well aware he and Alana drew more than their fair share of interest from the people they passed. He was taller than most Han Chinese, for one thing. And he didn't look Chinese. But cosmopolitan Hong Kong was used to British, Australian and American residents and tourists, so both of those things would have been quickly dismissed... if he hadn't been with Alana.

Young, delicately beautiful, with long, dark hair, which she wore down, and those unusual eyes. Did she know her resemblance to her famous cousin Juliana—long acknowledged as one of the most beautiful women in the world—made both men and women give her second and third glances? Covetous looks from the men, envious looks from the women. She didn't seem to be aware, and that intrigued him. He'd been with beautiful women before—his wealth drew them like bees to honey. But other than his mother and sister, he'd never known a beautiful woman who didn't trade on her beauty. Who didn't play it up every chance she had.

Until Alana.

She was wearing a simple lavender blue sundress today, which had been unadorned except for a simple silver locket until he'd bought her the scarf. Sandals on her slender feet meant lots of bare leg showing, which would have drawn comments of the wolfish variety in Cantonese...if Jason hadn't been at her side.

He'd brought her here to the Ladies' Market deliberately, although he hadn't told her that. This wasn't the same street from which she'd been abducted three weeks ago, but it was similar. And in a strange way Jason had wanted to make sure she wasn't afraid to return to the scene of the crime, as it were. Hong Kong was his city. He'd spent years in England attending an elite boarding school like his father before him, then studying at Oxford. But Hong Kong was his home, and most likely always would be. He didn't want one bad experience to taint Alana's perception of the city.

He'd considered bringing her here on their first date two Saturdays ago, but had rejected that as a bad idea since her abduction had been too fresh in her mind at that point. So he'd taken her to another tourist destination instead, the Tian Tan Buddha on Lantau Island. He'd been so—he couldn't think of a better word than *enamored*—of her after their first date that he'd invited her to spend the next day with him, as well...an invitation she'd promptly accepted.

She doesn't play games, Jason had reminded himself then and several times since, loving Alana's open delight in the sights she'd visited with him, as well as being in his company.

He'd monopolized her free time the past two weeks, but he hadn't so much as kissed her for one critical reason— once he started, he didn't trust himself to stop. And he'd promised her she'd be as safe with him as she wanted to be. She was a temptation he didn't want to resist, but he'd given her his word…and he always kept his word. Until Alana gave him the green light, it was easier not to start than to stop partway.

But that meant he'd spent nearly every moment with her in a constant state of semiarousal. Painful, but it wouldn't kill him. At least that was what he'd told himself…repeatedly. Problem was, the ache only grew stronger and more urgent the more time he spent in her company. Jason knew the day was not too far off when something would have to give.

They finally reached the end of the long street, and Alana said abruptly, "I'm hungry."

Jason smiled. "Not surprising, given how little you ate at lunch."

"Yes, well…" She didn't want to revisit that discussion. "All this walking has given me an appetite." She pointed to the McDonald's across the street and halfway down the block. "I'd like one of those taro pies. Do you mind?"

Alana stepped back on the sidewalk to allow three young women chattering away in Cantonese to pass them, and Jason did the same. Then she continued, "I know fried anything isn't all that healthy for you, but I don't care. I love the little fried apple pies at McDonald's in the US, but the taro ones here in Hong Kong are to die for." She put her hand on her purse. "My treat, okay?"

He'd just opened his mouth—probably to argue with her—when it happened. A white van screeched to a halt in the middle of the cross street, and the side door slammed open. Alana watched in horror as two men wearing black masks jumped out and grabbed the smallest and prettiest of the three women who'd just passed them on the sidewalk. One of the men held a white cloth over the woman's nose and mouth. She struggled for a moment, then sagged limply against her attacker. The other masked man pushed the woman's two companions to the ground, then he joined the first, and together they began dragging the unconscious woman toward the white van double-parked in the road with its engine running.

For a split second déjà vu held Alana frozen, then she darted forward. "Stop!" She grabbed the arm of one man and kicked at the legs of the other. "Let her go!" she screamed. "Help!"

She saw the fist aimed at her head and flinched, but it never made contact. Jason was there parrying the attacker's arm, then delivering a flurry of punishing blows to the man's midsection. The second masked man dropped the woman he was holding and produced a switchblade knife. He lunged at Jason, who danced back, out of danger. Then the man grabbed his fellow attacker and bundled him into the van, which roared away even before the side door was closed.

"Oh, my God, Jason, are you okay?" Alana launched herself at him, running her hands over his body to make sure the knife hadn't made contact. Reassured when she found no blood, she swung around to the unconscious woman lying in the middle of the street, whose two friends had already recovered enough to be huddling around her. One woman had her cell phone out, she saw with relief, probably calling for the police and an ambulance.

Suddenly Jason was there. "Let's get her out of the street," he said, and such was his air of authority that when he barked a command in Cantonese, two bystánders moved in to help.

Now Alana could hear police sirens in the distance, and the adrenaline that had allowed her to fight to prevent another kidnapping drained away, leaving her shaking and cold. The memory of her own abduction swamped her... especially those moments of near-despair on the cot in that horrible apartment, and she sank to her knees, hugging herself for warmth. "Oh, God," she whispered to herself. "Oh, God."

Jason had his back to her, but when she glanced up she could see he was talking into his cell phone. Then he turned around, saw her and disconnected almost immediately. He was at her side in an instant.

"Alana?" She knew he meant, "Are you hurt?" by the way his face contracted with concern, the way his hands touched her so gently yet with implacable purpose.

"I'm fine," she managed, trying desperately to catch her breath.

He drew her to her feet and pressed her head against his chest, then his arms closed around her. "It's okay," he soothed as if he realized exactly what she needed to hear. "Just breathe. That's right. Just breathe."

His body heat transferred itself to her, dispelling the chill. But it was his embrace that truly gave her what she needed. *Safe*, her frantic mind reassured her, just as it had during her dramatic rescue three weeks earlier. Jason's rescue. *You're safe.*

Jason took charge at the police station, refusing to let Alana be questioned and insisting Detective Inspector Lam of the Organized Crime and Triad Bureau be called in. "Miss Richardson was abducted the same way three weeks ago," he explained. "He's already working the case."

Alana allowed herself to be seated in the tiny interrogation room, moving on autopilot. A second of near-panic was dispelled when Jason dragged his chair over to sit next to her. His strong arm drew her to his side. "You're okay," he reassured her in the same calm voice he'd used in the aftermath of the attack.

She struggled against the fog that seemed to envelop her. "I know. It's just…remembering…" When his arm tightened around her shoulders, she added disjointedly, "The scene today. That's exactly… In broad daylight. In the middle of a crowd. I couldn't believe it. Couldn't believe it was happening." She buried her face against his shoulder. "I was terrified," she confessed.

"But you fought them. Three weeks ago and today." Admiration colored his words.

"But—"

He stopped her before she could continue. "No buts. You fought, Alana. That woman today is safe because of your quick thinking."

She shook her head slightly, unwilling to leave the comforting shelter of Jason's embrace. "No. She's safe because of you. I couldn't stop them. I just—"

"Delayed them long enough for me to intervene." Something brushed against her forehead, and Alana realized it was Jason's lips. *His first kiss*, her brain recognized, and she hugged that knowledge to herself like the precious memory it would always be.

"She's going to be okay, isn't she?" she asked.

"I don't see why not. Chloroform doesn't leave any lasting effects—you know that. She was taken to hospital, but I doubt they'll keep her once she regains consciousness." His voice roughened. "I'm sorry."

She raised her head to look at him. "For what?"

"For putting you through that experience again." The

corner of his mouth twitched against strong emotions held firmly in check. "I brought you there on purpose today, but I would never have done that if I had any idea…" When she just stared at him in incomprehension, he explained, "I didn't want one bad experience to color your perspective of Hong Kong."

She blinked. "Why?"

He didn't respond at first. Then, his dark eyes full of meaning, said, "Because this city is my home."

He didn't say anything more. It took her a minute, but eventually her eyes widened in dawning comprehension.

She almost blurted it out, but stopped herself in time, instead saying, "I'm glad you brought me there…whatever the reason. Yes, it triggered all those bad memories, but I'm *so* glad we were able to save another woman from being abducted. Remembering my own similar experience is a small price to pay."

Their gazes locked and held, and another nonverbal message was exchanged…this one momentous. Then a brisk knock sounded on the interrogation room door, breaking the spell, and the door opened to reveal Detective Inspector Lam.

Alana straightened and made as if to pull away from Jason, but he refused to let her go. She knew from the deliberately impassive expression on Detective Inspector Lam's face that he'd put two and two together, but had no intention of raising the issue since it wasn't germane to the situation.

"Miss Richardson, Mr. Moore," he acknowledged smoothly. "Sorry to meet you again under these difficult circumstances."

Two hours later Alana and Jason were free to go. Detective Inspector Lam ordered a squad car to take them back to where Jason's rented car was parked. "Home?" he asked her when they were standing on the sidewalk.

She shook her head emphatically. "Not unless you want to. I'm not ready for this day with you to end."

Pride in her surged through him. The same pride he'd felt during the attack today. The same pride he'd experienced listening to her steady answers to Detective Inspector Lam's questions, despite the latent fear he'd known still held her in its sway.

Pride? he asked himself suddenly. *Why pride?*

The answer, when it came, jolted through him like an electric shock. Alana wasn't his, but he wanted her to be. And that blew him away. *You've only known her three weeks*, the rational side of his brain protested. *You haven't even slept with her, for God's sake!*

But none of that seemed to matter. It was as if he recognized in her the mate he'd been searching for these past ten years. A woman who cared as passionately as he did about right and wrong, about protecting the innocent, no matter the cost. A woman who would sacrifice everything, even her own life. Not just for someone she loved, but for a stranger.

Just as he would.

Jason's smartphone sounded as he and Alana were sitting down in McDonald's with their somewhat-delayed taro pies, and he answered it with, "Wei?" He listened for a moment, then replied in staccato Cantonese too quick for Alana to decipher. She'd been taking lessons since she'd first arrived less than two months ago, but so far she'd only really mastered the basics that any tourist needed to know, like "bathroom," "train station," and "Star Ferry"—the most common way to cross from Hong Kong Island to the mainland if you were on foot. When Jason disconnected she raised her eyebrows in a question.

"The license plate on the van was stolen," he admitted.

"Detective Inspector Lam told you?"

"No."

Just the one word, but Alana wasn't stupid. "RMM." She nodded to herself. "That's who you were talking to on your cell phone earlier today, right after it happened. I should have realized, but I…I wasn't quite myself at that moment."

Jason didn't confirm or deny, but there was something in his eyes that made her feel she'd earned his approval again.

She opened the end of the cardboard container holding her taro pie and stared at it for a moment. Then she raised her gaze to Jason's. "Would you tell me something?"

He hesitated. "If I can."

"How did you become involved with RMM?"

Chapter 6

Jason froze. He'd known if he spent time with Alana, that question, or one like it, was bound to come up eventually. But just because he'd fallen hard for her didn't mean he was ready to reveal *all* his secrets. He wasn't about to tell Alana that RMM was his creation. That the money bankrolling the organization came from him. "Why do you ask?"

She considered him for a moment. "Because it's important to you," she said quietly.

"What did Dirk and Mei-li tell you?"

"Not much. Just what the initials stand for, and that the phrase comes from a quotation. That RMM does whatever it has to do to rescue the innocent." She paused for a second. "Oh, yes, and that RMM played a key role in rescuing Dirk's twin daughters when they were kidnapped last year. Were you involved in that?"

Jason nodded. "Mei-li asked for my help and I gave it."

"Just like when you rescued me three weeks ago. Mei-li asked and you said yes."

He nodded again.

"Does RMM ever say no?"

Jason allowed himself a small smile. "The organization doesn't get involved in solving every crime, if that's what you're asking."

She shook her head. "That's not what I meant. I know RMM isn't the police." An expression of—could it be frustration?—crossed her face. "I'm just trying to understand *you*," she said in a low voice.

He thought about what he could tell her. "You see...or maybe you don't...but my family didn't live in Hong Kong year-round. My father—perhaps you've heard of him? Sir Joshua Moore? He's a producer and director, pretty highly regarded in the movie industry."

"I've heard the name. Didn't Dirk do a movie with him? Isn't that why he came to Hong Kong in the first place?"

Jason smiled. "Yes. Well, as I started to say, we didn't live in Hong Kong year-round. My father traveled to the locations of his movies for three or four months at a time, and my mother and Mei-li accompanied him."

"Not you?"

"Only until I turned thirteen. That's when my father sent me to school in England." He named a world-famous prep school.

"That's a prestigious boarding school, right?"

He nodded. "My father went there. He wanted that for me, too." Just as Jason had never said anything to his parents about his experience there, he wasn't about to tell Alana, either. "But I spent most summer and Christmas breaks here in Hong Kong, with my mother's family. And mine, too, whenever my father wasn't on location."

Alana's eyes softened with compassion. "That had to be a lonely life for a teenage boy, growing up away from your parents. Your sister."

It *had* been a lonely life in many ways, although not all that unusual in the upper echelons of British society. His paternal grandfather's world. The world his father had tried not to impose upon his only son, except in this one way. "It wasn't too bad. I had two close friends growing up, Sean and David." Both Sean and David had been fifth-generation Hong Kong natives. But whereas David was Chinese, Sean had still been considered a foreigner by most of Hong Kong's residents. Their roles had been reversed in England, where David had been the foreigner; most of the students at the school had never let him forget it, and not just in subtle ways.

And then there was Jason. Never quite fitting in anywhere, despite his parents' best efforts. The target of jealous and malicious cousins who'd also attended the same prep school. But he wasn't going to share that with Alana.

"Both of my friends were born here in Hong Kong. And like me, they were both sent to the same boarding school in England when they were old enough." His school years would have been appallingly desolate if he hadn't had his two best friends with him. "We were the Three Musketeers. At least, that's how we thought of ourselves."

"Ahhh, I see." Alana smiled. "Where are Sean and David now? Are you still close to them?"

He'd let himself forget for a moment as he lived in the past, but the present came crashing down on him. "David, yes. He works here in Hong Kong, as I do, and I see him fairly often. But Sean…"

When he didn't continue, she prompted, "Sean?"

"Sean…died. He's the reason I…became involved with RMM."

Alana reached across the table and gently touched Jason's hand. "What happened?"

He didn't reply at first, as if it was difficult for him to talk about. Finally he said, "Sean was a great guy. I'm not just saying that because he was my best friend. He was also going to be my brother-in-law. He and Mei-li…" He cleared his throat. "Sean had fallen in love with my sister when she was sixteen and he was barely twenty, but he was a true gentleman. He never said anything. Never tried to put the moves on her or anything like that. He waited until Mei-li was eighteen before he asked her out. They became engaged a year later."

A long silence followed. "And?"

"Three days before the wedding, Sean was kidnapped. I don't know how much you know about kidnapping here in Hong Kong, but in many ways it's almost like a business. First rule of thumb is, if the ransom is paid, the victim is released unharmed. Which is why most people don't report kidnappings to the police until after the fact. Until after the victim is returned safe and sound."

"Isn't that what Mei-li does for a living? Private investigator and ransom negotiator?" Then it clicked for her. "That's why," she said softly. "That's why she went into that line of work. Because of her fiancé."

"Yes." Jason's voice roughened. "Sean's parents made the payoff, but there was a horrible screwup, and Sean was killed."

Alana's hand tightened on his, and tears filled her eyes. "I'm so sorry," she whispered, blinking hard, her throat aching for his obvious pain. "That's why you joined RMM."

"It was more than twelve years ago," he said, his voice harsh. "But I've never forgotten."

"I understand." And she truly did understand. Tragedy had never touched her life, but she could see that for a man like Jason, there was only one response to something so life-altering. "So…you and RMM…you do whatever you can to prevent this from ever happening again."

"Not just kidnappings, though that's how RMM—" He broke off, and Alana wondered what he'd been going to say. "But yes, that's why we do what we do. Every man in RMM accepts that he could die, because much of what we do is extremely dangerous. Barring that, we could also go to jail, because some of the things we do are illegal. Not *immoral*, but illegal."

Alana digested this. Then her brows drew together in a frown. "Only men?"

Jason cleared his throat. "Well...in the covert operations arm, yes."

"Hmm."

"It's not what you're thinking."

"You have no idea what I'm thinking."

"I do. You're thinking women have been deliberately excluded, and that's not true. If a woman such as Mei-li, for instance, wanted to join our ranks...if she trained as we train...if she was as dedicated to the cause as we are...

"But you have to understand this is a *highly* secret organization. We don't recruit people to join except in very circumscribed circumstances. Remember, *anyone* who is added to the organization is a risk to every one of us. So the members of RMM only recruit their trusted friends. And a man's friends are—for the most part—men."

"Hmm."

Jason laughed softly at her skeptical response. "You're severe," he told her. "But I'll admit there's a modicum of truth to your criticism."

"Yes, I know."

"So there is a...*slight*...bias against women in RMM. It's not forbidden, and we *do* have some women in the organization, just not..."

"I see." She thought about arguing further but realized the point was moot. She didn't know any women who wanted to belong. And she certainly wasn't about to criticize RMM just for the sake of criticism. Jason and RMM had saved *her*. She owed them the benefit of the doubt.

With that decision made, she changed the subject. "You reported the license plate number of the van this afternoon to someone in RMM, and they told you the plate was stolen."

"Yes."

"So there's no way to track down those men today. What about when I was taken?"

"What do you mean?"

"Mei-li explained about the tracking device I was carrying, so I know how you found me. But the driver of the van who took me back to the DeWinters' estate said that rescuing me was only part of the job—that you needed to *take care of* the men who kidnapped me." She hesitated. "Since the police didn't mention finding any bodies…I figure my kidnappers were long gone by the time you went back there."

"Astute of you."

Her gaze fell to her hand, still lying atop Jason's. Then her eyes met his. "Would…would you have killed them?" Then she held her breath.

"Not like that. If they'd come in while I was rescuing you and I had no other choice, yes. But not in cold blood. We're willing to break the law, if necessary, but we're not judge, jury and executioner. Yes, we want to shut this triad gang down, but we want to bring them to justice. Not mete out a death sentence."

She let her breath out in a rush. "I'm so glad."

"Did you really think…?"

"I didn't *want* to think it, but…I'll admit the thought had crossed my mind. And it worried me."

Jason didn't reply at first. Then abruptly asked, "Do you know what RMM stands for?"

"Dirk mentioned that the night I was rescued. 'Right Makes Might.' RMM."

"Yes. But I think if you know the context, you'll understand better. It's three words from a quote by Abraham Lincoln, a man who could put complex thoughts into simple words and phrases that touch the heart. The full quotation is, 'Let us have faith that right makes might, and in that faith let us, to the end, dare to do our duty as we understand it.' Which means RMM tries to do what's *right*. Not what's *expedient*. Always."

Jason turned his hand so it was clasping hers, and something in his face told her this was incredibly important to him. Not just what RMM would and wouldn't do, but for her to believe it.

"I understand," she whispered, needing to reassure him about this. "I do. I really do."

She *did* understand, maybe even more than Jason wanted her to. Because she suddenly knew Jason wasn't just a *member* of RMM; he had to be one of its founders. Which explained so much about him, and at the same time was incredibly appealing to her.

All her life she'd been ashamed of being her parents' daughter. Had desperately attempted to overcome her upbringing. Not wanting people to judge her for something over which she had no control, she'd tried to do the same, tried to judge people by the content of their character, as one famous orator had movingly stated, and not by any other yardstick. She hadn't always been successful, but she'd *tried*.

Here was a man who hadn't merely tried; he'd succeeded. He didn't care what the world thought of him. He didn't care he was risking his life. He didn't care if he went to jail for his actions. He did what was *right*. Always. That knowledge instilled in her a desire to emulate him. To be as fearless and true as he was. To be worthy of him.

* * *

Jason waited until Alana walked inside after he dropped her off that night before hitting speed dial on his smartphone. It rang and rang, but eventually went to voice mail. He frowned, then left a message to call him and disconnected.

He made the thirteen-plus kilometer trip in less than twenty-five minutes, despite the Saturday evening traffic, then pulled his rental car into the garage beneath his condo building. He inserted the key card and rode the elevator to the top floor—all his own. He was just walking into his condo when his cell phone gave off the ringtone reserved for Cameron Mackenzie, the Australian-born second-in-command of RMM.

"Cam?"

"You called?" a strong Australian accent said in his ear.

"Yes, about today."

"White van. Stolen plates. Which you already know. We've got *heung yau* out on the street," Cam said, using the Cantonese phrase that meant "fragrant grease," the polite Hong Kong euphemism for bribes. "But so far, nothing. It's like these chaps crawled into a hole and pulled it in after them."

"Have you checked the hospitals? It's possible I did some damage to one of them."

"Already done. And no, if you cracked his ribs, he didn't visit any of the emergency rooms for treatment." Cam's voice turned dry. "Of course, there's more than one doctor in Hong Kong who'll treat someone on the QT…for the right price."

"Understood." Frustration made him ask, "What about the women this afternoon? Any of them think they were stalked?" It was a long shot, but…

"No dice. Seems to be completely random, like the

woman who was abducted two weeks ago. Like Miss Richardson."

Something was niggling at the back of his mind, but Jason couldn't put his finger on it. "They're getting bolder," he told his second-in-command. "All the other cases were women on their own, weren't they?"

"So it would seem."

"Any traction on the other end? How the women are being smuggled into Macau?"

"No." Jason cursed under his breath, and the other man offered, "They'll slip up eventually, Jason. They're not that good—just lucky so far. But they'll slip up, and that's how we'll catch them. Mark my words."

"Would you make book on that?"

A chuckle sounded in his ear. "Making book's illegal in Hong Kong, mate...unless you're the Hong Kong Jockey Club. Ask me next time we're in Macau." With that, the other man disconnected.

Jason strode toward his home office and logged on to his laptop. As CEO of Wing Wah, he was never really "off the clock." While he had a legion of senior and junior vice presidents to help him manage the far-flung enterprise, there were still some things that could only be decided by the man at the top.

And then there were his RMM-related activities. There were three other ongoing covert operations in addition to the triad gang they'd been after for months on this prostitution thing, and all three demanded his attention.

The highest priority operation of the three was attempting to put a curb on certain kinds of pornography. Jason wasn't idealistic enough to think it could ever be eradicated completely—as long as there was a market for it, there would be people willing to meet the demand. But if the rumors were true, too much involved young women who were coerced into it by threats, drugs or other means. If RMM could make a dent in the supply business, he'd be happy.

Not quite two hours later he shut down his laptop and turned off the desk lamp. Then sat there in the dark for a moment, thinking about Alana.

Alana. So fragile, and yet...the heart of a warrior. Quick-thinking, too. He'd noticed that about her from day one, but if he'd needed anything to reinforce that belief, her actions today were proof. He prided himself on his reaction time, but Alana had been there before him, fighting to free the woman being abducted before their eyes.

God, was there another woman like Alana in the whole world?

Thinking of her made him need to hear her voice, and before he could tell himself not to, he'd called her cell phone.

"Hello?"

Out of the corner of his eye he saw the digital clock glowing red in the darkness. He hadn't realized it was so late, probably too late to call. But he'd already done it and Alana had already answered, so...

"Alana, it's—"

"Jason." His name on her lips sliced right through his defenses, and for a moment all he could think of was having her say his name exactly that way...in his bed. His imagination accelerated right into overdrive and he hardened in a rush, envisioning everything he wanted to do to her. Everything he wanted her to do to him.

"Jason?"

The question made him ruthlessly rein in his thoughts... though not without regret. "I wanted to thank you for today," he said when he could trust his voice not to betray his desperate need. "And to apologize again for putting you in a dangerous situation."

"You already apologized more than once—you really don't have to apologize again. How could you possibly know what would happen?" The firm note remained in her voice when she added, "And if one of us should thank the other, I should be thanking you. Not just for a mostly wonderful day, but for rescuing me again."

"I didn't—"

"Of course you did. I'd have a black eye, or worse, if you hadn't stepped in to prevent his fist from making contact with my face."

"Oh, that."

He could tell from her voice she was smiling. "Yes, that. And then afterward, when I was having a panic attack..." Her voice softened. "Thank you for holding me. How did you know that's exactly what I needed at that moment?"

Instinct, he thought, and knew it for the truth. But he wasn't sure Alana was ready to hear that he would always know exactly what she needed...because he knew her. Instead he said, "It seemed like the thing to do."

"You're right. It was."

For a minute neither said anything more. Then Alana asked, "Was there something else you wanted to say?"

"Are you free tomorrow? I'd like to make up for today."

"You have nothing to make up for. But yes, I'm free. Tomorrow's Sunday, remember? And I'd love to spend the day with you again."

"Is there any place in particular you'd like to go?"

"Other than the places you've taken me to, I've hardly been anywhere so far. To the Peak, of course, since it's just up the road. But other than that...I'm open to suggestion."

"No boat trips around the island?"

"No. Just the Star Ferry to the mainland."

"What kind of sailor are you?"

"I don't get seasick, if that's what you're asking."

He laughed. "That's exactly what I'm asking. How about a tour around the island, then?"

"Sounds like fun."

"Dress in layers—the wind can make it feel cold even if the sun is warm. Ask Mei-li. She'll know. Oh, and you'll want to do something with your hair."

Sunday dawned bright and beautiful, and Alana was up with the sun. Jason had told her to leave everything to him. "Don't even eat breakfast," he'd warned her. "I'll take you to my favorite *dim sum* restaurant before we set sail."

Following Mei-li's advice, she braided her hair and coiled it up, then took the hat Mei-li loaned her and fitted it into place. She was already dressed in an outfit that vaguely resembled boating toggery, with multiple layers as both Jason and Mei-li had advised, topping it off with a light jacket in her favorite lavender blue. At the last minute she tied the lavender and amethyst scarf Jason had bought her yesterday around her throat. It was beautiful and she loved it already, but she also remembered the look in Jason's eyes when he'd said, *It gives me pleasure to see you wearing my gift, Alana. Would you deny me that small enjoyment?*

The doorbell rang just as she was double-checking the contents of her purse. Alana rushed to answer the door, but Mei-li was there before her. Hand on the doorknob, Jason's sister said, "Just one thing before you go." She hesitated for a second, then continued on a rush, "You've been pretty much living in Jason's pocket for the past two weeks, and I'm glad about it. I am. Please don't misunderstand—there's nothing I want more for Jason than for him to find the kind of happiness I've found with Dirk, and I think you could be the one, Alana. I truly do. But Jason has been hurt more than you know. More than he'll ever tell you. So whatever you do, please don't break his heart."

Chapter 7

"You're awfully quiet over there." Jason cast a glance in Alana's direction before turning his attention back to Mount Austin Road.

"I…" She wasn't about to tell him what Mei-li had said just before she walked out the door this morning. *I'm not a femme fatale*, she protested in her mind. *I don't go looking to break hearts.*

Even the man whose proposal she'd turned down three years ago, the man whom she'd known genuinely cared for her—she hadn't broken his heart. She'd let him down gently and had never told anyone about it, not even Juliana. Then she'd introduced him to a close friend, one whom she'd known was perfect for him, and voila! The happy couple had become engaged a year later. He'd even thanked her afterward.

So what had Mei-li meant? *Jason has been hurt more than you know. More than he'll ever tell you…*

Looking at Jason now, so supremely self-confident, you'd never think he'd been emotionally wounded. And yet…what had he replied yesterday when she'd said it had to have been a lonely life for the boy he'd been?

It wasn't too bad. I had two close friends, Sean and David.

And all at once she realized exactly what Mei-li had been driving at. The British were notorious for understatement, which meant Jason would never tell her outright just how tough his childhood had been, or how much he'd depended on his friends…one of whom had died in heartbreaking fashion when Jason was only twenty-three. But he'd given her clues. Clues he probably didn't realize he'd dropped.

"Alana?"

"Oh, sorry." She schooled her features so her thoughts weren't reflected on her face. "I was…thinking of something."

"You're not reliving yesterday, are you? Or three weeks ago?"

"No. Oh, no. I'm okay. Really. I'm not as fragile as I look, honest." She gave a little laugh. "In fact, my cousin Juliana says I'm one tough cookie."

Jason slowed for a curve and shifted gears. "Really."

The disbelieving note in his voice made her say, "Really. She says it's because I don't crumble at the first sign of trouble."

He darted a look at her. "That's true. You don't."

"I might fall apart *afterward*, but—"

He removed his left hand from the gearshift and placed it over her right one momentarily. "I wouldn't call it falling apart. It's a perfectly normal physical reaction. Adrenaline allows the body to accomplish superhuman feats, but once the adrenaline rush wears away…"

"Has it ever happened to you?"

His answer was a long time coming. "Once."

"Would you…would you tell me about it?" She waited, almost holding her breath, and was eventually rewarded.

"It was a long time ago, shortly after I…joined RMM." *Founded RMM*, she translated in her mind. "Yes?"

"I killed a man."

A tiny gasp almost escaped, but she managed to hold it in. Jason had told her yesterday he didn't kill in cold blood, so despite the automatic reaction she couldn't help, she knew immediately that whatever had happened, whatever he'd done, had been justified.

"Tell me. Please."

He breathed deeply, then let it out long and slow. "It was a kidnapping. One of Mei-li's earlier cases. The seven-months-pregnant wife of a supposedly wealthy industrialist here in Hong Kong." Some latent emotion was reflected in his suddenly clenched jaw.

"And?"

"Mei-li came to me, begged me to lend her—" He broke off, then continued as if he'd never stopped. "She begged me for help, because the kidnappers were threatening to send the man his unborn baby in pieces if he didn't pay."

This time she couldn't suppress her gasp, and Jason glanced at her for a second, then turned his attention back to the road. "The man would have paid anything they demanded," he said, his voice hardening. "Problem was, he couldn't. He didn't have the money. He'd overextended and couldn't even come up with half of what the kidnappers were demanding. Mei-li had negotiated them down as far as she could, but then the kidnappers dug in their heels."

"So she came to you."

He nodded. "She knew about RMM, of course. I told her we'd help her, that RMM would come up with the balance of the ransom…if we could stake out the ransom drop, track the kidnappers and try to rescue the victim."

"I thought you said kidnapping in Hong Kong is almost like a business, and if the ransom is paid, the victim is released unhurt."

He slanted another look her way. "You remember everything, don't you?" Admiration was in his voice, and something else. But she couldn't figure out what that was.

"I don't remember every little thing, but the important things, yes. You were telling me about Sean, so naturally…"

"You're right. That *is* the case where professional kidnappers are concerned. But I had a feeling these weren't professional kidnappers, same as with Sean. And I was right."

"How so?"

"For one thing, only a little digging on their part would have revealed their target didn't have the kind of ransom money they were demanding. Ten minutes on the internet told me that much. If they were professionals, they'd have switched targets."

Jason pulled into a public car park, parked neatly and turned off the engine. Then he faced Alana. "For another thing," he said quietly, "the ransom drop they'd chosen. Only amateurs would have picked that site. Which told me it was very possible they weren't going to follow the rules."

"And they didn't," she hazarded a guess.

He smiled, but it didn't reach his eyes. "They didn't. They retrieved the money and were just about to slaughter their victim when RMM broke in."

"That's when you killed a man," she said softly, nodding to herself. She could envision it as if she'd been there. One or more of the kidnappers moving toward the woman with a knife…or a gun… A split-second decision by Jason that meant life for one, death for the other. "His life…or hers and her unborn child's. You had no choice."

"Yes."

"But then…"

"Right. But then." He breathed deeply again as if try-ing to dispel the tension talking about this engendered. "I'd never killed a man before. I'd known going in I might have to. I thought I could deal with it, no problem. And I *did* deal with it, long enough to take the other kidnappers into custody and turn them over to the police. To take the woman to hospital to make sure she and her unborn baby were okay. To call her husband to come be with his wife. Then I went back to my condo and…fell apart."

Mei-li had found him there. Shaking. Trying to process a reality that included watching a man's life fade away, his eyes locked open. Unblinking. Unseeing. And knowing he was responsible.

You did what you had to do, his sister had fiercely re-minded him. *You saved two innocent lives, one a baby not yet born.*

It hadn't really helped. Not then. Not until he'd visited the maternity ward two months later and held the kidnap-ping victim's healthy baby boy in his arms had he finally come to terms with it. *You're here, safe*, he'd whispered against the downy cheek. *The price I paid was worth it.*

But that wasn't something he would tell anyone. Ever.

"Jason?" Alana touched his arm. "Where are you? It's like you're a million miles away."

"Sorry." He forced his mind back to the present. "Where was I?"

"You were saying you fell apart after the killing."

"I eventually got over it, but yes, I'd say my first reaction counts as falling apart. Come on," he said, unbuckling his seat belt and changing the subject. "You haven't had *dim sum* until you've had it here."

* * *

A little while later Jason helped Alana into his Princess V62-S sport yacht, anchored at the far end of his private dock in Victoria Harbour near Causeway Bay. The dock housed three small speedboats, a launch, and *Night Wind*, a high-speed interceptor boat used by RMM, in addition to the yacht, aptly named *The Princess*. Not that he'd told her the yacht was his. But unlike switching his Jag for a less prestigious automobile, he couldn't see taking Alana on a cruise around Hong Kong Island in anything less worthy of her than *The Princess*. *A* Princess *for a princess*, he thought with an inner smile. Other than his mother and his sister, he'd never brought a woman on board his yacht before…as if he'd been waiting for Alana.

"When you said cruise, I thought you meant…you know…a cruise boat. With other passengers." Alana removed her hat and wandered into the main level salon as she spoke and made a complete rotation as if trying to take everything in. Then she said, "This is a *yacht*, Jason. Did you rent it just for me?"

Deception about just how rich he was was one thing, but he didn't want to out-and-out lie to her if he could help it. So he said, "What if I did? Don't you think you're worth it?"

"But…"

He moved until he was standing right in front of her. Until he could feel the rise and fall of slight breasts that for some reason turned him on big time, just as they had that first night and every moment since. "I want to make it up to you for putting you through yesterday. Can you understand that?"

"Oh, Jason, I already told you, you don't have to apologize or do anything to make it up to me. It wasn't your fault. It just happened."

The earnest expression in her amethyst eyes ringed by

those extravagantly long natural lashes did something to him. At first he couldn't figure out why, but then he realized her eyes were the windows into her soul. A soul untainted by those things that had scarred his own. And he knew beyond a shadow of a doubt that he needed Alana in some indefinable way. That with her he could lay down the burdens he'd carried so long, and rest. Truly rest. The slights and insults he'd suffered in his youth would lose their importance. Light would be shed on the dark corners of his mind. And his sins would be forgiven...if Alana believed in him.

"Who are you?" he whispered, brushing the backs of two fingers against her cheek. "How is it possible you've bewitched me with just a look?"

She gazed up at him. Solemn. Serious. "I haven't done anything."

"Oh, but you have. And I'll never be the same again."

Then he kissed her. Alana had been kissed before, by men who'd thought they were experts and by a man who'd truly cared about her. But she'd never been kissed by a man who embraced her as if she were his salvation, and her whole body went up in flames.

His arms were impossibly tight around her, but not tight enough. She wanted to crawl inside his skin to get closer. Wanted the fire he'd ignited to devour her. Driven by a need she'd never experienced before, she rocked against his hardness until he moaned her name and lifted her up so she could straddle him, so she could cradle that hardness where she needed it most.

In some distant recess of her brain she heard a whimper, then realized it was coming from her. She tore her lips from his. "Please, Jason," she pleaded, knowing what she was asking. "Please."

But it was as if her words had broken the spell enthralling him, because the next moment he'd lowered her to the deck. Unwrapped his arms from her aching body. And stepped back. Away from her.

All Alana could think of was how much being released hurt, really *hurt*, both physically and mentally. All she could say was his name in a needy voice she scarcely recognized. "Jason?"

His eyes squeezed shut as if he couldn't look at her and deny them both, and his lips thinned as if he were holding on by a thread. Then his eyes opened again, those dark, dark, mesmerizing eyes. "Don't look at me that way," he grated. "Do you know what we almost did?"

She swallowed hard, her throat working so she could get the words out. "I know."

"I didn't bring you here to seduce you, damn it!"

"It wouldn't have been a seduction." The words were out before she could consider the wisdom of them. But once they were uttered, she didn't care anymore. An eerie calm settled over her. "I wanted you, Jason. I wanted you that first night. I wanted you yesterday. I want you today. Here. Now. Is it wrong to admit it? I don't think so. I'm not married. Engaged. Pledged to anyone in any way. Are you?"

Shock flashed across his face, then he frowned. "Do you think I would have touched you if I was?"

She shook her head slowly. "So explain to me why you stopped, when I…I didn't ask you to stop."

"Because…"

"Because?"

"Because I didn't plan for this, understand?"

Puzzled, she replied, "No, I don't understand."

"No condoms. Is that plain enough? Unless you're on some kind of contraception."

Alana could *feel* the flush that crawled up her neck to

her cheeks. "Oh. No. No, I'm not." Having gone this far, she figured she might as well make a clean breast of it. She steeled herself, took a deep breath and admitted, "I'm not on contraception because I'm not...sexually active."

"You're not—" He shook his head as if to clear it. "Say that again."

"I know I told you I don't sleep with a man on the first date, but that was a...a slight understatement."

He opened his mouth as if to say something, then closed it, words unsaid. He swung around for a moment, away from her, the muscles of his back rigid. Then he faced her again. "You're a virgin." She nodded slowly. "You're a virgin," he repeated as if stunned, "but you wanted... want me."

She licked her lips and nodded again.

He muttered something under his breath. She figured the words were a curse, but she didn't catch it and she didn't ask him to repeat it. Then his face hardened. "That confession proves my point. I had no business touching you."

She took a step toward him and raised her chin. "So what you're saying is, if I'd slept around before I came to Hong Kong, then it would be okay to touch me?"

"I didn't say that!"

She took another small step in his direction. "Sounded like it to me."

"You're missing the point."

Another step forward. "Explain the point to me." Oh-so-politely. Now she was close enough to reach up and cradle his cheek with her hand. "Two weeks ago you said I was as safe with you as I wanted to be," she breathed. "But I don't want to be safe, Jason. Not from you. Please."

He groaned, then pulled her into his arms and kissed her again. And it was as good as the first time, or maybe a tad better. Because now she knew...and he knew...how explosive they were together. Now they both knew breathing was overrated.

Eons later Alana drew her lips from Jason's and whispered, "Tell me there's a stateroom on this yacht."

His voice was husky when he repeated, "There's a stateroom on this yacht."

"Tell me you're going to show me the stateroom."

"Alana…" If she didn't know better, she would have sworn he growled her name. "No condoms, remember?"

She smiled up at him with an invitation as old as Eve, one she'd never extended before. But she knew what she was doing. "My money's on you, Jason. I'm sure you'll think of something."

The stateroom was luxurious in the extreme, but Alana barely had a moment to look around before Jason's arms enfolded her. But he didn't kiss her. Instead he held her tight and gazed down at her, myriad emotions crossing his face. "Are you sure this is what you want?"

"Oh, Jason…" She was touched, but she didn't want a gentleman. She wanted the man who'd kissed her upstairs as if she were his salvation. She wanted the blazing inferno. The ferocious need. The essential man. She wanted…Jason.

But that wasn't going to happen this time. Not this first time between them. If she wasn't a virgin…maybe. If they had a condom…maybe. But she *was* a virgin and they *didn't* have a condom. Which meant they would have to be creative. Which meant there was no way Jason would let her unleash the animal in him again. This time.

Afterward Alana could never remember removing her clothes…his clothes. But she would never forget the expression on his face when one by one she removed the pins holding up her hair, uncoiled the braid, then slowly unplaited the strands.

"Let me," he said, his voice deep and low as he ran his fingers through her hair to finish the job. Then he gently pulled the silky mass forward, until it lay like a dark cloud on her shoulders. "I've dreamed of doing this. Of seeing you this way."

The boat swayed with the undulation of the water in the harbor as Jason drew her down onto the king-size bed with him. He was hard everywhere she touched…and she touched him everywhere. Smooth skin over muscle and sinew were a tactile sensation her fingers couldn't get enough of.

"What's this?" she asked, lifting the heavy gold medallion he wore on a gold rope chain around his neck. She couldn't quite make out all the details in the relatively dim light of the below-deck stateroom, but it was intricately carved with what she could tell was a dragon on one side and some kind of stylized, ornate bird on the other. "Is that a phoenix?"

He nodded. "A perfect pairing in Chinese mythology."

She didn't know how she knew, but the knowledge settled in without conscious thought. "RMM. This is the symbol of RMM, isn't it?"

A faint smile tugged at the corners of his mouth. "Brilliant as well as beautiful. A potent combination."

She reverently pressed her lips to the medallion, then lowered it back to his chest, and her hands continued their thorough investigation. Soon she was sighing a little, because she loved touching him and it turned her on. She wasn't shy about letting him know it, either, worshipping his body with her hands. Her lips. Brushing her long tresses over various body parts and eagerly watching for his reaction.

Just because she'd never slept with a man didn't mean she was a wide-eyed innocent. She knew enough. And even if she hadn't, Jason's quickened breathing, the harsh sounds of encouragement he made, betrayed him. All she had to do was be sensitive to the cues he gave her.

But Alana soon learned making love was a two-way street…and Jason loved to drive. He stopped her from taking him to the brink, then took the wheel. Her skin quickly became hypersensitized when large male hands stroked her curves, when firm lips suckled her slight breasts. But when his lips nibbled their way down, inch by excruciating inch, she caught her breath at the sensations coursing through her body.

Then his mouth closed over her. She arched upward like a bow and choked on his name. He gave her no mercy, driving her up and up, his tongue doing wicked things she'd only read about and dreamed of. The ache built with excruciating slowness, until the world condensed into one word. "Please. *Please.*"

She couldn't breathe. Couldn't even say his name. There had to be something wrong, because her body was coiling tighter and tighter like an overwound watch spring. And still Jason gave her no respite, no—

The sudden release of tension rocketed through her, and she sobbed. Just sobbed, her fingernails digging into Jason's shoulders all unaware. She never even noticed him moving up until he was holding her trembling body tight against his, bringing her down gently from the pinnacle.

Whispered words broke the silence, and she tried to understand; she really did. But her brain couldn't focus because the blood was pounding in her ears like the roar of the ocean, and all she could think of in that moment was there couldn't possibly be more to making love than she'd just experienced. Not. Possible.

When her heartbeat finally slowed, the words Jason was whispering still didn't make sense. They were just utterances, including something that sounded like *ngoh oi lei*, which he said more than once. Then she realized the words didn't make sense for a very good, nonorgasmic reason— they weren't in English.

Cantonese, she realized. *He's talking in Cantonese*. The idea sent a little thrill through her, because even though he looked and sounded like the upper-class British gentleman he was, she'd already deduced Cantonese was the language of his heart. She touched his cheek. "What did you just say?"

His eyes held secrets, but his smile was very male...and just a touch smug. "You don't want to know."

"I do. I really, really do."

He laughed softly. "I said you're exquisite when you come. And I want to watch you come again. And again."

Chapter 8

Warmth flooded Alana's body, and she couldn't think of a single thing to say except, "Oh."

"I told you, you didn't want to know."

There was absolutely no reply she could make to this. But then she remembered Jason had stopped her from taking him all the way earlier, and when her hands stroked over his body and down, she quickly ascertained he was primed and ready.

She was a little nervous about what she intended to do, because not only had she never done it before, she'd never imagined she would want to. It had ranked in her mind as one of those things men loved for some crazy reason and women barely tolerated because they wanted to please their men. But turnabout was fair play. And besides…she was curious.

So she did to him exactly what he'd done to her. Her lips nibbled their way down, her intent obvious. His hands caught her shoulders before she reached her final destination, holding her back. "You don't have to, Alana."

She raised her head and smiled slowly. "I know. But I want to." And when she said it, she knew it was the truth.

When her mouth closed over him he almost arched off the bed. And his guttural cry filled her with a sense of power. It didn't take her as long as it had taken him. Partly because he was already so aroused, and partly because Alana soon learned she loved doing this for Jason.

At first his hands twisted in the sheets as he writhed on the bed beneath her ministrations. Then, as if he just couldn't help it, one hand moved to hold her head in place. "Yes. Like that," he groaned. "Oh, Alana, like that. *Please.*" As if he feared she might stop. But she wasn't about to stop, not until she'd brought him the same pleasure he'd brought her.

When it was all over, she realized she'd been wrong. What she and Jason had done wasn't dirty. And it wasn't something she merely tolerated because he enjoyed it and she wanted to please him more than anything. If she was honest with herself, she'd admit she'd enjoyed it, too. Not just the feeling of power in a situation where she'd never expected it. But touching, tasting, hearing him—that had actually turned her on. And now she needed…

He knows, she thought as his fingers slid down, parting her gently, seeking and finding the source of her need. Then all thought fled and she could only feel…and gasp his name.

The rocking of the yacht in the wake of some passing boat woke Jason, and he immediately knew where he was. And with whom. Alana was draped across his chest like his personal blanket, although Hong Kong's semitropical climate made a blanket unnecessary at this time of year.

He lay there, unmoving. Enjoying the experience. Watching…*feeling* the slight rise and fall of Alana's chest as she breathed. Taking in the totally satisfied expression on her face.

And he *had* satisfied her both times, no question of that. He'd dreamed of her and him since the night they'd met, but that hadn't even begun to touch the reality that was Alana in his bed. He'd been stunned when she'd told him she'd never been with a man before—she was so beautiful, so desirable, it couldn't be anything other than her choice. But it was his own reaction that had blown him away. Some archaic, primitive part of him had savagely rejoiced that out of all the men in the world, she'd chosen him. *Him.*

And if that wasn't enough, she'd gone on to stagger him by how giving she was. Not just in what she was willing to do for him, but in letting him touch her the way he had. A woman who was still a virgin at twenty-six had to have a deep-seated reticence about sex. But she hadn't shown him any signs of it. It was as if Alana had some kind of on-off switch that had been firmly shut off…until she met him. And wasn't *that* an aphrodisiac?

His body hardened at the thought. She'd wanted him from the moment they'd met—she'd admitted as much earlier. Just as he'd wanted her. And now, whether Alana knew it or not, she belonged to him the way he belonged to her. Forever.

Then he let his memories wander back again. He hadn't been completely honest with her earlier, because what he'd whispered in her ear as he'd brought her down from her first orgasm with him hadn't *just* been the words he'd told her. He'd laid bare his heart…in Cantonese. Because he wasn't quite ready to tell her the truth. Because he wasn't sure she was ready to hear that he loved her…and always would.

The Eight Tigers had once again convened to discuss a failure. A failure that could have far-reaching consequences, because impossible as it seemed, the woman who'd been rescued from the Eight Tigers' clutches by RMM three weeks earlier had been instrumental in foiling their most recent abduction attempt.

Really, the High Tiger thought. *Two failures in little more than three weeks. Perhaps it's time to consider a change in leadership of that enterprise.* He listened impassively to the excuses that were forthcoming, then cut the man off.

"Yes, yes, the men were masked both times, as you say. And the license plates were stolen, of course, so it's highly unlikely the van can be traced. But are you aware the Hong Kong Police have the DNA of one of the men from the first abduction? And possibly from yesterday's attempted abduction, as well?"

Shocked silence met his words. Then, "How do you know this?"

The High Tiger stared impassively at the other man. Everyone at the table knew he had sources within the police department…and outside it. "I know," he averred. "Fortunately for this organization—and you—these two men's DNA is not in any database. Yet. So there has been no match. Yet."

The other man's eyes fell before his, but he continued mumbling excuses, and the High Tiger nodded internally. *Yes, a change in leadership is definitely on the horizon. I will need to meet one-on-one with the other six to discuss this possibility.*

Alana woke with the most wondrous sense of well-being she'd ever known. Not only was her body relaxed and boneless, but her mind had been scrubbed of every thought except one—Jason. How he'd kissed her. Touched her. The words he'd whispered to her in the language of his heart, which *had* to mean something important; she was sure of it.

"Good afternoon, *lang loi*." Jason's voice rumbled in his chest beneath her ear. "I'm glad you're finally awake."

She sighed with happiness, stretched sinuously for a moment, then settled back in Jason's arms. "What does that mean, *lang loi*?"

He laughed softly. "You want me to reveal all my secrets?"

"When they relate to me, yes. I've been taking Cantonese lessons, but I only know the basics so far." She recited the few words she'd memorized. "Speaking of which, does this boat have a bathroom?"

He laughed again and sat up, bringing her with him. "Yacht, not boat. And yes, of course there's a bathroom. More than one, actually. Only on board it's called the head."

When he stood, still holding her in his arms, she protested. "What are you—"

He deposited her at the bathroom door, saying, "I'll be in the galley. It's long past lunchtime, and I don't know about you, but I'm famished." He raised and lowered his eyebrows suggestively. "I've worked up an appetite."

Alana wasted a couple of minutes in the master bathroom—*the head*, she corrected herself with a little smile—marveling at the compact luxuriousness and the pristine condition. Like the stateroom, the bathroom looked to be meticulously maintained, unusual for a rental.

Her business finished, she located her clothes where she'd discarded them, dressed quickly in the bare minimum but didn't bother to put on her shoes, then wandered out in search of Jason. She found him where he'd said he would be, in the galley—*the kitchen*, she translated. Like her, he was barefoot but dressed, and she experienced a vague regret. It was a crime to cover a body like his with something as unnecessary as clothes.

A mouthwatering aroma was already floating in the air, and she teased, "A sex god and you cook, too? How come no woman has snapped you up yet?"

Jason turned at her words, a wicked smile on his face. "Sex god?"

"You must know you are." The expression in his eyes caused a hitch in her breathing, but she didn't look away. Neither did he, until the wok in which he was stir-frying something demanded his attention.

"My culinary skills are limited, I'm afraid," he tossed over his shoulder. "But anyone can stir-fry." Then he frowned and shot her another glance. "You're not allergic to shrimp, are you? I never thought to—"

"Oh, no. I love shrimp. And I can eat stir-fry anytime."

"Good." He picked up a bottle and shook some of the contents into the wok. "Do you know the secret to good stir-fry? Besides a superheated wok?"

"No. What is it?"

"Oyster sauce." He handed her the red-labeled bottle, and she dutifully looked at it. "Most people think soy sauce when they think of Chinese food, but oyster sauce is the real secret ingredient."

They ate at the dinette's corner table, and Alana was surprised to see a television on the wall facing her. "Wow, this yacht has just about everything you could imagine," she enthused. She leaned over and kissed Jason's cheek. "Thank you so much for going first class with this rental. My father has a cabin cruiser he takes out on Chesapeake Bay in addition to his sailboat, but nothing like this. It's amazing."

His quick smile didn't quite reach his eyes, and Alana wondered about it. Then she thought she knew the answer.

He doesn't like it when I thank him too much. As if I'm impressed by things, *when that's not the case at all.*

She took a bite of her delicious stir-fried shrimp that Jason had generously spooned over white rice. Chewed. Then swallowed. "I'm sorry."

"For what?"

Alana tried to put her inchoate thoughts into words. "It's…please don't get me wrong. I love this boat—"

"Yacht."

"Right, yacht. I love it. But…"

"But what?"

She segued slightly, hoping she wouldn't confuse him. "I don't know what Mei-li has told you about my background."

"A little."

She took a deep breath. "My parents have money. You probably know that. And I attended exclusive private schools from kindergarten through twelfth grade, schools that…that cater to the children of the wealthy." He didn't respond, so she forged ahead. "But that's not *me*. I mean… money, and…and…social status aren't anywhere near as important to me as they are to my parents." He still didn't say anything, so she added softly, "If those things were all I cared about, would I be here in Hong Kong, working as Dirk's executive assistant? That's a glorified title, but in some ways I'm really not much more than a secretary."

"Your point being?"

"Do you want to know the real reason why I'm still a virgin…and why I don't want to be a virgin anymore?"

His brows drew together into a frown as if he didn't get why she'd changed the subject again, but he said, "Why?"

"Because I was waiting for a man as idealistic as I was, and I wasn't about to settle for less."

He shook his head. "I'm not—"

"You are," she insisted. She placed her right hand over

her heart. "I know it here." She blinked back the unexpected tears that sprang to her eyes as she thought of all the things he'd done that proved it…and those were only the ones she knew about. How many of his other actions supported her claim? "So I wanted you to know…I don't need *things* from you, Jason." She drew another deep breath for courage. "I just need…you."

Jason's right hand tightened involuntarily on his chopsticks, and he had to force himself to loosen his grip and place them on the table. Alana couldn't possibly know… but somehow she did. Somehow she knew exactly what he needed to hear from her. What he needed to believe.

She had no idea how much his vast wealth had isolated him—more with every passing year—because she had no idea that fortune even existed. And he doubted she knew what his mother had sacrificed to marry his father. Which meant she also couldn't know he'd been searching for ten years for a woman who would count the rest of the world well lost if she had him.

But that was exactly what she seemed to be saying.

He closed his eyes momentarily, unable to take it all in. When he opened them again Alana was still there. That same yearning expression on her face that begged him to believe her. The one that matched the yearning in his heart.

He desperately wanted to believe, but at the same time he was afraid. He'd faced death without a qualm time and again, but when it came to his closely guarded heart he was still unsure. *Not* unsure he loved her; he'd slipped right over the edge this morning when she'd turned those innocent eyes on him and bewitched his heart and soul. But he *was* afraid because he needed her so much. Because she was almost *too* important.

He cupped her cheek with a hand that wasn't quite

steady, and her hand came up to cover his as she turned her face so her lips could brush his palm. Then she placed a kiss on his thumb, his forefinger and the other fingers in turn. Holding his gaze as she did so, before closing her eyes and cradling his hand against her cheek again.

He groaned and crushed his mouth on hers, pulling her into as fervent an embrace as the dinette table allowed. When he finally let her go his heart was pumping in erratic fashion, and her breathing was as shaky as his.

"You can't know, *lang loi*." His voice was husky and he was forced to clear his throat before he could continue. "You can't possibly know what that means to me." He pressed a finger against her lips when she started to disagree and added, "Someday I'll tell you…but not today." Someday, when he was sure of her love. Someday, when those last few doubts had been dispelled. "But when I do, you'll understand."

"I think I understand now." He shook his head. "Well, if you don't think I do and won't tell me why, will you at least tell me what *lang loi* means?"

He drew her against his shoulder. "That slipped out. I didn't mean to—"

"But you called me that once before," she argued. "When I woke up in your arms."

"It's an endearment." He grinned suddenly. "And when I call you that, you should respond with *lang jai*."

"Uh-uh," she told him. "I'm not using a phrase I don't understand."

"Literally it means *pretty boy*. But figuratively…it's an endearment…used between lovers."

"Then *lang loi* must mean…*pretty girl*?"

His arm tightened around her shoulders. "Literally… yes."

"So you think I'm pretty?"

He shook his head gently. "No. I think you're beautiful. But I can't be the first man to have told you that."

Serious all at once, she said, "No, you're not. But you're the first man I wanted to be beautiful *for.*" Then she laughed under her breath. "And if you'd known me in my early teens, you would never have believed I'd end up beautiful. I was the stereotypical plain girl in class until I hit a very late puberty, just like my cousin Juliana."

"That would be the Queen of Zakhar? The most beautiful woman in the world, according to the tabloids?"

"Mmm-hmm. She's six years older, and she's why I didn't despair when I was twelve. She was a late bloomer, and I was praying the same would hold true for me."

"It did." A lovely rose color tinted Alana's cheeks, and it fascinated him. But then, just about everything Alana did, said or *was* fascinated him.

She glanced down at her hands, then back up at him. "Juliana was a role model for me in other ways, too," she confided with a hint of shyness.

"How so?"

"She never…settled. Oh, I know rumors swirled around her when she was in Hollywood," she added quickly when he started to disagree. "But they weren't true. She'd fallen in love as a teenager with the man she eventually married. And even though there was a terrible misunderstanding that separated them for a time, she stayed true to him for the eleven years they were apart."

She twined her fingers together and stared at them for a moment, then looked up again. "I was twenty-three when she and her husband reunited nearly three years ago. I was *this* close," she said, holding her thumb and forefinger together as if to show him what she meant, "to accepting a proposal of marriage from a man I respected and admired."

The possessiveness that spiked through him came out

of nowhere, but he steeled himself to listen to Alana's confidences and not respond the way he wanted to…the way that just might frighten her into silence.

The need to touch was overwhelming, however, so he brushed a strand of hair away from her face and tucked it behind her ear as uncertainty reared its ugly head again. And he couldn't help wondering just how much in love Alana had been with this other man, until a sudden thought occurred to him.

"You almost married him…but you never slept with him." She shook her head solemnly. And though he believed her, there was *something* in her eyes that made him ask, "Why are you telling me this, *lang loi*?"

"Because all my life I've been holding out for a hero, even though I didn't know it. And I finally found him… *lang jai*."

The unalloyed truth in Alana's eyes as she bared her heart shredded his soul, because she'd been nothing but honest with him and he'd deceived her from day one. He'd thought himself justified in his deception, but it bothered him now. He just wasn't quite ready to end it. Not yet.

Chapter 9

Alana was hoping Jason would take her to bed again when he led her back to the stateroom, but he didn't. Instead of taking *off* the clothes she'd donned, he dressed her in the layers he'd warned her to wear out on the water. Piece by piece.

Being dressed by Jason was almost as erotic as being *undressed* by him. He smiled a knowing smile when she shivered and her nipples tightened until they were obvious even beneath her sweater, but he didn't say anything. Then he sat her down on the edge of the unmade bed, knelt and silently slipped her socks on her feet, followed by the espadrilles Mei-li had advised her to wear.

"There," he said as he rose and tugged his gray-green sweater over his head. "You're all set for the island tour I promised you."

"What about my hair? Mei-li said—"

"Damn! I forgot about that. Here, let me." He produced a

hairbrush from a drawer in the nightstand, but Alana fore-stalled him, pulling a small brush out of her purse. "I don't want to use someone else's hairbrush. Use mine."

Jason brushed her hair until it crackled, then swiftly divided it into strands and braided it. "Leave it down," he told her. "Please." The *please* decided her, and she left her hair down for him. Then, "Come on," he said, taking her hand. "Your hat's upstairs in the salon. You won't need it until later, but it's good you have one." His other hand came up to caress her cheek with a touch as delicate as a butter-fly's wing. "This complexion must be safeguarded from the strong Hong Kong sun."

It wasn't until she was upstairs that she suddenly won-dered how Jason had known there was a hairbrush in the nightstand. She was going to ask him about it, but he was outside throwing off the docking ropes and levering the yacht away from the dock with a boat pole. And when he came inside he immediately sat himself in one of the two chairs in the cockpit and fired up the engine.

He indicated the chair next to him. "Come sit by me," he invited in that British accent she loved, which was paired with one of his killer smiles. She sighed softly to herself and quickly complied.

Alana had barely settled into the seat, noting with a slight qualm there was no seat belt, when his hand moved on the throttle and the boat slid smoothly forward, soon leaving the dock behind as they headed west. She didn't want to interrupt his concentration, especially once they moved out into the shipping lanes, so she made a note to ask him about the brush later.

The cockpit and salon were enclosed, but Jason had the windows open to the harbor breeze, so Alana was grate-ful for her jacket and the not-quite-silk scarf he'd bought her yesterday.

"How far is it around the island?" she asked once they really got going.

"Twenty-six nautical miles, give or take." He darted a look at the watch he wore, which gleamed golden against his tanned skin. "We're a tad late in starting, but we should still be able to finish before sundown."

He pointed out the landmarks they passed, but she wasn't really concentrating. She was content to just listen to his deep voice with half her attention, while the rest of her was sorting through everything that had happened since Jason had dramatically entered her life.

She'd been enamored of him since the night of her rescue, of course. She'd known that immediately. And she'd heard his voice in her dreams ever since. She hadn't really expected to meet him again...but then she had. She'd seen his handsome features for the first time two weeks ago, and she'd fallen a little deeper under his spell as they communicated with just their eyes.

Then she'd spent nearly every moment of her free time over the past two weeks with him—living in his pocket, as Mei-li had so delicately put it. A whirlwind romance that was so unlike her she'd been stunned. Stunned, but unable to resist. Unable to call a halt, to take a breather. In fact, she seemed to have no willpower at all where Jason was concerned.

All at once a certain portion of her anatomy clenched at the memory of his lips. His hands. Driving her up and over that peak with seemingly effortless ease. Both times.

Willpower is overrated, she told herself now.

Alana stared at Jason's hands on the wheel, handling the yacht with the same light touch he'd used on her. And just like that she wanted him again. But he'd spent all that money on renting this yacht so he could take her around Hong Kong Island, which meant she had no intention of telling him. Of letting on in any way that she didn't care about this trip. That all she wanted was for him to take her back downstairs and make love to her again.

So she crossed her arms over her aching breasts, pinned an interested smile on her face...and forced herself to concentrate on what he was saying.

"Hold on a sec," he said after a few minutes, turning off his tour guide persona and pulling back on the throttle until the yacht was idling, practically dead in the water. He waited until the Star Ferry, chugging across the harbor from left to right, passed them before accelerating back to their previous speed. "Private craft must yield to public ones," he explained.

"You know, I never even thought to ask, but apparently you're a licensed, um, not sure exactly what it's called, but I'm sure you do."

"Yes, I do and yes, I am," he assured her. "I'm a licensed commercial pilot. It's called a Certificate of Competency." His voice dropped. "I would never put you at risk, Alana. Don't you know that by now?"

Their eyes met, and she couldn't look away from the dark intensity of his gaze. "Yes," she whispered, mesmerized. "I know that." Then she blinked and got herself under control. "So how do you know how to pilot a boat?"

"When you live on an island as I do, it helps if you can handle most boats that come your way." He hesitated for a moment, then added, "It's not just me. Every man in RMM is licensed for a variety of vessels—speedboats, cruisers, yachts. Some of our work entails trips to Macau...which is where they intended to take you when you were abducted. Prostitution is legal there, you know."

She shook her head. "No, I didn't know that about Macau."

"Macau is one of China's Special Administrative Regions, a SAR just like Hong Kong. But unlike Hong Kong, prostitution is legal there, although operating a brothel isn't. Doesn't mean they don't exist." His lips tightened into a thin line, and Alana knew without another word spoken that this issue bothered Jason a *lot*.

"Macau is a hotbed of human trafficking for the purposes of prostitution. Women are said to be brought there from all over Asia, and as far away as Russia and South Africa. Macau's even on the US State Department's watch list for human trafficking." Jason's body radiated anger held firmly in check, and his hands tightened on the wheel.

Alana touched his arm in sympathy. "Don't talk about this anymore right now," she said, making her voice as soothing as possible. "It upsets you. It upsets me, too, to think of women being forced into prostitution. And I'm so glad we intervened yesterday. If we can help even *one* woman…"

"Yes." He glanced her way, then turned his gaze back to the water in front of them. "Between you and the woman yesterday, that's two saved. But RMM—"

He broke off so abruptly that Alana knew RMM was somehow involved in trying to shut the whole operation down.

It was nearly dark by the time they finished circumnavigating the island. Jason cut the engine and let the boat's forward progress float them toward the dock. Alana followed him outside, thinking to assist him, but ended up just watching as he used the boat pole to loop the forward docking rope around the piling. He leaped lightly from the deck to the dock, secured the aft docking rope, then jumped back onto the yacht.

"I wanted to help."

He flashed a smile at her. "Next time."

She almost said, "But there won't be a next time," then stopped herself. Jason was obviously at home on the water. Which meant there very well *could* be a next time, although probably not on anything as big as this yacht. She didn't care about that, though. A rowboat or a dinghy was fine with her…so long as Jason was at the helm.

They strolled hand in hand up the dock toward land, Alana's borrowed hat swinging by its ties from her wrist as darkness settled comfortably around them. When they reached the parking lot, Jason unlocked her door and held it open for her, but blocked her entrance for a moment. "Dinner?"

She wasn't ready for her day to end, but she didn't really want to sit across from Jason in some restaurant, all the while wishing…hoping…remembering…

Maybe her eyes gave her away, or maybe he could read her mind, because his voice dropped a notch when he said, "I'd give anything I have to make love to you all night long…but not tonight."

Disappointment stabbed through her, sharp and deep. "Why not?"

"I have a previous commitment."

For just a second her heart panicked when she thought he meant he had another date, but then it came to her, and she said with certainty, "It's something to do with RMM." He hesitated, then nodded. "I understand."

She was grateful the gathering darkness hid the dismay she was already chastising herself for feeling. RMM was his calling, and she had to let him do what he needed to do. So she swallowed her disappointment and repeated, "I understand."

"I still have time for dinner."

Alana shook her head. "I'd rather not. That would just make it harder to say good-night to you."

"You're sure?"

She didn't trust her voice, so she merely nodded.

"Okay, then. I'll take you home."

Neither spoke for much of the drive, until Jason broke the silence. "Alana…"

"Yes?"

At first he couldn't continue. What could he possibly say? "Thank you for the best day of my life" sounded overly dramatic, although it was true. From start to finish this day would stand out like gold letters on a bright red background—the traditional Chinese colors of celebration.

As long as he lived he would remember Alana's eyes, her face, her voice, as she said, *I wanted you, Jason. I wanted you that first night. I wanted you yesterday. I want you today. Here. Now. Is it wrong to admit it? I don't think so…*

And then…as if his cup wasn't already running over… *I don't need* things *from you, Jason. I just need…you.*

All at once he remembered his tangle of thoughts when he'd woken with Alana in his arms, and he'd acknowledged he wasn't the twenty-first-century man he'd always believed himself to be. That it *mattered* to him Alana had chosen him to be the first. And if he had his way…the only.

He slowed and downshifted as they approached the turnoff for the DeWinters' estate, and he suddenly knew what he could say to her. "Thank you for choosing me."

She exhaled softly as if she'd been holding her breath, waiting for him to speak. "It wasn't so much a matter of *choosing* you as it was *recognizing* you were the one I'd been waiting for."

"However you want to put it, I'm…grateful it's me."

"I'm glad." And he could hear the truth of her words in her tone. "Glad it's you, and glad it means so much to you. I hoped it would." When she put her hand on his arm he felt it through all the layers of clothing, and his body responded in predictable fashion. *Terrific*, he thought with trenchant humor. *When I can't do a damn thing about it*.

He stopped in front of the gate and fished his key card out of his pocket. Before he was ready, he was parking in front of the main house.

"Thank you…for everything," she murmured and opened her door.

He caught her wrist and pulled her back inside. "Wait." Then she was in his arms and he poured everything he wanted to say but couldn't into his kiss. Eons later he came to his senses, whispering her name as his lips trailed over her face. "Oh, God, Alana, I can't let you go."

She made a little sound of protest deep in her throat, as if she didn't *want* him to let her go, either. But finally she pushed her hands against his chest to force herself away from him and stated firmly, "You have a previous commitment with RMM, remember? And I won't let you break it for me."

Jason drove away, prey to a mass of conflicted emotions. Hell yes, it had taken every scrap of self-control he could muster to let Alana step out of the car and walk into the house alone, when every male cell in his body was screaming to keep her with him. And as he'd told her earlier, he'd give anything to make love to her all night long.

But he hadn't been completely truthful with her…again. While it was true he had an assignation with certain of his men to follow up on a tip RMM had received about a notorious purveyor of pornography who was filming tonight, a man who was also rumored to use trafficked women in making his sex films, that wasn't the only reason he'd turned Alana down when her eyes had extended the invitation this evening.

The main issue was, where would he take her? His penthouse condo on Jardine's Lookout? Might as well take out an ad in the *South China Morning Post* or *The Standard* announcing who and what he was. If he still wanted to keep that part of his life secret from Alana—and he did, for complex reasons he hadn't had time to delve into—he'd have to think of a better solution.

He tried to marshal his thoughts as he drove, tried to enumerate his reasons for wanting to maintain the secrecy of his true identity a little longer. He trusted Alana, trusted she truly cared for him. Didn't he? So why…?

The only answer that came to him wasn't one he wanted to hear, because it was emotional, not logical, and Jason had always prided himself on his logical approach to the life he'd built for himself.

So he tried instead to bring order out of the emotional chaos today had wrought, but it was impossible. Too much had happened too soon, and he needed time to sort things out. Time he didn't have, because he really needed to concentrate on tonight's upcoming raid.

"You know better than to let yourself lose focus," he reminded himself, his voice harsh in the darkness. Resolving to put Alana out of his mind…at least for now. *An emotional man gets careless*, he remembered one of his covert ops teachers telling him years ago, *and a careless man gets dead real quick*.

The warehouse was located on the north side of the Hung Hom area of the Kowloon City District, and had seen better days. Its owner ran a thriving packing business during the day, but rented out sections at night for purposes he chose not to inquire about.

The film's producer stood behind the cameras with the director, smoking a pencil-thin cigar, while the arc lights were adjusted to illuminate the bed that was pretty much the entire set. A couple of actors wearing only bathrobes were casually perusing the scripts they'd been handed, but not really caring much. The dialogue wasn't all that important.

Two young women stood quietly to one side, conversing in a language no one else there understood. The arm of the older—that being a relative term, since she was only nineteen—was around the shoulders of the younger-by-two-years novice. "It is not so bad," Natalya whispered encouragingly in Russian. "It will soon be over."

Ludmilla shivered. "You have done this before?"

"Many times" came the reassuring reply. "They prefer it if you struggle to get away. And crying. That is good, too."

A note of desperation crept into Ludmilla's voice. "I don't want to do this. I want to go home."

Natalya understood all too well. She had never wanted to do this, either. Like Ludmilla, she'd been lured away from her home outside Moscow, thinking she was escaping the life of poverty she'd been born into by accepting the promise of a seemingly legitimate modeling job offer. Also like Ludmilla, the man she'd thought was her agent had turned around and "sold" her to the Eight Tigers triad for this very purpose because she was young, blonde and pretty.

Even though she'd been alone and defenseless in a foreign country where she didn't speak either Cantonese or English, she'd still resisted the first time she'd been brought onto the set of a porn movie. "Nyet!" she'd told them, appalled at what they'd wanted her to do. Only to have her very real and extremely brutal rape filmed and distributed worldwide.

Afterward, her new "owners" had made it very clear resistance was futile. Perform for the cameras and she would not be beaten or drugged. Refuse, and she would be taken to Macau, where even worse things would happen to her.

"Just be glad this is not a 'snuff' film," she told Ludmilla now. "I have heard rumors about this producer."

"*Snuff* film? What is that?"

"You do not really want to know. Just be thankful you will still be alive when it is over."

Jason double-checked the plastic explosives wired to the warehouse's back door, then nodded to the two other men with him garbed in black and disguised with camouflage face paint as he was, which RMM had long since determined was more effective than a mask. They backed off to a safe distance, and Jason handed the detonator to one of his companions. "Ready," he said into his radio transmitter, a word that sounded odd inside his head with the earplugs he wore that blocked most exterior sound.

"Roger that" came the muffled reply. "On three?"

"On three." He pulled his protective goggles over his eyes and cast a quick, questioning glance at his men, who both did the same before nodding their readiness. "One, two, three, go!"

Controlled explosions rocked the night air, and the back door to the warehouse was blown off its hinges. The three men burst through the door and raced toward the corner of the warehouse that had been screened off for the making of the film, just as three other RMM men converged on that section from the north, tossing stun grenades around the makeshift screens. These devices, commonly called flash-bangs, would produce a disorienting but nonlethal blinding light and intensely loud sound to temporarily incapacitate their targets, but hopefully nothing more dangerous than that. The same couldn't be said for the six RMM men, who were all hell-bent on one goal—putting this scum of the earth out of business for good.

It was over quickly. Their targets were clutching their

eyes and ears and writhing on the floor, having lost their balance from the impact the explosive devices had on the fluid behind their eardrums. Jason and his men swooped in and tied them all up with their hands behind their backs, except for the two young women.

Their plan was simple…yet fiendish. "Face" was everything to the Chinese. Men would go to great lengths to avoid "losing face." So while one of the RMM men hustled the women out of there, taking them to a safe house where they would be cared for and carefully questioned, Jason and the others stripped everyone involved in making this film naked, cutting off their clothes where necessary. They rifled through the men's pockets and found their identification cards, which they photographed. Then they hung signs bearing the words *Wolf's Heart, Dog's Lungs* in bold letters in both English and Chinese around each man's neck, stood them all up…and photographed them. Numerous times. From multiple angles. Making sure their furious and humiliated faces could be clearly seen each time over the deadly insult that meant these were cruel and unscrupulous men, guilty of a heinous crime.

While the other RMM members smashed the expensive movie camera equipment and confiscated whatever exposed film they could find, Jason held one of the digital cameras and sternly addressed the naked men in precise Cantonese. "You're out of the business as of this minute, understood? If we ever hear so much as a peep you're even *thinking* of getting back in, we'll publish these photos all over Hong Kong. And don't think we won't hear—we have eyes and ears everywhere."

He let his gaze wander over the naked men, lingering on their exposed genitals, and laughed softly. A laugh calculated to belittle and insult. It wasn't much payback for what these men had been planning to do to the two young women RMM had just rescued, not to mention all the others who'd been forced to participate in making this filth over the years, but it was something.

The producer lost his temper and blasted back, "Who the hell do you think you are? Do you know who I work for? The Eight Tigers will hear of this insult, I swear to you. They will—"

Jason stiffened at the mention of the Eight Tigers. This wasn't the first time the name had surfaced in an RMM investigation. But it was the first time someone actively involved in the criminal organization had invoked their name, and his voice sharpened. "What about the Eight Tigers?"

The producer trembled, obviously terrified he'd let the name slip. "Nothing. Nothing at all."

Jason got right in the producer's face, and in a voice as cold as ice and just as hard, said, "I don't care if you work for Lucifer himself. You. Are. Out. Of. Business."

Chapter 10

As always after a rescue, Jason was too wired to sleep. He followed his usual routine of a hot shower—especially hot tonight, as if he needed to eradicate the taint of what had been about to happen before RMM broke in— and a cold bottle of water.

Then, clad in just his boxers, he sought the comforting normalcy of his home office and collapsed into the chair behind his desk. He slumped back, closed his eyes and occasionally sipped from his water bottle as he tried to put tonight out of his mind.

He wasn't successful. He kept seeing the faces of the two women they'd rescued, especially their eyes. One had looked as if God's avenging angels had miraculously descended from heaven, saving her from a horrible fate.

But it was the other woman's eyes that had killed Jason, eyes that betrayed she'd already experienced the worst that could be inflicted on a woman...numerous times. That she had no faith in mankind, and even less in God. And he'd known then and there RMM was too late to save her.

He squeezed his eyes shut tighter, but moisture leaked from the corners. He impatiently dashed it away with a muttered oath, swallowing hard against the sudden constriction in his throat.

"You can't save them all," he whispered in the stillness, but the reminder helped only a little.

Weariness invaded his muscles and he craved sleep. But he knew it would be denied him. It would be hours before his exhausted body could conquer the vivid images in his brain, blot them out so he could get the rest he needed.

Desperate to think of something—anything!—that would erase the memory of those bleak eyes from the forefront of his consciousness, he suddenly remembered another set of eyes. Amethyst eyes. Guileless eyes. Innocent eyes. Eyes that had never looked upon the horrors he'd seen.

All at once he needed to hear Alana's voice. To know there *was* good in the world. Something clean. Something untouched by the sewers he inhabited as his alter ego. That there was a reason he kept subjecting himself to this mental torture.

Before he could talk himself out of it, he'd picked up his iPhone and pressed the speed-dial button he'd already set up for her. It wasn't until he heard her sleepy hello that he realized it was almost midnight.

"I'm sorry," he said quickly. "I shouldn't have called so late."

"It's okay." He heard her yawn, followed by, "Really, Jason, I don't mind." Then, with the unerring perception she seemed to have where he was concerned, she said, "Something bad happened tonight, didn't it." A statement, not a question.

"Yes."

Her voice was soft, soothing and unbelievably comforting. "Tell me."

He tried to marshal his chaotic thoughts, to weed through them to find the things he could tell her without destroying her innocence. "It was a lightning raid," he finally confessed. "Six of us went in with explosives and flash-bangs."

"What's a flash-bang?"

"A stun grenade. Blindingly bright light, deafeningly loud noise. Hence the nickname flash-bang. But unless you're careless, nonlethal."

"Oh, no. Was someone hurt? Killed?"

"No, no, nothing like that." *Just two more women touched by evil.* "We'd received a tip about…about a pornographer who had a shoot set up in an old warehouse." He could hear her sudden intake of breath through the phone, but she didn't say anything, so he continued. "Two young women, still in their teens. From the little we could get out of them—neither spoke much English—they'd both been trafficked into this."

"Oh, God." The distress in her voice was balm to his soul. "I'm so glad you were there to rescue them the way you rescued me."

He ran a tired hand over his face, wondering if he should admit his failure. Wondering also why it mattered so damn much she not know he'd failed. But then he said, "Not soon enough for one of the women. This wasn't her first time."

"Oh, Jason." There was such empathy in her voice, such caring. Not just for him, but for the woman he couldn't get out of his mind. "No wonder you can't sleep."

"I will…eventually. I just… I just needed to hear your voice."

"You need more than that, don't you." Again, not a question. "I wish I was there with you. I wish I could hold you in my arms and make the world go away. For a little while, at least."

Make the world go away. That's exactly what he needed. But he didn't want to use Alana that way. When he said as much to her, she surprised him. "You don't know very much about women, do you." Her third question that wasn't a question.

Jason's thoughts winged to the women he'd known in a physically intimate way—including Alana—and tried to suppress a chuckle at her naïveté.

But she must have heard him, because she said, "I'm not talking about sex. I don't think there's a man on this planet who knows more about a woman's body than you do. How to…you know."

"Right. I'm a sex god." He could almost see the blush he figured was tinting her cheeks.

"You are, but that's not what I'm talking about."

"Then what?"

Her voice softened. "When a woman lo—*cares*—about a man, she wants to take his pain away, however she can."

His heartbeat kicked up a notch at what she'd nearly said. *Love?* Had Alana almost admitted she loved him? Part of Jason thrilled to that idea. But the scene in the warehouse tonight was a vivid reminder of the precarious nature of the world he inhabited. She would never be safe if he let down his guard and let her into his life.

Problem was, he didn't want to keep her at a distance even though he desperately wanted to keep her safe. And those conflicting emotions threatened everything he'd thought he understood about himself.

Then he forced his mind back to what she was saying.

"Sometimes that means giving him the shelter of her arms. Holding him tight. Letting him know she's there. Sometimes that means just letting him talk as I'm doing now." She drew a deep breath and exhaled softly, a gentle sound that did things to him. "And sometimes it means giving him the comfort of her body. Whatever he needs to take away his pain." There was a tiny pause, then, "That's how I feel about you, Jason."

"Alana...*lang loi*..." He couldn't find the words to tell her how moved he was by her admission, but she didn't seem to need the words.

"I honestly thought you already knew."

He shook his head, even though she couldn't see him. "No. I hoped. But I wasn't sure."

"What did you think today was all about? Just sex?"

"No! God, no. But..."

She made a little sound that could have meant anything. "Don't misunderstand, the sex *was* fantastic. But I wasn't looking for a lighthearted romp between the sheets, and I don't think you were, either."

"I wasn't."

"We have something special, Jason. And I for one want the chance to see where this takes us." He could hear the deep breath she drew, as if she was gathering up her courage to make a momentous declaration, but then she said, "I...care about you." The slight hesitation made him suspect she'd originally intended to use another word, but had changed her mind at the last minute. Was she unsure?

"No! Don't say anything," she commanded when he started to speak. "I didn't tell you this to try to force your hand. I told you because I believe in honesty between two people who respect and trust one another."

All unknowing, she'd slipped a knife right between his ribs with that last statement. Because while she'd been honest with him from the get-go, he'd deceived her. Deliberately. And he intended to continue deceiving her. Didn't he?

But there was one thing he couldn't lie about. Not now.

"I care about you, too." He more than cared, but if Alana wasn't ready to admit she loved him, he wasn't about to put his heart out there, either. Not yet. "I want what you want—the chance to see where we go from here."

"When? When did you know you...cared?"

Jason couldn't help but smile because this was one of the things he loved about her. Direct. Forthright. But also a little shy in unexpected ways. "I was intrigued that first night, of course. And the way you looked at me at dinner the following Friday, I knew I was in trouble. Then yesterday, I was so proud of the way you handled yourself during the attempted abduction and the interrogation at the police station, I privately acknowledged I wanted you for my own."

"You were? You did?"

"I was. I did."

He could almost hear her brain humming as she digested this. "But..."

"But I was still blind," he admitted.

"So when *did* you know for sure?"

"When I apologized on the yacht this morning for what happened yesterday, and you said I didn't have to."

"Then? You knew then? Before I told you—" The abrupt way she stopped made it obvious what she meant.

"That I'd be the first? I won't lie to you—" *not about this anyway* "—I'll admit a part of me...a primitive part of me...found that knowledge incredibly appealing. But I'd already gone down for the count by then. It was your eyes," he said obscurely.

"My eyes?"

"Yes. When you looked at me on the yacht, I realized I've never seen eyes so earnest and innocent. Windows into a soul untouched by evil." He closed his own eyes fleetingly as everything he'd felt in that moment came back to him. "I've seen so much evil in my life, Alana," he confessed in a low voice. "Can you understand why I knew in that instant I needed you to wipe the slate clean for me?"

"I understand." And the beauty of it was, he believed she *did* understand. "But I'm far from perfect, you know. I don't want you to think that I—"

"Not perfect. Just perfection…for me." Then, being the man he was, he had to know. "When did you…?"

"I was intrigued that first night, too. But I never thought I'd see you again, so I tried not to think about you…too much."

"But you did."

"Yes. That next morning, I…"

"You what?"

Her voice was faint and he had to strain to hear. "I realized you were the kind of man I wanted as the father of my children."

Of all the things he'd imagined she would say, he'd never imagined this. But he suddenly saw Alana in his mind's eye with a baby in her arms. He knew in his heart she'd be a wonderful mother, just as his own had been.

Hard on the heels of that thought came another, from the primitive side of him—he didn't want any other man fathering Alana's children. Which meant her children would have to be his…if he allowed himself to have any, which he'd long ago vowed would never happen.

He shook off that thought, because he wasn't ready to discuss it with Alana. He would have to eventually, but not right now. "So you were thinking about me three weeks ago," he said, pretending she'd never mentioned children. "Then what?"

"When I met you again on that Friday, I…I was strongly attracted to you. Again. But it wasn't until yesterday, when I realized you're one of the founders of RMM, that I knew you were the man I'd been waiting for."

Once again Alana had floored him. "I never said that."

Tender amusement was evident in her voice. "You didn't have to. But I knew." Words spoken with such assurance, he didn't bother trying to deny it.

"And that's why you fell for me? Because I founded RMM?"

"I told you yesterday, I was waiting for a man as idealistic as I was. And I was holding out for a hero like the ones I dreamed about when I was a teenager. You're a knight in shining armor, Jason, whether you admit it or not. And you can't get any more idealistic than RMM. Case in point—the raid tonight."

"I barely told you anything about it, so how can you say that's an example of RMM's idealism?"

"Oh, Jason." Tenderness was back in her voice. "I'm not as naive as you think I am. I know what goes on in the world. I know that shutting down one pornographer who preys on women is just a drop in the bucket…but it *is* a drop. Most people just turn a blind eye. But not RMM. Not you. You can't save everyone, but you save the ones you can."

Jason's throat closed and he couldn't have spoken to save his soul. But Alana wasn't done. "You saved one woman tonight. That's *one* who was spared the evil no woman should ever have to endure. And I heard your pain when you said this wasn't the first time for the other woman. It's tearing you apart you couldn't save her. But what you don't realize is, you *did* save her. This time. That's one less time this abuse was inflicted on her." There were tears in her voice by the time she finished. "Oh, Jason, don't you see what a hero you are? How could I not care for a man like you?"

It was nearly 1:00 a.m. when the phone rang in the penthouse apartment of the High Tiger, waking both his wife and him. He answered it after the fourth ring, and when he heard the name of the man calling, said, "I'll call you back from my office."

He curtly told his wife, "Go back to sleep," and made his way to his office without turning on the hall light.

He flicked on the desk lamp, picked up the phone and stabbed out the number of the man who'd just called him, a number he knew by heart. When the phone was answered by the enforcer in charge of pornography, the High Tiger said, "What is so urgent you must call me at this time of the morning?"

He listened without interruption for several minutes, then said harshly, "So you lost some expensive equipment. So what? Easily replaced from profits. So two women have disappeared. What information can they possibly supply except the names of the men who are already known to this vigilante group? So the producer and director and various other hirelings are wavering on whether they will go back to work tomorrow. This is not the first time we have had to deal with recalcitrant men.

"I am sure you know what needs to be done, so why do you come to me? This is your bailiwick. Deal with the problem."

Then he slammed the phone down in its cradle and headed back to bed, mumbling to himself about incompetence.

Jason's sudden yawn took him by surprise, and he glanced at the clock. Just over an hour had passed while he'd been talking with Alana, but he was already relaxed enough to know he'd sleep like a baby.

Which meant Alana was spot on when she said he didn't know much about women. Because just *talking* with her had taken the load off his shoulders, had let him unwind in this relatively short time the way it normally took him hours. Which meant she was exactly what he needed.

But just because he knew he could finally sleep didn't mean he was ready to say good-night. For the last ten minutes he hadn't said much, he'd been content to just listen to Alana's sweet voice in his ear. Soothing. Calming. So like his sister in certain ways, including that way she had of handling high-strung men.

Not that he considered himself a high-strung man as a general rule. Just in the aftermath of an RMM operation. Success or failure didn't really make a difference—he was always wound tight afterward.

He'd never sought out a woman after an RMM raid. Had never trusted himself that much because his control was iffy at best in the aftermath, and he prided himself on his control. But he wondered now, would it be different with Alana? Would he still need to be in control 24/7? Or could he relinquish it to her when he couldn't be sure of being strong on his own?

He didn't know…but he damn sure wanted to find out.

Another yawn warned him his body was about to shut down, but he still wasn't ready to end the conversation. He knew he should. She had a job and she needed her sleep. So when she reached the end, he said, "I should let you go, *lang loi*. I don't want to say good-night, but—"

"It *is* late, but I can sleep a little later in the morning, if necessary. Dirk lets me set my own hours, you know. As long as the work gets done, he doesn't really care. But what about you? Don't you have to work tomor—I mean, today?"

"Yes, but I'm used to working on very little sleep. I never know when I'll be called out for something related to RMM. That comes first for me, but I still have a—" *company to run*, was what he'd almost said. He quickly substituted, "Job. I still have a job."

"You never told me what you do for a living."

Guilt stabbed through Jason at the ongoing deception he still wasn't quite ready to end, and he considered what he could say without outright lying to Alana. "I work for a multinational electronics firm, Wing Wah Enterprises. Nothing exciting, but it pays the bills." *RMM's bills, too*, he considered adding, but didn't.

He wandered into his bedroom as he spoke, then collapsed on top of the king-size bed and dragged a corner of the coverlet over him, still holding his phone to his ear.

"Engineering? Finance? Sales?" she asked with the air of someone who really wanted to know and wasn't going to let him off the hook.

"Management." He quickly reviewed his scholastic history and figured there wasn't anything there he couldn't reveal. "I have dual management and engineering degrees from Oxford."

"A double major? Wow, impressive. I just have a major in history and a minor in communications."

"I knew when I graduated I'd be working for the electronics company I still work for," he explained. "So it seemed appropriate." He yawned a third time, and this time she heard him.

"You're exhausted, poor baby. You're the one who needs sleep."

He could barely keep his eyes open now, and his words were starting to slur together. "You were right, *lang loi*. Talking *did* help. Thank you."

"You're very welcome. Good night and sweet dreams, Jason."

"*Lang jai*," he corrected.

"Right," she said, and he could almost see her smile. "Good night and sweet dreams…*lang jai*."

Chapter 11

Jason woke at his normal time. No matter how late he was up the night before, his circadian clock was staunchly set for 6:00 a.m. And once he was awake, he was awake. He couldn't turn over and go back to sleep again.

Coffee and breakfast he'd grab on the way to work, as usual, and he'd showered the night before, so all he needed to do was dress, pack up his laptop in its leather briefcase, pick up his keys from the credenza in the foyer—a creature of habit, he always left his keys there—and find his smartphone. But it wasn't on his bedroom nightstand. And it wasn't in his office next to his laptop, the only other place he could imagine it might be. He stood staring for a moment, his brow furrowed. Then he remembered.

He strode back into his bedroom, impatiently tossed the top sheet to one side and there it was…still in his bed. Where apparently he'd fallen asleep with it pressed to his ear, something he'd never done before in his life. He checked, but the phone was off. So either he'd disconnected at the very end of his conversation with Alana last night, or the phone had shut itself off after an extended period of time with no usage.

He pocketed it with a soft smile of remembrance, a smile he refused to glance at in the dresser mirror because he figured it made him look sappy—although he didn't care— and headed down to the basement and his Jag.

It was raining, which wasn't uncommon for this time of year. Because it was a more scenic drive and he wasn't pressed for time, he took the Stubbs Road route to the Wing Wah Enterprises office tower, the gleaming steel-and-glass monolith the company had occupied for the last five years. He wanted the scenic route because thinking of Alana, who'd occupied his thoughts almost constantly since he'd woken this morning, filled him with an almost euphoric sense of well-being. And the lovely vistas—even in the rain—seemed apropos.

Alana. He couldn't relegate her to the back of his mind the way he'd relegated all the other women he'd been involved with over the years…and he didn't want to. She'd become the most important person in his world in less than a month, and he loved it.

The Jag's Bluetooth system rang for an incoming call on his cell phone, and after a glance at the display, he hit the button on the steering wheel. "Good morning, David. You're up with the birds. Since when do you—"

His best friend cut him off. "I don't suppose you've seen the news this morning."

The grim way this was delivered was a huge red flag something had gone down between last night and this morning. Something which David suspected involved RMM… and him, so he answered cautiously. "No, I haven't."

"Ten men were found murdered this morning, in various districts of the SAR," David said.

"That's rather a lot for one day." As soon as the words left his mouth the number ten took on special significance. *Weren't there that many involved in the RMM raid last night?* He counted them up in his mind and nodded to himself. Yes, ten. Producer, director, two cameramen, a pair of actors and four others, who he'd figured were makeup, wardrobe and a couple of grips. But they'd been alive when RMM had left. Humiliated. Naked. But alive. *This couldn't have anything to do with—*

"The SAR doesn't get that many murders in a *quarter*, much less one day." David let that statement hang there for a moment before adding, "And preliminary reports indicate they could be connected. One of the men was a notorious purveyor of pornography, with unsubstantiated rumors surrounding him about even less savory pursuits. The others were part of a film crew he often used, including the director and a couple of male porn stars."

Jason's mouth tightened. *They were alive the last time I saw them*, he reiterated in his mind. Then the name the producer had threatened him with in anger last night materialized, and he knew he had to share this with David. "The Eight Tigers."

"What makes you think it was them?" Jason said nothing. "You wouldn't know anything about a vigilante raid that took place in a warehouse in Hong Hum last night, would you? From all accounts a movie was being shot there. The doors were blown off, movie cameras wrecked and the place was trashed." Jason didn't answer, knowing David would take his silence as a tacit admission. "Damn it, Jason…"

The throttled anger and frustration in his friend's voice

made him say, "They were alive when we left. That's all I can tell you."

"Damn it, Jason," David repeated. This was followed by a weighty silence. Then, "Where are they?"

He knew David wasn't referring to the dead men; he was referring to the women who had to have been there last night, the subjects of the film. The police obviously wanted to question them about the dead men and everything that had led up to last night. Not that David thought the women might be responsible, but it was always possible the murders were the work of an enraged boyfriend or relative.

"They're safe. And they're not involved, not in any way."

"How do you know?"

"Trafficked from Russia, both of them. No family here. No boyfriends. Lured away from their homes with promises of modeling careers, then 'sold' to the highest bidder—you know how that business operates."

"I want to hear it from them." A demand, not a request.

Jason sighed softly. "I'll see what I can do."

He was about to disconnect when David said, "If the Eight Tigers are involved, I have to ask. Is this related to the abducted women?"

"We haven't made a definite connection between the two, if that's what you're asking. Not yet anyway."

"That's what I'm asking."

"But you know as well as I do, word on the street is the Eight Tigers *are* involved in both abductions. They have brothels in Macau, which is where we're fairly confident the women are being transported."

His friend's voice was hard and implacable. "I need to know what you know, Jason. I need whatever evidence you have. And I need it now."

"We don't have any evidence you don't have. All we have is hearsay. Nothing that can be used in court."

"Would you tell me if you did?" That was a bow drawn at a venture, but it found its target. In essence, David was calling him a liar.

"My word as a gentleman," he said evenly. "This is too important for me to give a damn who shuts this triad down, you or us."

Alana's alarm woke her at seven. She considered hitting the snooze button and going back to sleep for five minutes, then decided against it. She made quick work of dressing before heading downstairs to breakfast. It was eight on the dot when she walked into Dirk's office and checked on the threshold because Dirk was there at his desk, scrolling through something on his computer.

"Hi," she said. "I thought you were filming this morning."

He flashed her the smile that had won him millions of female fans, including her before she'd come to work for him. Not that she wasn't still affected by his brilliant smile; she was. But things were somehow different now that she knew him personally. Now that she knew what a…a *normal* guy he was. Down to earth. And an utterly devoted family man.

"Change of plans. Supposed to be an outside shoot today, but this rain means they're scrambling to rearrange the schedule and shoot some indoor scenes instead. They won't need me on the set until this afternoon, so I thought I'd try to make a dent in the emails you flagged for me." A guilty expression reminiscent of a little boy crossed his face. "I know I said I'd do it yesterday, but Mei-li and I took the twins to Stanley Market instead."

Alana seated herself behind her desk and turned on her computer. "That sounds like fun. Did they enjoy it?"

"Did they ever. I'm a sucker where the girls are concerned, and they know it. They've got me wrapped around their little fingers." He chuckled. "Good thing Mei-li knows how to rein me in. Otherwise I'd spoil them rotten."

"It's hard to say no when you can afford to buy just about anything," she commiserated. Her parents had done their best to spoil her by giving her everything her heart desired, she remembered. *Thank goodness I had Uncle Julian to keep my feet planted firmly on the ground. To realize my privileged life wasn't the way most people live.*

"Yeah," Dirk said in response to her statement. "I try not to spoil them, but it's difficult. So how was your day on the water?" he asked, changing the subject. And when she raised her eyebrows, questioning how he knew, he added, "Mei-li happened to mention you had another date with her brother, this time to take a trip around the island."

Alana pretended to be distracted by something on her computer so she wouldn't have to look at Dirk until the betraying flush had time to subside. Then, in as casual a voice as she could muster, she said, "Lovely. Absolutely lovely, from start to finish."

Dirk hesitated as if he was of two minds about what he was about to say next, but something decided him. "Please don't take this the wrong way. And if I'm crossing some kind of employer-employee line, I'll apologize up front. But Juliana is the best friend I have in the world. She entrusted you to Mei-li and me, and I'd be remiss if I didn't speak up to warn you."

That sounded ominous. "Please don't say anything against Jason."

He shook his head. "Not my intention. Jason is…well, I'm sure you've already discovered for yourself, but he's just about the best man I know. I admire him tremendously. But he's an extremely complicated man with a lot of emotional baggage. A hell of a lot more than he's ever let on to Mei-li or me."

"She said…" Alana searched her mind for Mei-li's exact words yesterday. "She said Jason has been hurt more than I know. More than he'd ever tell me. Then she practically begged me not to break his heart." She glanced down at her hands for a moment, remembering yesterday and the love she'd shown Jason with her hands, her lips. Her heart. Then she looked up at Dirk. "I would never do that, you know. Break Jason's heart."

"He's her brother, so of course she'd look at it from his perspective. But you're Juliana's cousin, and my first loyalty is to you. I'm less concerned with you breaking Jason's heart than I am with him breaking yours. Not that I think he'd do it deliberately," he quickly interjected when she opened her mouth to leap to Jason's defense. "But any woman who gets involved with him has to know up front it could happen."

She didn't respond at first. Then said quietly, "Because he's a very complicated man with a lot of emotional baggage, right?"

"Right."

"Are you saying this because of his involvement with RMM, or because he founded it after his best friend was killed?"

Dirk looked thunderstruck. "He told you?"

Alana shook her head, a faint smile touching her lips. "Of course not. He confided in me about Sean's murder, but that's all. I figured it out, and when I told him I knew, he didn't deny it."

"It's more than just that. More than just RMM. There's something riding him he'll never tell a soul, but I know it's there. So does Mei-li."

"Do you mean the man he killed? He has an extremely

stern conscience, and I know that still weighs on him, even though it was completely justified."

If anything, Dirk's expression turned even more thunderstruck. "He told you about that, too?"

"Just the bare facts, but I extrapolated from there."

Dirk shook his head. "It's something deeper and more basic than that. There's a gaping hole in Jason's psyche, and I don't know if the woman exists who could fill that void. Who could love him enough to heal him."

She'd known. Hadn't she known there was a darkness in Jason, secrets he'd never confide? But Dirk didn't understand. That knowledge just made her love Jason more because she knew he needed her in some elemental way, more than anyone else would ever need her.

"You don't have to worry about me." She smiled to reassure him. "I know what I'm doing." Despite her confident words, however, a sliver of self-doubt refused to be quelled.

As soon as Jason arrived at the office he called the safe house where the women RMM had rescued had spent the night. He got a full report from Soo-Ying Kwan, the social worker who ran it, after asking, "Other than the little they told us last night through the interpreter, have they said anything at all?"

He listened to the response, closing his eyes momentarily as a pang struck in the region of his heart. When Soo-Ying finished, he asked, "In your professional opinion, are they in any condition to be questioned by the police?"

"That depends, *laoban*," she said, using the Cantonese word for *boss*.

"On?"

"Not alone. I'll consent to it only if I can be there *and* if I can immediately stop any line of questioning I feel is inappropriate. And *not* at the police station. Not here, of course—we don't want the police knowing our location—but somewhere neutral."

He thought about this. "I'll make those nonnegotiable terms. And I'll arrange to have a barrister there representing the women. They're victims, not criminals, and I won't let the police treat them as such."

As soon as he hung up he called David. After some heated debate, his friend conceded to his terms, and Jason said, "I'll make the arrangements and get back to you when everything's lined up."

He then called an acquaintance who agreed to legally represent both women as well as to hold the interrogation at his offices that afternoon. Two more phone calls, to the social worker at the safe house and to David, and everything was set.

The rest of Jason's day passed in a blur of meetings, overseas conference calls and a not-totally-unexpected decision to shut down an unprofitable venture in Egypt. They'd take a loss, but it would barely register as a blip on the bottom line. And the company's name hadn't been on that venture, so the media fallout would be minimal.

In between times, whenever he had a moment, he texted Alana.

Thank you again, lang loi.

She texted back, My pleasure, lang jai. Did you sleep well?

Like a baby, thanks to you.

And this.

Are you free tonight?

For you, yes of course. What did you have in mind?

A wicked chuckle escaped him when he read that, because she *had* to know what he had in mind. She'd offered him a gift yesterday, one he had every intention of accepting at the earliest opportunity.

But that wasn't the only reason he wanted to see her tonight. In fact, it wasn't even tops on his list. Okay, it was second, but it wasn't *first*. So he texted.

Dinner, and...?

Then he laughed out loud when he read her response, and he was glad he was alone in his office at that moment.

As long as there's an "and" on the agenda, I don't mind dinner.

His office intercom buzzed. "Your two o'clock appointment is here, sir."

He glanced at his watch and saw it still lacked five minutes to the hour. He toggled the switch and said, "Give me two minutes, then send them in." Then he texted Alana.

"And" is definitely on the agenda. 6:00? Dressy?

As soon as he hit Send, he realized he still had no place to take her for "and." It wasn't that he didn't want to take Alana where he'd made love to other women, because he'd never taken a woman to his condo. Too dangerous. He didn't want his secret life to become known, and there was always a risk the woman might see or hear something she shouldn't. So he'd always maneuvered things so they spent the night elsewhere.

No, his condo was out because it would be a dead give-away. He hadn't lied to Alana; he just hadn't been completely forthcoming. His reasons had been compelling at the time, and they still were to a certain extent. But would she understand? She might walk out if she thought he'd been deceiving her. Or worse, that he was playing her for a fool.

No, he couldn't risk it. Not yet. He had to bind her to him first. Mentally. Physically. Emotionally. Then, when it no longer mattered, he'd tell her the truth.

But if he couldn't take her to his condo, where could they go? She didn't have her own apartment—she lived with his sister and brother-in-law, for Pete's sake!—and what excuse could he come up with for a hotel room? "My apartment's a mess," was too lame.

His iPhone buzzed for another incoming text.

I love dressy. See you then.

He picked up the phone and dialed his executive assistant. "Hold off on sending them in. Can you come here for a moment? And bring your notepad."

The door opened, and the diminutive, gray-haired employee he'd inherited from his grandfather walked sedately in and quietly closed the door behind him, not bothering to take a seat. "Yes, sir?"

"I need you to find me a small, furnished apartment. Price is no object, so long as it's meticulously clean and available by five tonight. That means keys in my hand no later than five."

His exec never batted an eye. "Yes, sir. How many bedrooms? And how long will you be needing it?"

That stymied him for only a second. "Number of bedrooms is immaterial, so long as it's not an efficiency. And

I'll take a month's rental, with an option for an additional month."

The man made a few notations on his pad. "Any particular location?"

"Something on the north side of the island, if possible, but immediate availability trumps location."

"Yes, sir."

"You may send my two o'clock appointment in now."

His exec unbent enough to smile faintly. "Of course, sir. I'll get on this right away."

Alana hummed Billy Joel's "Until the Night" to herself as she dressed for her date with Jason. She'd shaved her legs yesterday morning, but she did it again when she took a bubble bath because she wanted to be silky smooth for the "and" Jason had promised her. She creamed her elbows and feet, applied just a hint of her favorite lilies-of-the-valley-scented perfume at her pulse points, and dug out the risqué bra and thong she'd bought when she'd first arrived in Hong Kong but had never worn yet. She'd hidden them at the back of her underwear drawer, hoping someday she'd have a reason to wear them. Now she did.

She'd known what she wanted to wear for Jason the minute his "Dressy?" text had arrived. Red. It had to be red, the Chinese color of celebration. And she only had one sufficiently dressy dress in that color, a red silk *cheongsam* embroidered with dragons and phoenixes in gold thread. The dress was new, too, bought here in Hong Kong. It hadn't looked like much on the hanger in the boutique Mei-li had taken her to that first week, but when she'd tried it on she couldn't resist it, and now she was glad. For all its seeming modesty, with its cap sleeves and high neckline, it was form-fitting and quietly seductive.

But there was another reason she wanted to wear the dress.

Dragons and phoenixes. She hadn't known it at the time, of course, but they were the symbols of RMM. How beautifully apt for the man who'd made RMM his life's work!

Jason was the hero she'd been waiting for all her life. With every fairy tale she'd read. With every entry in her diary. This was her knight in shining armor. And like her secret teenage crush, the Chevalier de Bayard, whose real-life story had fired her imagination at the tender age of twelve, Jason was *sans peur et sans reproche*.

She brushed her nearly waist-length hair until it gleamed. She considered leaving it down, but remembered the erotic thrill of Jason unbinding her hair yesterday, so she braided and coiled it the same way.

Silk stockings held up by the laciest of garters and red heels completed her ensemble. She didn't care for lipstick—it never stayed intact anyway and she hated having to constantly check it—so she brushed on lip gloss instead. She added the antique ruby earrings set in gold her uncle Julian had given her when she graduated summa cum laude from Tulane, earrings he'd inherited from his mother, the grandmother she barely remembered. Then she was ready. Ten minutes early, in fact, something she confirmed with a quick glance at the clock on her nightstand.

She closed her eyes and pressed both hands to her chest, trying to calm her suddenly racing heart. She wasn't the slightest bit nervous about her first time; she already knew Jason was an exquisitely tender lover, so she had no qualms there. An apropos line from Chaucer suddenly came to her. Jason was her *parfit, gentil knight*, as well as *sans peur et sans reproche*. She'd waited for him all her life, and now she was fiercely glad she had. But she so badly wanted tonight to be perfect—not for her, for him. *Oh, God*, she prayed. *Let me never hurt him in any way.*

Then the doorbell rang.

Chapter 12

Jason unlocked the door of his rented apartment near Causeway Bay after dinner, and flicked on the light with a tinge of trepidation. There hadn't been time to swing by and check on the apartment before picking up Alana, but once inside he realized he needn't have worried. His executive assistant had outdone himself, and he made a mental note to augment the man's Christmas bonus.

The apartment was immaculate and smelled faintly of lemon oil. The furniture had clean lines and was almost Spartan in appearance. And there were no personal touches. No *feminine* touches to upset Alana with the thought there were other women in his life.

On a hunch he moved into the kitchen and opened the refrigerator. Sure enough, there was his brand of bottled water stacked neatly on the top shelf. And on the shelf below reclined two bottles of Bollinger 1996 Vieilles Vignes Françaises, an exquisite Blanc de Noir champagne, with two crystal wine-glasses nestled beside them.

He didn't drink alcohol often, but his executive assistant knew his tastes. He'd also apparently figured out why Jason wanted the apartment, and had efficiently and discreetly supplied what he might need.

Jason's first reaction was that he shouldn't wait for Christmas, that he should thank his exec with a bonus now. But then, out of the blue, distaste whipped through him for what this said...about him.

He'd wined and dined women in the past. Not hundreds, but enough. And he'd had his assistant make reservations at Hong Kong's premier dining establishments, as well as arrange for flowers, Godiva chocolates and other gifts to be delivered to those women, both when he was wooing them and when he was bidding them a fond farewell.

He'd never consciously thought about it before—that was just the way things were done in his world. Which meant his exec had also made all the reservations for the little out-of-the-way restaurants he'd taken Alana to since they'd started dating. Not to mention the flowers he'd requested his exec send her after their first date. And their second. And their third.

So the bottles of Bollinger were a silent indictment of him...and his intentions in setting up this rented apartment in the first place.

But he wasn't here to enact a grand seduction scene. And the *last* thing he wanted anyone to think—least of all Alana—was that he thought she would be influenced by his wealth. That he thought she'd be impressed with the expensive wine, the costly trinkets, the trappings of luxury other women had accepted from him without demur.

Except...that was *exactly* what he'd thought. He'd deceived her from the beginning, and he'd gone on doing it. Even renting this apartment so he wouldn't have to take her to his condo and she wouldn't figure out who he really was, because he'd been afraid she might be like all the other women who hadn't been able to separate the man from the money.

Be honest, he told himself ruthlessly. *It's not just that. Not anymore. It was at the beginning, but not now. The truth is, you want a woman who will sacrifice everything for you, the way your mother did for your father. And if she knows who you are, how would you ever know?*

He closed the refrigerator door with a decided thud, then turned to face Alana. So beautiful in her red *cheongsam*, which she'd already confessed at dinner she'd worn for him because "Red is the Chinese color of celebration, and I'm celebrating." Followed by a soft, almost shy, "Dragons and phoenixes, too. Did you notice?" So sweet. So loving. So innocently *trusting*. And he was treating her the way a man might treat his mistress...not the woman he loved.

His voice was harsh in the stillness. "This is a bad idea."

"What?"

He grabbed her hand and pulled her toward the front door. "Come on, I'll take you home."

"Jason, why? What did I do?" The bewilderment in her voice, her immediate assumption that it was *her* when it was him, all him, shamed him to the core. He turned to face her and—because he couldn't help it—caressed her cheek, thrilling to the sensation of soft skin beneath his fingertips...and despising himself for it at the same time. "I'm a right bastard for bringing you here, and I'm putting an end to it. Now."

All Alana could hear in that instant was Dirk saying, *There's a gaping hole in Jason's psyche, and I don't know if the woman exists who could fill that void. Who could love him enough to heal him.*

And just like that she knew Jason's abrupt decision was somehow, someway, related. Her lips tightened with determination. "I'm not leaving, *lang jai*. You promised me 'and.' I'm staying until you keep your promise."

His eyes closed and pain slashed across his handsome face, a face already so impossibly dear to her. She didn't know where the pain had come from, but she remembered her prayer earlier. *Let me never hurt him in any way.* When his eyes opened they were filled with torment, those inner demons she'd already sensed existed. And she knew it was up to her to dispel them.

Her heels gave her added height, allowing her to pull his head down to where she could reach his face. She pressed her lips to the corners of his mouth…first one side, then the other. "I'm not going anywhere without you," she breathed. "Please don't ask me again." Then she kissed him.

He groaned and his arms wrapped around her. All at once she remembered yesterday, and the way he'd kissed her as if she were his salvation. *That's it*, she exulted, deepening the kiss and pressing her body all along the length of his, *that's exactly what I am*. She didn't know why, but it didn't matter. Someday he'd tell her. Someday…

When he finally raised his head she whispered with a husky catch in her voice, "Tell me there's a bedroom in this apartment."

He didn't answer at first, then reluctantly admitted, "There's a bedroom in this apartment."

"Tell me you're going to show me the bedroom."

"Alana…" Such yearning in his voice. Such need.

"Tell me you brought condoms this time."

He laughed softly, in the manner of a man who didn't want to but couldn't help it. He pressed his forehead against hers and whispered back, "I brought condoms this time."

She smiled an invitation at him. "Then what are you waiting for?"

* * *

Unlike yesterday, where she couldn't remember how their clothes had disappeared, she knew she'd always remember tonight, and the reverent way Jason unbound her hair until it spilled over her shoulders, then kissed her after each article of clothing was removed.

The *cheongsam* went first. "Beautiful...but in my way." Leaving her wearing a bra, half-slip, those bits underneath and red high heels that suddenly felt wobbly for some reason. He brushed a kiss against her stomach, then slipped his fingers beneath the elastic waistband, and the half-slip slithered down to pool on the floor. Jason's eyes widened at the barely there thong revealed, but he didn't say anything. Alana deliberately leaned against his chest as she stepped out of the silky circle and smiled to herself at his sharply indrawn breath.

He sat her down on the edge of the bed and knelt before her. "Someday I'll make love to you while you're wearing those heels...and nothing else," he said, his voice rough with pent-up desire. "But not tonight." And the shoes were whisked off and away.

One by one he slid the lacy garters off and rolled down her silk stockings with a care she wouldn't have expected from a man. His warm hands on her thighs, her calves, her ankles, made her shiver with erotic anticipation. Then he kissed the inside of each knee, and her whole body quivered.

It was a little unnerving being nearly naked while Jason was fully clothed, and she experienced a moment of panic. But somehow he must have read her mind. "Don't go shy on me now, *lang loi*." His deep voice did things to her insides. "Do you know how much it turns me on you dressed for me tonight? Especially these?" Long fingers stroked over her red satin bra cups, which barely covered her nipples. Then those same fingers trailed down, down, until they passed over the matching red thong and lingered for agonizing seconds at the crux of her thighs, so she'd know—as if she didn't!—exactly what he meant.

She barely suppressed a whimper, and she melted. Just melted. He had to know what he was doing to her, but she said it anyway. "Jason, please. I don't know how much more I can take."

"Patience, *lang loi*, patience." His smile was wicked. "Haven't you heard? Everything comes to those who wait." He drew her hand to the front of his dress slacks, where she could feel him hot, hard and obviously ready for her. He let her stroke him, measure him through his clothes for long moments, then he stopped her and brought her hand up to his mouth for a lingering kiss. When his lips touched her palm she felt it everywhere.

He put his hands on her shoulders and gently pressed her down on the bed. Then he parted her thighs. His big hands stroked slowly up and down, up and down, coming ever closer each time to where she was desperate to feel him. "I told you yesterday you're exquisite when you come," he said in his deepest voice. "And that I want to watch you come again. Which is exactly what I'm going to do now... if you'll let me."

Permission? He was asking for *permission* to drive her insane with those things he'd done to her yesterday? He couldn't possibly expect her to say anything but "Yes, please." Which she did. In her company-manners, oh-so-polite voice.

He laughed as if she'd amused him, then stood and stripped out of his clothes in nothing flat. Naked and aroused, he was magnificent. Those lean muscles in his arms, chest and thighs she'd first felt as he'd held her during his dramatic rescue of her were as tempting tonight as they'd been yesterday on the yacht, and her hands itched to glide over the smooth, tantalizing skin that covered them.

Before he came back to the bed, he felt in the pocket of his trousers and pulled something out, which he dropped on the nightstand. Alana craned her head to see what—oh. There seemed to be an awful lot of them, though.

He saw the direction of her stare and reminded her, "All night long. I told you last night I wanted to make love to you all night long. Can't risk running short."

That forced a laugh out of her, despite the yearning ache that still had her body humming. "Yes, please."

His smile faded, replaced by a curiously intent expression in his dark eyes. "Oh, I'm going to please you, *lang loi*. Trust me. I'm going to please you until you weep from pleasure. Then I'm going to start all over again. And again. Until you beg me to stop."

She drew a shaky breath, unbearably excited by the prospect. "Yes, please."

Jason had never made a promise he hadn't kept. Never. But never had keeping a promise meant more to him than keeping the one he'd made to Alana. And when she said, "Yes, please," he knew that even if the walls came tumbling down around them, he would still fulfill his promise. Somehow.

He was already painfully aroused from just looking. Touching. That was secondary, though. It would take every ounce of willpower he had, but he had faith in himself. He would indulge Alana's senses with so much pleasure that when he finally took her innocence there would be no pain. None. Just more pleasure.

He lay beside her on the bed, making concentric circles on her abdomen with one hand until she shifted restlessly. Then he slid his hand down beneath the thong he'd refused to let her remove. Yet.

She was already wet, and he smiled with deep satisfaction. Alana was so incredibly responsive it seemed impossible she was still a virgin, but when his middle finger parted her and slipped inside, he found the way blocked before he'd gone very far, and he knew she'd been telling him the truth. Not that he hadn't believed her. But still…

She made a tiny sound that wasn't a moan but wasn't pain, either, so he delved a little deeper, testing the strength of the barrier. Assured it wouldn't take much, he withdrew and located the source of her pleasure, stroking it patiently until he was finally rewarded. She stiffened and gasped his name, but he never stopped until she arched up against his hand and cried out.

That's one, he thought, smiling to himself, though it didn't count against his promise to make her weep with pleasure. But it was a start.

The High Tiger disliked clandestine night meetings. But with this man they were always at night. He also disliked going to locations not of his choosing. But with this man that was the norm, because he was highly suspicious that his actions might be observed, and therefore ultracautious. Such was his value to the High Tiger that he willingly put up with most of the man's idiosyncrasies.

The High Tiger had taken a bus and two subways, and had been forced to walk five blocks to reach this destination. And that was the one thing he resented. He had a luxury limousine and a chauffeur to drive him everywhere he needed to go, so he wouldn't have to be subjected to the crowds and other inconveniences most Hong Kong residents took for granted. But the man insisted no one other than the High Tiger could know of their meetings, which meant the chauffeur as well as the bodyguards had to be left at home. And since the High Tiger had never learned to drive, that also meant utilizing public transportation for these meetings.

He collapsed into a chair next to the man with whom he was meeting, who was casually reading a newspaper and pretending he hadn't been watching the High Tiger's approach. He had, which the High Tiger knew all too well.

After a moment the man folded the newspaper in thirds and placed it on the table. That was the signal. Unfolded or folded in half would mean the man suspected something, and the two men would not speak.

"So what do you have for me?"

The man glanced once more to the left and right, then leaned forward and spoke in an undertone. "The High Dragon of RMM," he said, referring to the head of RMM by the euphemism the man always used. "And the woman with whom he is enamored. This is the first chink in his armor in all the years I have known him. Now he is vulnerable." The man smiled, and even the High Tiger was chilled by the absolute malevolence in that smile. "Now we have him."

Alana had heard there was sometimes pain, but not for her. Not with this man. She'd steeled herself against the possibility until she realized he wouldn't *let* there be pain for her with his loving.

Jason had fulfilled his pledge...by fulfilling her. Numerous times. She'd lost track somewhere along the way, but that didn't seem to matter in the slightest. No, the only thing Jason seemed to care about was the tears she'd shed when the pleasure was too great—as he'd promised she would. And because she sensed it mattered to him, she hadn't held the tears back as she would otherwise have tried to do. She wasn't ashamed, and she wanted him to know. She wanted to give him that small triumph.

She was floating in pleasure-dazed euphoria after the last time, when Jason reached over to the nightstand and grabbed one of the little packets there. She watched as he rolled the condom on over his impressive erection, then moved between her thighs.

"Open for me, *lang loi*," his husky voice whispered in her ear, and she eagerly complied. This was what she'd been waiting for after all. Everything else had been a prelude to this.

Then he slid inside. Not quickly, painfully, but slowly, inexorably. There was one instant when her body refused his entrance, but his fingers caressed the little nub until her body softened in surrender. Only then did he flex his hips and fill her to the hilt. She caught her breath in wonder at the sensation of having this man so tight, so deep, within her; it was as if for one brief moment they were one. And she knew from the inarticulate sounds issuing from his throat she was giving him the same pleasure he was giving her.

She raised her knees and arched her hips, taking him impossibly deeper…and he loved it. Then she tightened her pelvic muscles, wrenching a groan from him. He growled, "Do that again and I won't last, *lang loi*." So of course she did it again, and he lost all control, driving into her hard and fast.

The orgasm took her by surprise. She hadn't thought she was capable of another—but then it hit and she throbbed around him and sobbed his name. Hers preceded his by mere seconds. A brief flurry of thrusts and then he came, too, her name on his lips.

Alana was floating again. She hadn't lost consciousness because she was all too aware when Jason drew away, and she wanted to protest. But she knew he needed to deal with the condom, so she contented herself by squeezing him one last time with her inner muscles as he withdrew.

She was shocked out of her lethargy when Jason muttered a pithy Anglo-Saxon curse, and her eyes flew open. "What? What's wrong?"

His mouth was a thin line and guilt wove its way over his features when he confessed, "The condom broke." As if it was a disaster.

A dart of unthinking panic was quickly replaced with the once-shocking thought that it wouldn't be the worst thing she could imagine. She'd always known she wanted children. Not just because she wanted a chance to be a better parent than her own had been, but because she couldn't envision a life *without* them someday. And she couldn't imagine anyone other than Jason as her children's father. She loved him. He loved her—at least, she was pretty sure he did. So why was he so upset?

She sat up, drawing the sheet over her bare breasts and touching his arm in comfort. "Does it matter that much to you? I mean, okay, it's not something we planned. The odds are against it, but it wouldn't be the end of the world, you know, if it *did* happen."

His face hardened. "Yes, it matters. It matters more than you can imagine."

A tiny chill feathered down her spine and she blinked. "Why?"

He didn't answer, just rose from the bed and disappeared into the bathroom with the defective condom. She heard the shower running briefly, then he emerged a minute later, a towel wrapped around his hips. And the closed expression on his face warned her something was going on here, something she didn't understand.

"Why, Jason? Why does it matter so much?"

Then he dropped a bombshell. "Because I don't want children. Ever."

Chapter 13

Jason watched as the warm color drained from Alana's cheeks, leaving her face white and pinched. And he knew he'd just delivered a body blow.

"Not even with me?" Her voice wobbled a bit, and her eyes…her eyes slayed him. But he couldn't lie to her about this.

"Not even with you."

"I…see." Her fingers tightened on the sheet. "I see." She averted her face as if she didn't want him to see how it affected her, and that ripped a hole in his heart. Alana hadn't been ashamed of anything they'd done in bed. Not yesterday, and not tonight. But he knew she was ashamed now.

Still without looking at him, she asked quietly, "May I have my clothes, please?"

"Alana, I… You don't understand." The words were on the tip of his tongue to suggest she obtain a doctor's prescription for the morning-after pill, which wasn't yet available over the counter in Hong Kong. But her reaction told him the request would devastate her even more than his admission, and the words died unspoken. "It's not—"

The face she turned to him was as fierce as her voice. "Don't you dare say, 'It's not you, it's me.'"

"Why not, when it's the truth?"

Her eyes glistened suddenly, and she bit her lip. "Because if you really cared for me—"

"I *do*."

She shook her head in denial. "You can't possibly." Her voice was scarcely above a whisper.

He sat on the bed and reached for her, grasping her upper arms and shaking her a little. "Don't say that, *lang*—"

She pulled away sharply. "And *don't* call me *lang loi*, because you don't really mean it."

His arms dropped to his sides. "You're deliberately misunderstanding the situation."

"What about me?" The tears in her eyes and her voice were a dagger in his soul. "*I* want children. *Your* children. You're not willing to consider it? Not even at some point in the future?"

More than anything in the world he wanted to be able to say yes. But memories flooded his consciousness, reminding him why he'd vowed years ago he'd never put any child through what he'd endured. "No."

"Why? Will you at least tell me that much?"

He couldn't tell her, but he couldn't say the word *no*. Not again. His throat closed and he couldn't speak. So he just shook his head slowly, watching the faint hope in her eyes die.

Her lips trembled, then tightened, and she nodded her acceptance. "I see," she said for the third time. "So what you're saying is, you don't care about what I want."

"I *do* care." He briefly considered asking why children

were so important to her, but decided against it because there was no point. No matter her response, he wouldn't change his mind. Instead he said, "Ask me for anything else. *Anything*. But not this."

"Then may I have my clothes, please?" Politely. As if there was nothing between them. As if they were strangers.

His hands tightened into fists and he fought the primitive possessiveness that swept through him, the possessiveness that insisted Alana was *his*, and he would never let her go. He clenched his jaw against the sudden urge to keep her here by force, if necessary, until she admitted she belonged to him. Making love to her until she agreed never to leave him.

She seemed to divine his thoughts, though, because she said in a tight, little voice, "You can't keep me here against my will, Jason. And I…" She caught her breath as if it hurt her to say the words that were the death knell to his dreams. "I don't want to be here…with you."

Alana didn't cry as Jason drove her from Causeway Bay to the DeWinters' estate on Victoria Peak. She desperately wanted to, but she knew her tears would devastate Jason, and she couldn't do that to him. Dirk's words kept coming back to her, like a filmstrip on a repeating loop. *I'm less concerned with you breaking Jason's heart than I am with him breaking yours. Not that I think he'd do it deliberately. But any woman who gets involved with him has to know up front it could happen.*

Her heart *was* breaking. But she didn't know why. There was an explanation, though. There had to be an explanation that made sense to him, even if she couldn't see it now. Even if he refused to tell her.

It wasn't that she just wanted children, and any man

would do. She would have been married long since if that was the case; she'd had plenty of opportunities.

No, her dream had been of a future with the man she loved, including children created from their love who would grow up in a caring, nurturing home, unlike the one in which she'd been raised. A dream that now lay in ashes.

But she wasn't ready to give up. She loved Jason; tonight would never have happened if that wasn't the case. So even though part of her wanted to lash out at him, wound him as he'd wounded her, she couldn't do it. He'd flinched when she'd told him earlier she didn't want to be there with him. He'd hidden his reaction behind a stoic front almost immediately, but he hadn't been able to prevent that initial instant's betrayal of pain her words had caused. Alana knew he *did* care for her after all. And she'd already hurt him enough.

Which was why, when he parked the car in front of the DeWinters' house, she reached over and turned off the engine. Then waited for his puzzled gaze to meet hers, a question in his eyes.

"I have something to say, and I'd appreciate it if you just listen quietly and don't speak. Okay?"

"All right. But only if I can say what I have to say after."

She nodded, then took her courage in both hands and said, "I still—" She stopped abruptly, unwilling to reveal her love in the face of Jason's outright rejection. "I still care for you. I know it might not seem that way after what I said earlier, but I do. I just need time by myself to think about this." *To come to terms with your edict*, she almost said, but she didn't want to make promises she might not be able to keep. She wasn't sure she could ever come to terms with it, but she was going to try.

She touched his cheek. "That's it. That's all I wanted to

say. I still care, even if I can't…" She reached for the door handle, but he stopped her.

"You've had your say, and now it's my turn."

"I'm sorry, I forgot. What did you want to tell me?"

He was silent for a moment, then said, "If it was any woman, it would be you. I want you to know that."

By which Alana knew Jason meant if he ever had children, he would want her as their mother. She was so moved by the admission tears threatened again, but she held them back with a superhuman effort. "Thank you."

Tenderness for this man, so obviously wounded in ways she still didn't understand, washed through her, and she knew she couldn't leave things like this. She leaned over and brushed a kiss against his cheek, murmuring, "Good night, *lang jai*. Thank you for making my first time so wonderful."

Jason jolted awake much earlier than normal the next morning. His heart pounding. His breath coming in gasps. Then he collapsed back onto his pillow, struggling to bring his body down from the nightmare that had woken him.

It didn't happen, he told himself firmly. *It was just a bad dream. Alana wasn't taken to a brothel in Macau. She wasn't raped, then forced with threats, drugs and beatings to service the men who would pay handsomely to—*

But other women had been. He and RMM had rescued Alana, but what about all the other women? RMM had to shut this triad down. Which meant he needed to stop obsessing over her and focus on the job at hand.

Easier said than done, especially now. Now that Alana had sealed herself to him in the most elemental way. Now that she'd shown him how much she loved him.

She hadn't said the words, but nothing else made sense.

Alana would never have slept with him otherwise, no matter what she said about "wanting" him.

And she still loved him, despite what he'd confessed last night.

Hadn't he known, though? Hadn't he told himself Sunday night that if Alana truly loved him she'd accept children weren't in the cards? Even though she'd been shocked and devastated at first, she'd left him with hope that all wasn't lost. That his dream of a life with her was still a possibility.

We could have a good life, he thought now, *even without children of our own.* There were numerous child-related charities crying for volunteers. He quietly supported numerous charities with money, even though he didn't have the time to devote to them, since RMM took all his free time. *If Alana married me, she could spend her time however she chooses. If she needs interaction with children, volunteering would be the perfect outlet.*

He would never subject a child of his to what he'd suffered growing up. *Not happening*, he reiterated in his mind.

He'd never told his parents. Had never told his sister, either. Those wounds went too deep, and he couldn't bear to have them touched. The only person alive who knew was David, and he was sworn to secrecy.

But that didn't mean he planned to live his life alone, especially now that he'd found Alana. In his mind's eye he already saw them married, taking their places in society in both his worlds.

His parents would love her; that went without saying. And her cultured background and royal connection to the Queen of Zakhar would play well to his paternal relatives, members of the British upper class who seemed to momentarily expect Jason to introduce an outsider into their midst, even though he'd always kept that part of his life completely separate. "She's not our kind, darling," had never been addressed to him—he'd made damn sure of that!—but he'd heard it said often enough about others…including his beloved mother. It had infuriated him, but paradoxically had also inculcated in him a steely determination that no one would ever be able to say that about his wife.

But right in the midst of his fantasies about his future life with Alana, a picture surfaced. One that had briefly appeared to him Sunday night, although he'd immediately suppressed it at the time—Alana with his baby in her arms. No matter how hard he tried to suppress it now, the picture…and the longing it engendered…refused to be completely dispelled.

Alana woke forty minutes before her alarm clock went off, and she tried to go back to sleep without success. So she lay on her side in bed, one hand tucked beneath her cheek. Thinking. Trying to figure out why, something she'd dreamed about off and on all night long.

Why wouldn't Jason want children? It didn't make sense. It wasn't that he didn't like children—he was a beloved stepuncle to Dirk's twin daughters. Children were pretty perceptive. Linden and Laurel wouldn't adore their "Unca Jason" if he didn't love them first and willingly spend time with them.

A sudden thought occurred to her. Was it possible Jason *couldn't* father children? Some men who were sterile pretended they didn't want children rather than admit their sterility, which they saw as a reflection on their manhood.

She dismissed that idea just as quickly as it popped into her head. Jason wouldn't have been upset about the condom breaking if that were the case. In fact, he wouldn't even have needed a condom in the first place.

"That can't be it, stupid," she murmured to herself.

So what *could* it be?

* * *

The first thing Jason did when he arrived at his office was call the social worker at RMM's safe house. "So how did the interview with the police go yesterday?"

"Not too bad. I only had to stop the questioning once."

"Were they able to supply any information the police or RMM can use?" She was a trained RMM operative; Jason knew he could trust Soo-Ying to know what was and wasn't important in that regard.

"Sorry, *laoban*. They didn't even know all the names of the men making the film. The producer and director, of course, and they picked them out of a photo array, but that doesn't tell you anything more than you already knew. And since those men are dead…" She let Jason fill in the blanks.

After a moment's reflection he changed the subject. "Has the doctor seen them yet? And what about the therapist? I notified them right away."

"The doctor arrived shortly after your first phone call yesterday. They appear to be in good health, all things considered, but the doctor is running some lab tests. Those will take a little time before we know the results." Unspoken between them were the words *sexually transmitted diseases*, a definite worry where one of the women was concerned.

"And the therapist saw each of them yesterday, after the police interview. Separately, of course. His opinion? Only one needs counseling." She didn't have to say anything more. Jason knew who…and he knew why.

Soo-Ying was one of a handful of people who knew of Jason's philanthropic endeavors in addition to his work with RMM. Anyone who'd suffered abuse was eligible for free counseling at one of the fifteen clinics Jason sponsored throughout the SAR. Sadly, there was often a waiting list, and Jason was in the process of opening five more to handle the demand.

"Make sure she moves to the top of the list," he told Soo-Ying.

"Already done, *laoban*." There was a tiny trace of smugness in her voice. "I knew you would request it."

He laughed ruefully. "You know me too well." Then he hung up.

He stood and strode restlessly to one of his office's floor-to-ceiling windows, the one facing Victoria Harbour. He ran a hand over his face, then propped his elbow on his other arm, which lay across his chest, tapping a finger against his lips. Lost in thought.

This high up the view of the harbor was incredible. But Jason didn't see the vessels plying the open waterway between Hong Kong Island and Kowloon on the mainland. All he saw was that woman's eyes on Sunday night.

Alana intended to keep as busy as she could all day. Which, given her workload, wouldn't be that difficult to do. She really didn't want to dwell on last night—early this morning, actually. She'd already racked her brain trying to figure out what Jason could possibly have against the idea of children. His children. To no avail.

She tried to imagine a life with the man she loved *without* children, but she couldn't. Juliana's mother had died before Alana was born, but the close parent-child relationship between her uncle and her cousin had set the standard for her, and she'd dreamed of having that with her own children ever since she was old enough to remember. Could she give that up? Was it even possible?

Jason didn't call or text, but then she hadn't expected him to. He'd unequivocally stated his position. The ball was now in her court, and he wasn't the kind of man who'd try to influence her one way or the other. If she wanted Jason without children, all she had to do was tell him. Problem was, she wasn't sure she could do that.

She was tempted to tell him okay, she could accept his terms while at the same time praying she could eventually change his mind. But that wouldn't be fair to either of them. Not to Jason, who had a valid-in-his-mind reason for his "no children" fiat. And not fair to her, either. Because if she went into a long-term relationship with him, thinking she could alter his stance and wasn't successful, she'd become bitter. Resentful. And she didn't want to become that woman. Ever.

Alana had just fired up her computer when Mei-li wandered in. "Hi there. I thought I'd catch you at breakfast," she said, leaning against the side of Alana's desk. "But…"

"Oh, I…I wasn't all that hungry for some reason, and I have a lot to do today. I'll be at lunch, though."

"Good. Hannah gets upset when anyone misses a meal—I think she thinks we'll starve." The tongue-in-cheek way this was delivered made Alana smile because she'd already been on the receiving end of a "just because I care about you" lecture from Hannah about eating regular meals. But her smile was erased when Mei-li said softly, "I heard you come in, you know."

She didn't reply, because Dirk had been quite insistent when he'd hired her and offered her room and board at the estate that her free time was her own. That she could come and go as she pleased, and he and Mei-li wouldn't try to run her life. This statement from Mei-li seemed unwarranted interference.

The other woman's lips twitched into a faint smile. "You're thinking it's none of my business how late—or early—you come in."

"Dirk said I was free to—"

"I know. And you are. This isn't about that, I assure you."

"Then why are you telling me this?"

"Because Jason texted me yesterday afternoon not to expect you home at all last night, and not to worry because you'd be with him. And that he'd bring you home this morning."

Alana gawked at Mei-li. "What?"

"You didn't know? I thought not."

"Why would he do that?"

Mei-li's smile turned rueful. "Because Jason is a protector by nature, and he can't help it. He thought I might worry if you didn't come home. And—" she chuckled beneath her breath "—he didn't want me to activate your electronic transmitter beacon, either."

"Oh," Alana said blankly. "I never thought of that."

"Yes, well…Jason did." Mei-li straightened. "So I guess this probably isn't the best time to tell you he texted me about you early this morning, too."

Alana felt as if she'd somehow wandered into the middle of a play without a script. "Why?"

"To make sure you're okay."

She blinked. "He drove me here. He watched me walk in the front door. He knows I made it home safely."

"That wasn't exactly what he's worried about."

She couldn't imagine what the other woman meant. "Then what?"

Mei-li made a face. "So this is where you're going to be furious with Jason, but remember what I said about him being a protector. He can't help himself. Which means he's something of a control freak and he worries about *everything*."

An idea suddenly occurred to her, so preposterous that when she opened her mouth to blurt out a demand that Mei-li tell her it wasn't *that*, she closed her mouth, words unsaid. The two women's gazes met, a silent question asked and answered, and warmth surged into Alana's face. "I'll kill him."

"I'll hold your coat when you do." Amused understanding was in Mei-li's voice.

"Oh, my God." She was so flabbergasted she couldn't get the words out fast enough. "I can't believe… How could he… He *told* you?"

The older woman nodded. "In his defense, he's worried about you, because…apparently…you left right afterward."

"Oh, my God." She felt like a parrot repeating the same thing over and over. "I'm fine." Then she muttered beneath her breath, more to herself than to Jason's sister. "*More* than fine, actually, because—"

Mei-li held up a hand to stop her. "I…really don't need to hear the rest of that." Her lips twitched as if she was trying to hold back a smile. "It was bad enough I couldn't stop Jason from telling me, because that's between you and him and nobody's business but yours. But he *texted* me. Once I started scrolling, it was too late. I couldn't unread what I'd already read."

Alana wanted to pull a pillow over her head and pretend this conversation had never happened. She wanted to crawl into a hole and never come out. But she couldn't do either of those things. It was a struggle, but finally she asked with as much dignity as she could muster, "What exactly did Jason say?"

Mei-li pulled her smartphone out of her pocket. "Why don't you just read it for yourself?" She unlocked the phone, scrolled, then held it out to Alana, who took it as gingerly as if it were an unexploded hand grenade.

"'Calling in a huge favor,'" she read, noting that just like the texts Jason had sent her, he didn't use the abbreviations most people used when texting, those she hated and never used herself. Everything was precisely spelled out, though the meaning was somewhat ambiguous. "'Last night was Alana's first time. Something happened and she left upset. So kill me later, just check on her please?'"

"I'm going to assume you're okay," Mei-li said, "unless you tell me otherwise, because I know my brother. He would *never* hurt a woman."

"He didn't." *He made it beautiful for me*, flashed into her mind, but she wasn't going to say that out loud. "So if you're not here because of that, then what?"

Mei-li breathed deeply. "You're probably going to tell me it's none of my business, and in a way it isn't. But I feel responsible, because I'm the one who asked Jason to mobilize RMM for your rescue. He might never have met you if not for me."

Alana could read between the lines. "You think I hurt him, don't you?" A spurt of anger shook her. "Well, I didn't. It's the other way around, actually."

Chapter 14

Mei-li frowned. "You just got finished saying—"

"Not physically. You're right. Jason would never hurt a woman that way."

"Then what *do* you mean?"

At first Alana was going to tell Mei-li that this was between Jason and her, and much as she appreciated the other woman's concern, she wasn't going to discuss it. But then she realized maybe Jason's sister could tell her why… So she stated flatly, "He doesn't want children. Ever."

Mei-li's first reaction was a severe disappointment to Alana—she blinked. "He doesn't?" This was followed by a growing expression of incredulity. "He told you that last night? That's why you got upset and left?"

Alana nodded. "I was hoping you could tell me why."

Mei-li still looked stunned. "I had no idea. Truly. I mean, he loves Linden and Laurel. You should see him with them."

"I don't have to see them together to know that. The

twins talk about him a lot, and I can tell from what they say that he's special to them. So I can't understand…"

Then a curious thing happened—an arrested expression flashed across Mei-li's face. "It can't be that," she whispered to herself.

"What?" The question was sharp and urgent. "What can't it be?"

Shock held Jason's sister immobile for a moment, then she shook her head and blinked as if coming out of a trance. Her eyes met Alana's. "It can't be." But the note of uncertainty said whatever she suspected just might be the reason.

Alana's throat was suddenly too dry to speak, and she swallowed hard. "Please tell me."

"I *can't.*"

"Why can't you?"

Mei-li bowed her head and covered her face with her hands. Breathing deeply as if she was trying not to cry. Eventually she raised a tearless yet ravaged face and whispered, "Oh. My. God. All this time I didn't know." Her voice was desolate when she spoke directly to her absent brother. "I'm so sorry, Jason. I never realized. Please forgive me."

"Tell me," Alana begged. "Please tell me."

Mei-li's gaze met Alana's, and she slowly shook her head. "It has to come from him. If I'm right—it seems impossible, but I can't imagine what else it could be—he has to be the one to tell you."

Suddenly her heart-to-heart with Dirk about Jason made sense. Crazy, illogical sense. "Dirk said…" She tilted her head and gazed off into the distance, trying to remember his exact words. "He said there's a gaping hole in Jason's psyche, and he didn't know if the woman existed who could fill that void."

"Dirk said that?"

"Mmm-hmm." Alana's voice wobbled, then firmed. "He also said he didn't know if any woman could love Jason enough to heal him." Her eyes met Mei-li's again. "Whatever it is that's so terrible you can't tell me, that's it, isn't it." It wasn't a question; she was as sure as sure could be. "That's what Dirk meant." Then the words poured out of her. "I love your brother. I haven't told him yet—I meant to last night, but…"

"But you never got the chance."

She nodded. "I don't know if I can heal him, though, if he won't tell me. He wouldn't tell me last night, and I asked him point blank. All he would say is that he doesn't want children ever. And if I care about him, I'll agree to do as he says." Her voice broke. "I just don't know if I can."

Lunchtime came and went, but Alana never left her desk. She had no appetite anyway, and she didn't want to sit at the kitchen table with Dirk's daughters, listening to their childish babble—too poignant a reminder of what she *didn't* want to think about. What she might have to sacrifice if she couldn't convince Jason to confide in her. If she couldn't heal him.

She worked steadily until midafternoon when her smartphone dinged for an incoming text. Her heart jumped, thinking it might be from Jason, and she was bitterly disappointed when she saw it was from Juliana.

Text me when you're free, please, so I can call you. I have a favor to ask.

But then she realized maybe Juliana was exactly the person she needed to talk to. They were cousins, but as only children they shared a special bond. Juliana had been something of a big sister to Alana during her teen years, and if she could confide in anyone other than Jason's sister the terrible decision confronting her, that person would be her cousin. So she texted back.

Free now.

The phone rang in less than a minute. When she answered, the world-famous voice filled her ear. "Alana?"

She quickly calculated the time difference in her mind and said, "Good morning, Your Majesty."

"*Would* you cut that out!" Juliana exclaimed. "You're picking up bad habits from Dirk."

"You've got to be kidding, right? Mr. Perfect? The man's practically a saint!"

Juliana laughed. "So how's the new job going?"

Alana expounded at length, then concluded, "I guess you can figure out I love my job, Jules. And I love Hong Kong, too—it's so different from what I'm used to, but I'm getting acclimated. I can never thank you enough for the referral."

"I knew how desperate you were to—" Juliana broke off suddenly, and Alana filled in the rest of the sentence. *Distance yourself from your parents.* "Well anyway, I knew you wanted a complete change, and I also knew Dirk needed someone who wouldn't…well…" She cleared her throat, and Alana knew what she meant. Dirk's last two executive assistants hadn't worked out because they'd both crushed on him to the point where it had become embarrassing for the devoted family man.

They chatted for several minutes more before Alana asked, "So what's the favor you want to ask me?"

Juliana's musical laugh made her smile. "Oh, Lord, would you believe I forgot?" Her voice softened. "How would you like to be a godmother?"

Alana gasped with joy. "A baby? You're having another baby?"

"Mmm-hmm. It hasn't been officially announced yet. Andre and I," she said, referring to her husband, the King of Zakhar, "we wanted to at least wait until I passed my first trimester. Now that that's safely behind me, the announcement's going out next week. But I wanted to tell you myself before the rest of the world hears the news, and ask you to be one of the baby's godmothers."

As was the norm with royal children, Juliana's firstborn had more than one set of godparents, so Alana wasn't surprised Juliana's second child would, too. "I'd be honored. So do you know what you're having, a boy or a girl?"

"Andre refuses to let the doctors tell us, and he says he doesn't care, he just wants the baby to be healthy. But I know he dreadfully wants a daughter. I won't say he always gets what he wants, but..." Her tone was droll. "I would never bet against him."

Alana laughed. "And since you do everything in your power to give him what he wants," she teased her cousin, "my money's on a girl."

A sharp pang suddenly hit her—an actual physical pain—as the memory of Jason surfaced, and how much she yearned to give him everything he wanted, too. Only...

She gripped the phone tighter and blurted out, "Jules, can I ask you something?"

The day dragged interminably for Jason, with no word from Alana. A dozen times he picked up his smartphone to text her, but every time he forced himself to stop. He wasn't going to pressure her in any way.

He touched base with David midmorning, who thanked him for making the women available for questioning and confirmed Soo-Ying's assertion that the police had learned nothing helpful in their investigation. "But we had to cross that off our list, Jason," David said. "You know we did."

"I know."

"So I'm going to ask you one more time. Are you holding anything back? Ten murders," David reminded him. "The pressure from the top to solve this quickly is intense."

That's putting it mildly, to say the least, Jason thought.

"There have even been delicate 'inquiries' from Beijing," his friend added, which made Jason sit up with a jerk. "One country, two systems," the constitutional principle behind the SARs of Hong Kong and Macau, was great in theory. But the ruling government in Beijing had a habit of flexing its might when something happened in the SARs to which it took exception.

"I know nothing more than what I already told you," he reiterated. "The name of the Eight Tigers was invoked during the…conversation. But those men were alive when we left."

After he hung up with David, he made a call to his second-in-command at RMM. "The Eight Tigers," he said without preamble. "What do we know about them?"

"Some people don't like children," Juliana reminded her. "I'm not one of them and neither is Andre, but…"

"It's not that," Alana insisted, going on to tell her cousin about Jason's close relationship with the twins, whose godmother Juliana was. "And until I mentioned it to Mei-li, she had no clue her brother didn't want children."

"Then why—" Juliana began.

"That's just it. He won't tell me why, even though I asked him. But Mei-li had an epiphany when we were discussing it earlier. She thinks she might know, but—" frustration was evident in her voice "—she won't tell me, either. She says if she's right, it has to come from Jason."

"Then I think you have to ask him again." Juliana gave a rueful little laugh. "Not easy, I know, asking a tough question like that and *making* him give you an answer." She sighed softly. "I can't tell you what to do, honey. You have to make the decision for yourself. All I can do is give you the benefit of my own experience and let you take it from there."

"What do you mean?"

"You know the 'misunderstanding' that separated Andre and me? I should have confronted him when I was eighteen, when I thought he'd repudiated me. I didn't. And I paid a bitter price for eleven years."

"I'm not sure I follow."

"It wasn't Andre's doing—it was all his father. But I didn't know that. Neither did he. He actually thought—can you believe it?—that I'd decided I didn't love him after all. It wasn't until he lured me back to Zakhar with a starring role in *King's Ransom* that we finally figured it out. But…" Juliana hesitated. "Eleven years. Eleven *years* we wasted being apart because we let our pride get in the way."

Alana saw the parallel Juliana had drawn. And she knew what she had to do…as soon as she got up the courage. Jason had shot her down once when she'd asked the question. But he *had* admitted she would be the woman he'd choose as his children's mother if he ever had a family. Which meant he loved her, even if he couldn't bring himself to say the words. Now all she had to do was convince him to confide in her.

Jason signed the lengthy contract his executive assistant had brought in and handed it back to him. Wing Wah Enterprises had just acquired a controlling interest in a British firm that was already making a name for itself in cyber technology, which would nicely round out Wing Wah's portfolio and add a tidy little profit to the bottom line. His investors would be happy.

"I've already alerted the flight crew about your trip to London, sir," his executive assistant said, referring to the crew of the company's Gulfstream G550 corporate jet. "They filed a flight plan and have advised me there's a window of opportunity for a six-forty-five takeoff this evening. That means you'll have time to go home and pack a bag."

Barely, Jason thought privately with a quick glance at his Rolex, a present from his parents and cherished for that reason.

He didn't always use the corporate jet when he flew, but in this case it was warranted for two reasons. First, the last-minute nature of the trip, since he hadn't been sure until the company's attorney had given him the green light to sign the contract this morning that there'd be a reason to go. And second, his entire executive team would travel with him, including an attorney and the head of personnel.

The last thing he wanted to do was leave Hong Kong right now, with things not yet resolved with Alana. But he knew it was necessary to visit the cyber tech firm and reassure its employees he had no intention of making sweeping changes, something everyone feared when the company for which he or she worked was taken over by a multinational firm like Wing Wah Enterprises. *Especially* one based outside their home country.

He'd thought he'd have the opportunity to tell Alana personally about his pending trip to London, although he hadn't known last night it would be today. But the disastrous end to their evening—from the broken condom to having to confess he wanted no children, now or ever—had put paid to that possibility.

His exec handed him a portfolio containing a detailed itinerary. "I booked you and the executive team into The

Savoy, sir. I know you prefer The Dorchester or The Connaught," he explained quickly when Jason frowned, "but The Savoy is in Covent Garden, a stone's throw from where you'll be spending the next week. Much more convenient, sir."

"Thank you." He gave the man his best smile. "What would I do without you?"

Jason texted his sister from the company's jet just before he shut off his smartphone.

London on business unexpectedly, he typed. Not avoiding you. Not avoiding Alana. Staying at The Savoy. Call me if…

He knew he didn't have to be specific. Mei-li was smart enough to know what he meant.

After takeoff he accepted a cold bottle of water from the smiling flight attendant, one of two who were part of the Gulfstream's flight crew. Then he reclined in his leather seat and stared out the window. Brooding over Alana.

Eventually he dozed. He hadn't had a lot of sleep last night—for which Alana was responsible, both directly and indirectly. First, the incredible evening with her…right up till the end, which had *not* gone as planned. Then the abduction nightmare that had woken him far too early this morning, after which he'd been wide awake…and thinking of her.

Without realizing it, Jason drifted into REM sleep. His heartbeat kicked up a notch. His respiratory rate increased. His brain waves altered. And he dreamed. Vividly.

At first he dreamed of Alana, from the moment he'd carried her out of that hellhole of an apartment to the tears that had glistened in her eyes last night when he'd admitted, *If it was any woman, it would be you. I want you to know that.*

Then, in the way of dreams, he was thirteen years old, he and David joining Sean at the prestigious boarding school outside Windsor, England. Sean, their staunch defender, who'd started there the year before when he'd turned thirteen himself.

No one alive except David, who'd shared some of the same experiences, knew what Jason's life had been like those years between thirteen and eighteen, when he'd matriculated and had headed off to Oxford. No one alive except David knew the worst, too, the scars inflicted on Jason's psyche much earlier by both his grandfathers. And he wanted to keep it that way. Sean had known, but Sean was dead.

Jason wasn't even aware when his dreams segued to Sean. Sean…and RMM. Receiving the gut-wrenching news about Sean's murder. Holding Mei-li as she wept her heart out in his arms over their loss. The vow he'd made over the grave, to be the man Sean never had a chance to be. To fight injustice the way Sean always had, to protect the innocent. The earliest years of RMM and the heartbreaking failures. Then he'd learned. And success had soon followed upon success with RMM. Until recently.

Jason stirred restlessly in his sleep, but it didn't disturb the dream.

RMM's success rate was still incredibly high, given all the uncertainties revolving around the things they did, both legal and illegal. But the occasional failure bothered him because there never seemed to be a cause he could put his finger on. And with no root cause there could be no corrective action. You couldn't fix something if you didn't know how it was broken.

Curiously, it was only those covert ops he was personally involved in—though certainly not all—that failed for one reason or another. As if he was careless. Or as if someone had a personal animus against him. But that didn't make sense. No one was more prepared than he when they went on an op, and who hated him enough to want him to fail?

And yet…that was the only explanation he could come up with. An explanation he refused to admit except in the deepest recesses of his soul because he trusted every man in RMM with his life. But the only thing that made sense was…sabotage.

Which meant RMM had a traitor in its midst.

Chapter 15

Alana texted Jason right after dinner. "Juliana's right," she muttered to herself as she typed.

We need to talk.

But Jason didn't call, and he didn't return her text. So she messaged him again.

It's important.

After more than an hour with no response, Alana turned off her smartphone in a fit of pique. If he called, it would go right to voice mail. *Serve him right*, she thought with righteous indignation. Then almost immediately a possible explanation popped into her mind, and guilt swamped her. What if Jason couldn't respond because he was on some kind of mission involving RMM? That thought made her scramble to turn her phone back on again.

But her phone didn't ring and it didn't ding for an incoming text. It stayed stubbornly silent well past her normal bedtime. She finally gave up and went to bed, only to be startled awake in the wee hours by the shrill of the landline.

It was answered on the third ring, so Alana turned over and tried to go back to sleep. Three minutes later she was roused by soft tapping on her bedroom door and Mei-li's voice urgently calling her name.

She grabbed her bathrobe and was still struggling to tie the belt when she opened the door. "Mei-li?" Her voice was middle-of-the-night hushed. "What's wrong?" Her heart clutched at the distress and concern on the other woman's face. "Jason. Please don't tell me something's happened to Jason." Her mind was racing frantically as she remembered her theory why he hadn't called her that evening, and she stumbled over her words. "Something to do with RMM?"

"No. No. Not Jason," Mei-li rushed to assure her. "It's your cousin, Juliana."

"Juliana?" Coldness enveloped her. She'd just been talking with her cousin earlier today. What could have—

"Her husband called Dirk. Juliana's in hospital and she's asking for you."

"Oh, my God." She stared blankly. "What—"

"Your cousin tripped going down the Grand Staircase in the palace and fell almost to the bottom. She started spotting and was rushed to hospital. They got the bleeding stopped but they're still afraid she might miscarry."

"Oh, no." A sick feeling settled in the pit of her stomach. Juliana's precious baby. Her goddaughter-to-be, the daughter her cousin's husband was praying for.

Suddenly Dirk was there in the dark hallway beside his wife. "The king's chartering a plane to take you to Zakhar.

Mei-li and I will drive you to the airport. How quickly can you be dressed and packed?"

"Twenty minutes, max." Then she realized… "But I can't just leave you in the lurch like this. I—"

Dirk cut her off, his face grim. "If Juliana's asking for you, it's serious." And Alana suddenly remembered Dirk had lost his first wife in heartbreaking fashion when his daughters were born. "I'd charter a plane myself to get you there if I had to."

The rest of that night passed in a nightmarish blur for Alana. The nerve-racking ride to the airport. Being practically thrown aboard the jet, which taxied down the runway almost before she got her seat belt fastened. The endless flight, during which she slept only in snatches when her body practically shut down, forcing sleep upon her. Sporadic prayers. *Please, God. Don't let her lose the baby. Please.*

The time difference between Hong Kong and Zakhar meant it was still nighttime when they landed, which was somewhat disorienting. A military escort met the plane, and Alana was hustled into a waiting limousine, which sped out of the airport preceded and followed by military police on motorcycles, sirens blaring.

They arrived at the hospital in no time at all. A tall blonde woman with sharply watchful eyes was waiting for her. "Miss Richardson? I am Captain Mateja-Jones, head of the queen's security detail."

"How is she?" Alana had heard nothing for hours, and she was desperate for news. "How's the baby?"

"It is touch and go." The captain quickly escorted Alana toward the elevator, her face reflecting the same unspoken dread Alana herself felt. "The queen is calling for you. There is some fever and her blood pressure is sky-high.

The doctors say calm is essential at this time, but something is weighing on her mind, and she will not rest until she speaks to you. If you could put her mind at ease…?"

"Whatever I can do." Alana couldn't imagine what Juliana wanted to tell her, but she knew ill people sometimes stressed over the oddest things, things which didn't always make sense. Whatever her cousin needed to calm her down, Alana would promise.

A nurse was standing right in front of the elevator doors when they opened. Flanked by the nurse and the captain, Alana was taken to Juliana's private room and ushered inside.

The room seemed to be full of people, she noticed right away. A private nurse, a technician monitoring the plethora of medical equipment surrounding the bed, and two men who looked for all the world like bodyguards. *Which they probably are*, she mused.

The captain moved to the bedside and bent over the petite, dark-haired woman in the bed. "Your Majesty? Your cousin is here." She held out a hand to Alana and wiggled her fingers, indicating Alana should move closer so Juliana could see her.

"Alana? Oh, thank God! I've been waiting and waiting."

Alana ignored everyone, cradled her cousin's face in her hands and leaned over to kiss her cheek in comforting fashion. Then she smoothed back the long, dark hair, so like her own, from the flushed face. "Hi, Jules," she said, hiding her incipient fear behind a confident smile. "You called, I came. Just like you came to my homecoming dance when I asked you, remember?" Making light of her urgent summons to Juliana's sickbed by comparing it to that lighthearted invitation nearly nine years ago. "And wasn't Darlene's nose put out of joint when my famous cousin came *all the way from Hollywood* to see me crowned homecoming queen!"

Juliana laughed as Alana had intended. "Oh, Lord, I remember that. And then the homecoming king—what was his name?—had the gall to ask me for a date!"

"Tommy Cooper. Captain of the football team. Senior class president. With an ego the size of Texas." She winked at her cousin. "I'd already shocked him by saying 'No way!' when he tried to sweet-talk me into bed two weeks earlier, and he was still smarting from that rejection. Guess he was just trying to show me up by asking you out."

Juliana laughed again, and Alana was heartened by the obvious lessening of stress in her cousin's face, not to mention the steadily dropping line on the blood pressure monitor near the bed.

She glanced around the room, looking for a chair, and that was when she saw her cousin's husband, Andre, standing in one corner, apparently leaning casually against the wall, his hands in his pockets. Then she saw the tenseness in his muscles and the terrible anxiety radiating from the green eyes set in an otherwise stoic face, and she knew he was far from casual.

Before she could ask, the captain was pulling up a chair for her. She sat and took Juliana's hand in hers. "So you got me here by scaring the living daylights out of everyone, including me. What's up?"

Juliana's head tossed restlessly on the pillow. "I can't talk with all these people in the room," she fretted.

Alana's meaningful gaze swung to the other occupants of the room, who quickly and silently exited. All except Andre. "Not while breath remains in my body," he said evenly, and after a moment Alana nodded her understanding.

"Okay, Jules," she said, stroking the hand that seemed far too warm. "It's just you, me and your husband."

"Andre?" The surprised wonder in Juliana's voice came

as a shock. Her cousin had to be far more ill than Alana had originally thought if she hadn't been aware her beloved husband was in the room.

"Forget him for a moment, Jules, and tell me why I'm here."

Juliana's hand tightened on Alana's. "Bree died," she said obscurely, mentioning the name of the woman Alana knew had been Dirk's first wife. "She was my best friend in all the world, and she died."

"I know." Alana's voice was very gentle. "I remember how devastated you were when it happened."

"Dirk loved her so much, and when she died, he—he went a little crazy, I think. He didn't even want to have anything to do with Linden and Laurel at first. Almost as if he *blamed* them for being alive when Bree was dead."

Alana hadn't known this. Dirk adored his daughters *now*. She couldn't imagine he hadn't always. But all she said was, "Okay." Waiting for the rest.

"Andre loves me so much," Juliana confided, and Alana knew that in her fevered state her cousin had already forgotten her husband was right there in the room. "If something happens to me, I…I don't think he'll be able to bear it."

Alana darted a glance at Andre. From the burning eyes in a face that had lost most of its color, she knew Juliana was more accurate in her assessment than she realized. And for no reason at all a memory of Jason surfaced. Jason gazing down at her in the instant before he'd kissed her for the first time. The expression in his eyes that—as blasphemous as it sounded—said she was his salvation. And she knew beyond a shadow of a doubt Jason loved her with the same all-encompassing love Andre had for Juliana. The same way she loved him.

She brought her attention back to her cousin with an effort, just as Juliana was saying, "I'm so afraid he'll react the way Dirk did. So I need you to promise me…"

"Anything, Jules. You know that." The calm assurance in Alana's voice seemed to help Juliana.

"Raoul didn't mean to trip me," she said, referring to her twenty-month-old son. "I was in a hurry and he was fidgety and I…you know how little boys are."

Alana didn't, but she desperately wanted to. And the little boys she wanted to know were Jason's sons. She wanted to know his daughters, too.

"So if anything happens to me, please don't let Andre blame Raoul," Juliana said on a rush. "I'm so afraid… I love them both so much and I couldn't bear it if…"

Alana sighed with thankfulness that Juliana had finally been able to voice the great fear weighing on her mind, the thing preventing her from getting the rest her body sorely needed. She stood and leaned over to kiss her cousin's cheek again. "I won't let Andre blame Raoul, Jules. I promise. And you know I always keep my promises. Now you have to promise me something in exchange."

"What's that?"

"Promise me you'll sleep now and won't worry anymore." She touched a gentle hand to the slight bulge that was the baby Juliana carried. "My goddaughter needs her rest. And she needs her mother, too." She forced a lightness into her voice she was far from feeling. "I want you to remember how you do everything in your power to make your husband happy," she teased, "and get some rest. So five months from now you'll be placing his daughter in his arms."

Six weeks later Juliana was completely recovered and her pregnancy was safely out of harm's reach—all signs indicated she would easily carry her baby to full term. And

Alana was finally packing to leave Zakhar now that her cousin no longer needed her. The maid the master of the household had assigned to her had offered to do her packing, but she'd politely declined, preferring to do it herself.

The king had intended to send Alana back to Hong Kong in his private jet, but Alana had adamantly refused. Charter a jet to get her here quickly when Juliana's life seemed to hang in the balance? She could understand that. But there was no earthly reason to fly an entire plane to Hong Kong and back for one person.

"I'll just take a commercial flight," she'd insisted. And the king's personal secretary had subsequently hand-delivered Alana's first-class one-way ticket for Friday morning. "The limousine will take you to the airport in plenty of time, Miss Richardson," the man had assured her. "Please ring for someone to bring your luggage down when you are ready."

As she packed, Alana thought of the work waiting for her when she got back. She'd done her best to keep up as much as possible long distance—email and the internet helped greatly in that regard. But some of Dirk's older fans still put pen to paper when writing to him, and those letters had probably piled up in her absence, along with a few other things.

Dirk had insisted she stay in Zakhar as long as Juliana needed her. How many bosses out there would be so understanding about a six-week hiatus? He'd still paid her full salary, too, which, considering she hadn't worked for him all that long before her emergency trip to Zakhar, put Dirk right up there next to sainthood where bosses were concerned.

"No wonder his fans love him," she murmured to herself as she tucked her panties in a corner of her suitcase. "He's such a sweetheart."

When she was completely packed except for what she'd need tonight and tomorrow morning, Alana sat on the bed next to her suitcase and contemplated for the umpteenth time what she'd done her best not to think about while she was here in Zakhar...and had failed miserably at doing.

Jason.

Jason and his "no children ever" stance.

He'd texted her that next day.

Sorry I missed your text, lang loi. I was on a plane to London. I'll be back next week, and we can talk then. Glad you see things my way. Yours always, Jason.

He'd obviously misunderstood. He'd seemed to think that because she'd tried to contact him she was conceding he was right. Which wasn't the case at all. Before she could formulate a response, however, and text him back, another message had popped into her inbox.

Mei-li told me about your cousin, lang loi. You and she will be in my thoughts and prayers. We'll talk when you get back. Missing you already. Yours always, Jason.

It wasn't possible to say what she wanted to say in a text—that medium wasn't designed for eloquence. She'd seriously considered calling him immediately to discuss it, because at least then he would understand how important this was to her. But she'd decided against it because she wanted to see his eyes when they talked. And she wanted him to see hers.

But the days in Zakhar had turned into weeks, the weeks into a month, and still Juliana wasn't completely out of the woods. There'd been one mini-scare after another, and Alana had had no intention of leaving her cousin until she was confident Juliana and the baby she carried were 100 percent healthy.

Jason had called her every afternoon at four on the dot. Which, considering the six-hour time difference between Hong Kong and Zakhar, meant it was already ten o'clock for him. So at first Alana had tried to keep their phone calls brief—no more than fifteen minutes. But after the third time he'd wormed the reason out of her. And from then on he'd refused to let her hang up until they'd talked for an hour or more.

Every morning she'd promised herself that the next time he called, she'd ask him again why he didn't want children. But her courage had failed her every time. Instead they'd talked of inconsequential things…her day, his day. And not-so-inconsequential things…how much they missed each other. Alana had even confided in Jason about her strained relationship with her parents, and why, hoping that would prompt him to open up to her about his past.

That hadn't happened, although occasionally he'd shared with her the progress RMM was making on the various cases they were pursuing, including the one that had almost ensnared her. Not the *details*, but still… She'd cherished those moments, because it had indicated a level of trust she knew was difficult for him.

Every day away from Jason was subtle torture, though, because just hearing his voice on the phone made her knees weak, made her stomach quiver and evoked intimate memories of all the things they'd done for and with each other. Now she knew what she was missing. Now she knew he could arouse her with just a look. A touch. And his smile? He had a thousand smiles, but the wicked one, the one that said she could trust him to satisfy her completely, she craved that smile the way she craved him. Alana had never so much as experimented with illegal drugs, but now she was addicted…to Jason. He was her drug of choice, and she never wanted to kick the habit.

The problem was, she might have to. Unless she could reach him somehow, unless she could help him conquer whatever deep-rooted fear prevented him from wanting children, unless she could *heal* him as Dirk had so bluntly put it, she would have to. Because she already knew she was carrying his child.

Chapter 16

That night Alana finally broke down and confided in her cousin. Not just about her pregnancy, but about the terrible dilemma she faced where Jason was concerned. Her flight was departing the next morning, and she desperately needed advice and moral support before she left.

"You're sure?" were the first words out of Juliana's mouth. "It's not just the stress over what happened to me? You know, stress can play havoc with a woman's system, and—"

"I'm sure. I took a home pregnancy test…three times. Positive across the board."

"Oh, honey." Juliana hugged Alana tightly for long minutes, then stepped back and asked, "Have you seen a doctor?"

"Not yet. But I will when I get back to Hong Kong. I promise."

"What are you going to do…about Jason?"

"I don't know. If I don't tell him, it's totally unfair to him. But if I *do* tell him, I know what he'll say. What he'll probably try to talk me into doing."

"You never had a chance to ask him again why he doesn't want children?"

Alana shook her head. "I was going to, but he had to fly to London unexpectedly and then I got the urgent call about you, and…well…no. And it wasn't the kind of conversation I wanted to have over the phone." She hesitated, then admitted in a low voice, "I love him so dreadfully, Jules. But I want this baby, even if he doesn't. Am I wrong to feel this way?"

"You're not wrong. At least…I don't think so." Juliana sighed. "I never told you, never told *anyone*, not even my dad…but I…I faced something of a similar situation when I was eighteen."

"You did?"

"Andre and I…well, he had reason to believe I might be pregnant when I started college. His father found out and sent agents to see me, pretending Andre had sent them. They handed me an envelope stuffed with cash, saying I could use it to have an abortion, or if I wasn't pregnant, I should consider it my farewell gift from him."

"What?" Alana couldn't believe it. "Did you throw the money back in their faces?"

"That's exactly what I did. As I told Andre years later, I wasn't pregnant, but even if I had been I could never… I loved him with all my heart, Alana—still do, as you know—but when it came right down to it, I could never destroy his child. *Our* child."

"I can't do it, either," Alana confessed. "Even if…" She gulped. "Even if he makes it a choice between the baby and him."

"So what are you going to do?"

* * *

Alana had plenty of time to think about Juliana's question on the flight back to Hong Kong. As she'd told her cousin, on the one hand she had to tell Jason. On the other, she shrank from telling him. Because she wanted him to want their baby, and she was so afraid…

So what are you going to do?

From that question for which she had no answer, she moved into the blame game. *You shouldn't have relied on just a condom for protection. Why weren't you on birth control? You know condoms aren't perfect, even if they don't break.*

But then she answered, *What are the odds? What are the odds I'd get pregnant on my very first time?*

Oh, she'd known ever since sex-ed in sixth grade that it only took once. Hadn't her teacher hammered the message home that unprotected sex was like a game of Russian roulette? But still…it wasn't as if they hadn't used protection at all. It was only afterward that…

She sighed and readjusted the pillow the flight attendant had provided her with when she'd taken her first-class seat on the plane. Then, because the seat next to her was vacant, she raised the armrest and stretched out across both, draping the blanket she'd also been given over her legs. Her first-class seat on the jumbo jet from DC to Hong Kong had converted into a horizontal bed, but the morning flight from Zakhar on the smaller plane wasn't long enough for the airline to think it was warranted.

What are you going to do? What are you going to do?

Jason checked Alana's flight status on the Arrivals board in Hong Kong International Airport. He'd rescheduled three appointments to meet her flight, but he hadn't even had to think twice. He hadn't seen her in forever. Hadn't kissed her. Hadn't held her. Hadn't breathed in the scent that was uniquely associated with her in his mind. He'd been strongly tempted to fly out to Zakhar every time there'd been another postponement of her return, but things were heating up with the covert operations RMM had going, and he couldn't justify it to himself. He was needed *here*. Absenting himself at this time would be selfish. *I want* just didn't cut it.

He pulled out the little box he'd been carrying around in his pocket for the past month and flicked it open. Then stared at the ring it contained, a flawless three-carat princess-cut diamond ringed by amethysts in a platinum setting. It wasn't the largest stone he'd looked at, but he'd known this was the ring the moment the jeweler had brought it out of the back room and placed it on the black velvet display card…the amethysts complemented Alana's eyes. There were matching wedding bands, too—he had every intention of wearing one—back at his condo.

He had no reservations about asking Alana to marry him. None. Her absence had left a black hole in his existence these past six weeks. Not just a physical ache but a deep yearning for the simplest things: touching her hand, watching her slow smile. Their phone calls had made her absence bearable. Barely.

And she'd been the one to contact him first, despite knowing how adamant he was about not having children. That had to mean she accepted it.

He had big plans for tonight, more than just the proposal. More than just making love to Alana. Tonight, after she accepted his proposal, once she was wearing his ring, he intended to tell her who he really was. What he was. And explain why he'd deliberately deceived her. If she loved him, she'd forgive him the deception. He couldn't fathom a scenario where she wouldn't.

He saw her before she saw him, and a jolt of adrenaline shot through his veins. She walked through the wide customs doorway, overnight case on one shoulder and pulling her wheeled suitcase behind her, then stopped and looked around expectantly. He waved from behind the barricade to get her attention, and when she spotted him she smiled and practically ran to meet him.

He'd waited forever; he couldn't wait a minute more. He wrapped his arms around her, even though the metal barricade stood between them. Then he lifted her over the barricade despite her laughing protests. "Jason! You really shouldn't. Won't we get into trouble?"

His mouth found hers, silencing further protests. And when she dropped her purse and overnight case at their feet and her arms stole around his neck, he deepened the kiss. Alana filled his senses, and the sights and sounds around him faded into nothingness.

Eons later he finally broke the kiss. Then just stared down at the woman who'd become his world so quickly he'd been blindsided. Heart pounding. Pulse racing. Lungs desperately trying to make up for lack of oxygen.

She smiled the smile he'd only seen in his dreams the past six weeks. "I think you missed me, *lang jai*," she murmured. "Almost as much as I missed you."

"More," he assured her. He kissed her soft mouth one last time because the urge was too great, then reached over the barricade, grabbed the handle of her suitcase and lifted it to their side. He strapped her overnight case to her other bag, handed her the purse she'd dropped and wrapped his free arm around her waist, drawing her to his side. "Come on, *lang loi*. Let's get out of here. I have so much to tell you, but—" he glanced around at the teeming swarms of people waiting for their loved ones to exit from customs "—not in this crowd." His eyes sought hers, letting them speak volumes about love and longing and who missed the other more.

Surprising him, her smile dimmed. "I have something to tell you, too." Her eyes turned soft and vulnerable. "But you're right—this isn't the place."

In the terminal's adjacent parking structure, Jason stopped beside a gleaming fire-engine-red Jaguar and clicked the key fob to unlock the doors and pop the trunk. He stashed Alana's luggage inside, then held the passenger door open for her.

Startled and a little concerned because owning a car in Hong Kong, *any* car, was an expensive undertaking, not to mention a Jaguar, she asked, "Is this new?" Hoping he hadn't bought the luxury vehicle just to impress her.

He hesitated. "Not new, no." He accurately interpreted the expression on her face and said gently, "No, *lang loi*, your worries are unfounded. I'm not trying to impress you. And yes, I can afford to run a Jag here in Hong Kong."

When it appeared he was going to explain further, she blurted out, "I'm not trying to…to pry into your finances, honest. I just don't want you to think…" She fumbled for the words. "I told you once before, but maybe you didn't really believe me, so I'll tell you again. I don't need *things* from you, Jason. I just need you."

His slow smile made her heart melt. "I believe you, *lang loi*. That's why—no," he said, shaking his head. "We're not having this conversation here." *But soon*, his eyes promised her.

Alana had hoped Jason would take her back to his apartment near Causeway Bay, and was disappointed when he pulled into the valet lane of one of Hong Kong's premier hotels. "Why are we—"

"This is a special occasion, *lang loi*, and the restaurant here is one of the best. But it's not just the food. The restaurant is on the top floor of the hotel and it rotates, giving its diners an incredible view of Hong Kong. The perfect setting." He didn't say the perfect setting for *what*, but Alana's pulse kicked up a notch, wondering if…

A sudden realization hit her. "But I'm not dressed for anything fancy." She'd known Jason was picking her up at the airport, so she'd selected an outfit with that in mind. But still…she was wearing a poppy-patterned sundress made from an uncrushable fabric that would withstand wrinkles, pairing it with a solid poppy-red jacket she could take off if she got too warm. Nowhere near dressy enough for an exclusive restaurant.

"You're beautiful in anything," he assured her. Then his smile turned wicked and his voice deepened. "But you're most beautiful when you're in my bed wearing nothing but a welcoming smile."

Alana didn't have time to respond before the valet opened her door, but she promised herself she'd have something to say to Jason in the elevator going up to the restaurant.

A promise she wasn't able to keep after all, since another couple got into the elevator with them. The man was wearing a business suit, same as Jason, but the woman was wearing sequins and four-inch high heels.

Jason laughed softly when Alana cast an accusatory look his way, obviously correctly interpreting the message she was sending. He leaned down to whisper in her ear. "She can't hold a candle to you, *lang loi*, no matter what you're wearing." A statement which mollified her somewhat, but at the same time sent a tinge of warmth to her cheeks as she remembered what he'd said in the car.

Alana couldn't help but notice the golden-brown color of the folded bill Jason discreetly handed the hostess who seated them at a table on the outer ring, right next to the window, and her eyes widened when she translated that into US dollars. Hong Kong currency was printed in different colors and different-sized bills for the various denominations, and golden brown was five hundred dollars HK. Not quite sixty-five dollars US. And that wasn't the tip for the *meal*, just to seat them.

She started to say something, but the waiter materialized before she could. He handed Alana a menu, then dexterously shook out the folded linen napkin on the table in front of her and tenderly laid it across her lap. He handed another menu to Jason, saying, "Our specials of the day are Lobster Cardinale, prawns in a delicate garlic sauce, and abalone steak, breaded and pan-fried, served with our chef's unique cocktail sauce."

Alana made a little face at this last item. She knew abalone was an Asian delicacy, but not for her. She noticed the waiter also didn't mention the price before concluding with a smile, "I'll give you and the lady a few minutes, sir. If you have questions, just signal."

When she opened her menu to make her selection, she was shocked to see the waiter had given her a "Ladies' Menu." Which was the old-school practice of printing a menu without prices for the man's female companion, so as to not sully her mind with anything as unimportant as the cost. She leaned across the table and hissed, "Jason! This is my father's kind of restaurant. You don't have to compete with him, I told you. So what are we doing here?"

He merely smiled at her, and all at once the wine steward was there. Jason didn't even consult the proffered list, shaking his head to decline it. He glanced across the table at Alana, then told the wine steward, "Champagne, I think. The Bollinger '96."

"Excellent choice, sir. I'll bring it right out."

As soon as he left, Alana glanced to the left and to the right, then leaned across the table again to whisper, "I meant what I said, Jason. You don't need a restaurant like this to sweep me off my feet." She'd tried so hard to build a life apart from her parents and their moneyed world, and at first it bothered her Jason might think he needed to impress her this way. Then her ever-present sense of humor bubbled up, and she chuckled suddenly. When Jason cocked a questioning eyebrow she explained, "My feet are already swept."

His answering smile was so tender Alana lost her train of thought. Then he extended his right hand across the table, palm up. An invitation. She placed her left hand in his and clasped it, pleading, "It's a lovely gesture, Jason. Please don't think I'm unappreciative. But it's not necessary, I promise you."

He raised her fingers to his lips. "I know what I'm doing, *lang loi*," he murmured. "Please just sit back and enjoy the meal and the surroundings." He gestured toward the window, and for the first time Alana let herself focus on the incredible night view.

The lights of the city twinkled like diamonds, rubies, emeralds and sapphires on black velvet, and she sighed her appreciation. She was well aware the darkness and the lights cloaked the seamier sections of the city, but from up here it was easy to forget anything one didn't want to think about.

"The Lobster Cardinale sounds good to me," Jason said judiciously. "I feel the same way you do about the abalone steak, and—"

"How did you know?"

A faint smile touched his lips. "You have an expressive face." Then he returned to his original topic. "I don't know about you, but I'll pass on anything with even a hint of garlic tonight, so the prawns are out."

Alana had been thinking the same thing. "I'm not all that fond of lobster, either," she confessed, quickly perusing the menu in front of her. She didn't recognize many of the offerings, and without the prices... She loved steak, but she knew it was prohibitively expensive in Hong Kong. In most of Asia, actually. So she wasn't going to order steak.

"They do an excellent shrimp in lobster sauce here," Jason volunteered. "And no, there's no lobster in the lobster sauce."

She raised startled eyes from the menu. "There isn't?"

"Nary a scrap," he reassured her, grinning. "The lobster sauce is actually made with egg whites, but shrimp with egg white sauce doesn't have the same cachet."

His grin was contagious, and she just had to smile in return as she closed her menu with a little snap. "Then I'll have that. I love shrimp."

"I know."

And just like that, his suggestive tone made her thoughts wing to the day they'd spent on the water. Jason cooking stir-fry shrimp for her...and everything that had preceded it.

She was grateful for the interruption provided by the wine steward bearing a silver bucket in one hand, a stand in the other. He set up the stand, then reverently withdrew the champagne bottle nestling in the crushed ice. He popped the cork without wasting a drop and handed it to Jason, who sniffed it lightly, then nodded. A small amount of champagne was tipped into a crystal wine flute for Jason to sample.

"Excellent."

It wasn't until the wine steward went to fill Alana's glass that she suddenly remembered. "None for me, thank you," she said, holding her hand over the top.

The steward shot a shocked glance at Jason, who merely tilted his head in a gesture of dismissal. The man replaced the bottle in its bed of ice and quickly departed.

"You don't care for champagne?" Jason's voice was quiet. "I could have ordered something else."

"It's not that." This was the perfect opportunity to tell him about the baby, and she opened her mouth. But the words wouldn't come. *How do you tell a man who's adamant about not wanting children he's going to be a father, whether he likes it or not?*

"Then…" His voice was even quieter than before. "You don't feel we have anything to celebrate?"

"Oh, no!" she rushed to assure him. "It's not that, either. It's…" She took a deep breath preparatory to telling him, but was frustrated by the return of the waiter. Placing their order seemed to take forever, and when they were finally alone again she heaved a tiny sigh of relief. She slid her hand across the table, palm up, just as he'd done earlier.

When he took her hand, she said softly, "You know I love you, Jason, don't you?" She'd never actually said the words to him before, but he had to know.

A wary expression stole over his face, almost as if he feared what was coming next. "Yes."

"I love you, but…I can't agree with your 'no children' rule. I'm sorry, but I just can't."

His hand was sharply withdrawn, and its loss made her heart ache. "I thought you'd changed your mind. When did you decide this?" The icy tone in which this was delivered caused her to shiver.

She took another deep breath. "Almost from the beginning."

"So when you texted me that we needed to talk…this was what you meant?"

Jason's face was an expressionless mask, but his eyes…

all Alana could think of to compare them to was the eyes of a lost and bewildered boy who didn't understand why he was being abandoned, and her heart broke for him. "No. Not exactly. I wanted to ask you why. That's all. I thought I deserved to know why." She bit her lip, but she knew she had to finish. "Then later on I realized why you felt that way didn't matter, because I couldn't go through with it."

"So all this time," he said with deliberate slowness, "all this time when we talked on the phone…when I confided in you things I've never told a living soul…you never had any intention of building a life with me."

"No! That's not true!" Alana desperately wanted to cry, *needed* to cry—for Jason and herself. But she couldn't. Not here. Not in a crowded restaurant. "I want to be with you more than you'll ever know, but I…I was praying I could change your mind."

Jason shook his head, and Alana's secret dream died. But she forced herself to ignore the pain and say as calmly as she could, "There's a reason you don't want children. There has to be. Some crazy reason that makes sense to you. Won't you tell me what it is? Please?"

She'd never seen a colder, more cynical smile than the one on Jason's face when he said softly, "If you loved me, my love would be enough."

Alana flinched as if he'd struck her, and all the warm color faded as it had done once before, leaving her face pale and still. Jason wanted to retract the words, but it was too late. He'd intended to wound as he'd been wounded… and he had.

Her lips parted as if she was going to speak, but then she closed them again, pressing them tightly together as if to hold in words she'd regret. Finally she said, "I won't dignify that with a reply."

She lifted the napkin from her lap, folded it precisely, then placed it on the table. She seemed preternaturally composed, but Jason noticed the slight tremor in her hands. "I'm not very hungry after all," she said in that civilly polite tone she'd used on him once before. The one that pretended they'd never lain naked in each other's arms. "I'll take a cab, but my luggage is in your car."

He signaled for the waiter. "I'll take you home."

"I'd rather—"

Fierce anger slashed through him, and he wanted to shake her. But he contented himself with an implacable "I'm taking you home."

Chapter 17

You don't die from a broken heart, Alana told herself during the interminable ride home. *You just want to.*

Neither she nor Jason said a word the entire time—what was there to say? They'd said it all in the restaurant. Jason had drawn a line in the sand, saying, in essence, "If you love me, you'll do this for me. You'll give up the idea of having children."

She could never tell him about the baby now. Maybe it wasn't fair to him, but that no longer mattered. *You have to think about what's best for the baby.* Which meant more than just raising her child on her own. If she wanted to keep the secret from Jason, something she had to do at all costs, she'd have to quit her job and move away, someplace where she'd never run into him. Because if she stayed working for Dirk, Jason would inevitably learn she was pregnant when she started showing. And it wouldn't take a rocket scientist to figure out he was the father.

She tried to make plans, but her brain wouldn't function. All she could think about were the questions for which she had no answers, like where could she go? She'd rather beg on the streets than go home to her parents. No way would she expose her child to their prejudices, especially since that child's father was Eurasian.

What would she live on? Her parents were wealthy, but she wasn't. She had a small inheritance from her grandmother, the one whose ruby earrings her uncle Julian had given her for graduation. But the principal was tied up in an unbreakable trust, and the income wasn't enough to live on. Not to pay for her own medical expenses and those of a baby. Unless she put her pride in her pocket and appealed to Juliana for assistance, something she was bound and determined not to do except as a last resort, she would have to have a job. *Other women do it all the time*, she told herself stoutly. *You won't be the first single mom juggling raising a child and holding down a job. You can do this.*

Only…what would she tell Dirk? What excuse could she give him for leaving? She didn't want to lie to him—he'd been too good to her for her to do that. But if she told him the truth, he'd know Jason was the father. And Dirk being the honorable man he was, he'd insist Jason needed to live up to his responsibilities. Meaning he'd tell Jason, which was the last thing she wanted now.

If you loved me, my love would be enough.

The backs of her eyes suddenly ached when those words replayed in her mind, and she knew tears weren't far away. But not for herself. For Jason. Because she knew with unshakable conviction he would never have said those words…unless he no longer believed she loved him.

It was nearly dawn when Jason walked into his penthouse and laid his keys and cell phone in the Ming bowl on the credenza. The need for speed had possessed him after watching Alana walk away from him, but there was no way he would put someone else at risk by racing the Jag on the streets of Hong Kong. So he'd driven to his private dock near Causeway Bay instead. He'd changed on board his yacht into one of the all-black outfits he wore on an RMM op, then had strode back up the dock and had taken one of the RMM speedboats out on the water. He'd donned one of the life jackets stashed beneath the seat the minute he realized he'd forgotten the first rule of boat safety, and once he was clear of the shipping lanes he'd opened her up and let the horses run.

As did all the RMM boats, this speedboat had the latest high tech electronic gadgetry, courtesy of Wing Wah Enterprises, and he'd set course for Macau. Not that Macau held any appeal for him as a general rule. He never gambled… except with his life. And prostitution was anathema to him. But it was a destination. And he'd figured while he was there he could also surreptitiously check out the Eight Tigers' casinos and brothels. Part of him had known it was the longest of long shots, but he'd theorized at least it would take his mind off Alana, which he'd desperately needed to do.

He'd returned home exhausted, covered with dried sea salt from the ocean spray, and unsuccessful…in putting Alana out of his mind. But he *had* uncovered something that might be helpful about the Eight Tigers. He needed to turn that info over to the others in RMM working this investigation with him, see if they agreed.

A quick shower took care of the sea salt. A cold bottle of water and a protein bar revived him. But there was nothing he could do about his craving for Alana except suffer.

He rifled through his clothes before stuffing them in the laundry hamper and pulled out the little ring box he'd transferred there earlier from the suit he'd left on the yacht.

He'd had some crazy idea of heaving it overboard on the way to Macau, but something had stopped him at the last minute. *Not* because he still believed they had a future; that belief had died in the restaurant. No, the only reason he hadn't chucked the ring was because he knew he could turn around and sell it back to the jeweler, then donate the money to one of the philanthropies he supported.

That the amethysts matched the color of Alana's eyes had absolutely nothing to do with his decision.

He collapsed naked on his bed. Moonlight streamed through the blinds and across the bed, reminding him he'd left them open on purpose. He'd told the maid who maintained his condo in pristine condition on a daily basis to change the sheets. But he'd been the one to arrange bowls of gardenias at strategic points around the room so their erotic fragrance would fill the air. And he'd opened the blinds before he'd left for the airport, to welcome the moonlight into the room for when he brought Alana back here after dinner. After he'd proposed. After she was wearing the ring he'd so painstakingly chosen for her.

Alana. He'd had such plans for her. For them. Plans that meant nothing, now that he knew the bitter truth.

He turned over abruptly, cursing himself for a lovesick fool.

If you loved me, my love would be enough. The words replayed in his mind as they had off and on all the way to Macau and back. Alana hadn't denied them. She hadn't insisted he was wrong, that she *did* love him enough for any sacrifice.

And yet…

He couldn't forget how pale and still she'd gone when he'd thrown that accusation at her. Couldn't forget the stricken expression in her lovely eyes. As if he'd mortally wounded her. As if he'd been her judge, jury and executioner.

Shock held him immobile. Was that what he'd done? Hadn't he told Alana he was willing to break the law, but he couldn't kill in cold blood? That he wanted to bring the Eight Tigers to justice, not deliver a death sentence?

But wasn't that exactly what he'd done tonight?

And where was his much-vaunted compassion for the innocent when it came to Alana? *Nonexistent*, his stern conscience answered. In his anger and pain over not being loved the way he selfishly demanded she love him, he'd lashed out at a woman he'd never wanted to hurt. A woman so beautiful inside and out she could have had her pick of men, but she'd chosen…him.

And why had he accused her of not loving him? Because she wanted his children. Not a crime any way you looked at it—most women felt that way when they loved a man. His own sister had confided she and Dirk were trying for a baby. "Don't misunderstand," Mei-li had said. "I love Linden and Laurel as if they were my own. But…"

Hadn't he understood what Mei-li meant? Hadn't he seen the wistful expression in her eyes, the desire to express her love for Dirk by creating a child from their love, to bind their lives together in this unique way?

So why had he condemned the same desire in Alana? Because of wounds more than twenty years old?

The High Tiger laid out his plan. "RMM has interfered with our endeavors once too often and must be taught a lesson."

"And how do you intend to do this?" queried the enforcer in charge of running the Macau casinos.

The High Tiger smiled slowly. "I have a source who tells me the High Dragon of RMM is enamored of a woman."

A chorus of "aahs" went around the room as most of

the men there immediately grasped the cunning nature of the plan.

Only the enforcer in charge of prostitution inexplicably didn't seem to get it. "What?" he asked, glancing left and right, then seeking elucidation from the High Tiger. "How does this knowledge help us teach RMM a lesson?"

He must go, the High Tiger vowed silently. *How did we ever think this man could be trusted with one of our most profitable undertakings?* "He is vulnerable through this woman," he explained patiently. "Therefore all of RMM is vulnerable through him. We do not know who the members of RMM are…but we know who this woman is. We could not strike before because she was out of the country, but she has now returned."

It took a minute, but understanding finally dawned. "You mean…?"

The High Tiger nodded and allowed himself another smile. "After she has spent time in one of our brothels in Macau…after we have taken photos of her with the men who will pay lavishly to pleasure themselves with her, the same way RMM took photos during their raid on our porn film…after we kill her and leave her naked body exposed, with the photos as a warning. Then RMM will get the message that the Eight Tigers will not brook interference."

Then he added silently, *Yes, and after we take care of this woman and RMM, we will take care of you, my friend.*

Even though it was a Saturday, and was technically one of her days off, Alana threw herself into the work that had piled up in her absence, and not just to keep from thinking about Jason. Loyalty to Dirk, who'd gone above and beyond in proving his loyalty to Juliana and her, made Alana determined to catch up as quickly as possible.

She was just laying the tidy pile of printed responses to

the hand-written fan letters on Dirk's desk for his signature when he walked in. "Hey, today's Saturday. You're not supposed to be working."

Alana had already scanned all the letters Dirk had received so they could be stored electronically—Dirk's office would need to be twice as big if they stored everything on paper in filing cabinets—and she'd queued up a couple of really sweet ones on his computer so he could read them. She looked up and smiled. "I know it's Saturday. But you've been paying my full salary the entire time I was gone, even though I was only doing three-fourths of the work. I figured the least I could do was read and answer these fan letters right away—some are almost six weeks old." She pointed to his computer. "Oh, and there are a couple you might like to read. I think you'll be as touched as I was."

Dirk sat and made short work of signing what Alana had prepared for him, saying as he did so, "Everything okay with Juliana and her baby?" He glanced up. "I assume so or you wouldn't be here." But there was a note of concern in his voice she rushed to allay.

"Everything's fine. She sends her dear love and heartfelt thanks for letting her keep me with her for so long."

He waved a dismissive hand. "That was nothing."

"Not nothing," she insisted. When a discomfited expression crossed his face she added, "But I won't embarrass you by going on and on about it," and noted his look of relief.

All at once she thought of Jason. Jason, who'd never looked for thanks, either, when he'd rescued her. Jason, her quiet hero.

Dirk's voice broke into her thoughts. "Mei-li and I would have picked you up at the airport yesterday, but Jason said he'd do it." He hesitated. "I got the impression we shouldn't expect you back until Sunday night." Buried in that statement was a question Dirk wouldn't ask outright, but he was obviously concerned about finding her here this morning.

"We went out to dinner, but we…had a difference of opinion, so he brought me home." A vast understatement, but she really didn't want to tell anyone what had transpired. It was between Jason and her. She didn't want Dirk to worry, though, so she said, "I'm okay, really."

"So why do you look as if you haven't slept for a week?"

Her hand involuntarily touched her cheek. She'd used a little more makeup this morning than she usually did, but apparently not enough to hide the emotional ravages of last night. "Oh, I…" she stammered. "I don't like flying. So I didn't get a lot of sleep the night before I left." Both of which were true statements. They just weren't the *only* reasons.

"Hmm." She could tell Dirk wasn't completely convinced, but he didn't press her on the issue, for which she was thankful.

They worked in quiet harmony until Alana's smartphone buzzed at an incoming text. Her heartbeat immediately ratcheted up a notch, and didn't slow back down when she swiped a finger over the touch screen and saw who the text was from. Her first instinct was to read what he had to say, but she forced herself to ignore it. He'd hurt her enough last night. And he'd been quite clear she couldn't change his mind. She couldn't imagine what he had to say to her, and she wasn't going to open herself up to more pain.

Ten minutes later her smartphone sounded the special ringtone she'd set up when she was in Zakhar so she'd know when Jason was calling her. And like his text, she ignored his call.

"Aren't you going to answer that?"

Thank goodness Dirk doesn't know it's Jason on the

other end, she thought as she shook her head. "It's not important. Whoever it is can go to voice mail."

Sure enough, a couple of minutes later she heard the little ding indicating she had a voice mail message. She dug the fingernails of one hand into the palm of the other beneath her desk as she fought the urge to listen to it. *Don't go there*, she warned herself. *You both said everything there is to say last night.*

The minutes crawled by. Alana tried to concentrate on the latest posts to Dirk's Facebook page, but her attention wasn't on her job and she had to read one of the longer posts three times before it made sense and she could click "Like" on Dirk's behalf.

Then the office phone rang.

"Oh, for Pete's sake!"

When Dirk slanted a questioning look her way, Alana realized she had no idea if Jason was on the other end of the line or not. She'd automatically assumed it was because he was on her mind, but it could be anyone. Still… she couldn't bring herself to answer the call, so Dirk picked up the cordless phone.

"Dirk DeWinter. Oh, hi, Jason," he added almost immediately, fixing his gaze on Alana. "Yes, she's right here. Hold on a sec."

She shook her head vehemently. "I don't want to talk to him," she whispered.

Dirk held the mouthpiece against his chest so Jason couldn't hear what he had to say. "If you had a difference of opinion last night, apparently he's calling to apologize."

"It can't be that."

"So you *didn't* have a difference of opinion last night?"

"We did. But—"

Dirk rose and handed her the cordless phone. "I'll give you some privacy," he said as he headed toward the door.

He paused with his hand on the doorknob. "Don't make him grovel." A tiny smile touched his lips. "You might be tempted, but don't. Men like Jason don't handle it well." There was a decided twinkle in his eyes when he tacked on, "I, on the other hand, have perfected groveling to a fine art," as he closed the door behind him.

Which meant Alana was laughing when she held the phone to her ear, because "Dirk" and "groveling" didn't go together any more than "Jason" and "groveling" did. "Hello?"

When he didn't respond she said, "Hello? Jason?"

"You were laughing."

The hint of gladness in his voice wasn't lost on her, but she quickly clarified, "Not at you. Something Dirk said."

"I'm glad, *lang loi*. Glad you can still laugh after what I said to you last night."

She closed her eyes against the waves of pain mixed with joy that swept through her when Jason called her *lang loi*. She would never forget his deliberately hurtful accusation, *If you loved me, my love would be enough.* But although he'd meant it in that instant, the Cantonese endearment proved he didn't now. She was still his dearest love…and he knew he was hers. Now she was fiercely glad she hadn't said any of the things she'd wanted to say last night, including, *If you loved me, you'd understand how I feel.* Because he'd already been hurt enough in his life, and he'd hurt himself as well as her last night.

"I should have told you—there *is* a reason, *lang loi*. And I shouldn't have accused you of not loving me when I know you do."

"I do."

Neither said any more for the longest time, as if what they were feeling in that moment transcended mere words. Then Jason asked, "Are you free tomorrow? Would you spend the day with me?" Before she could reply, he stated,

"I'd planned to spend the entire weekend with you, *lang loi*—I'd cleared my calendar—but something has come up with one of RMM's investigations, and I couldn't say no."

He'll never be able to say no when RMM calls, she acknowledged privately. And strangely enough, instead of being upset that RMM took precedence over spending time with her, a tidal surge of love and pride washed over her. A perfect man? Hardly. But he would never let what *he* wanted be more important than doing what needed to be done. And wasn't that one of the things she loved most about him?

"Yes, I'm free tomorrow. And yes, I'd love to spend the day with you."

"Is eight too early?"

"Eight's perfect. I'll be ready and waiting."

A half-dozen men were already seated around a spacious conference table in an isolated RMM hideaway not far from Repulse Bay when Jason walked into the room that afternoon and took his place at the head of the table. He stood there for a moment, his gaze moving from one man to another, silently assessing each one, fighting to suppress the insidious little voice in the back of his head that whispered, *One of these men could be a traitor.*

Every man there he trusted with his life. And every man there had proved himself worthy of Jason's trust at one time or another, some of them numerous times. *Not possible*, his rational brain insisted. *Not possible. It can't be any of these men.*

Cam Mackenzie, his second-in-command, and Cam's twin brothers, Luke and Logan. His maternal cousin, Shuài "Patrick" Chan, whom even Mei-li didn't know was a member. Trevor Garrett, the only paternal relative he respected, a man who'd taken a bullet meant for him on another RMM op and had nearly died. And Chao Jin, whom he'd known practically forever—Chao's father had worked for Jason's grandfather—and who'd been one of Jason's first recruits.

If he was wrong, what he was about to say could be a death sentence for himself and others in the room. *But I'm not wrong. Could there be a traitor in RMM? Anything's possible. But not these men.*

His sudden conviction vanquished his last, lingering doubts and he heaved a quiet sigh of relief. Without preamble he stated, "I think I know how the women are being smuggled into Macau."

Alana woke at six, excitement and anticipation making it impossible to sleep any longer. She dressed quickly in one of the jogging outfits she'd bought in Zakhar, tucked her hair under a hat and donned her sunglasses. She grabbed a bottle of water from the kitchen, then headed out for a run. She had plenty of time to still be back to shower and dress for her day with Jason.

She hadn't told anyone except Juliana, but she'd started serious physical training while she was in Zakhar. She was up to four miles a day now, and though she knew Dirk had all the workout equipment anyone could ask for in his exercise room, equipment she was free to use, she much preferred jogging outside to using a treadmill. The sun was shining and it bade to be a glorious day. Too nice a day to jog indoors.

She'd been lifting weights, too. She could bench-press her own weight now—not much compared to what she was sure Jason could do, but a substantial improvement over where she'd started out six weeks ago.

Not to mention the weapons and hand-to-hand combat training she'd received from the head of Juliana's security detail. Alana had even earned a few cherished words of praise from Captain Mateja-Jones with how quickly she'd mastered certain skills, including, *You are a natural with a pistol.*

And she loved her toned new look. It wasn't obvious in her clothes, but she was hoping Jason would approve when he saw her naked again.

She hadn't said a word to him when they'd talked on the phone, though, because she wanted to surprise him with how ready she was…when she asked to join RMM. She could still hear his deep voice in her mind, stating, *If a woman such as Mei-li, for instance, wanted to join our ranks…if she trained as we train…if she was as dedicated to the cause as we are…*

That was her goal. She'd have to take time off from training when she had the baby, of course. She wouldn't do anything to jeopardize her pregnancy, so she'd have to see what her obstetrician had to say about it.

Which reminded her; she needed to find a good one here in Hong Kong, now that she didn't have to hide her pregnancy from anyone. She was only a little more than six weeks along—she knew exactly when she'd conceived!— but it was never too soon to consult a good ob-gyn. She'd done her research as soon as she discovered she was pregnant, so she knew she wasn't putting her baby at risk by jogging. But she wanted confirmation before she did anything more strenuous than that.

Alana had passed The Peak a short time before, heading for the very top of the mountain. Then she'd rest for a few minutes; jogging uphill was a lot tougher than on a level, and her legs were feeling the strain. But after that it was all downhill from there. *A nice relaxing shower*, she promised herself. *And then…*

She'd noticed the van that had passed her a mile back along with two other cars, but she hadn't really given any of them a lot of thought, just made sure she was far enough off the pavement so they didn't accidentally hit her.

Until she rounded a bend and saw them lying in wait.

Chapter 18

Alana whipped around and ran as fast as her tired legs would take her, back in the direction from which she'd come. A surge of fear-induced adrenaline gave her added speed, but then she heard engines roaring behind her. Closer and closer. She feinted left and darted right, heading for one of the few houses along this section of the road. A car swerved in front of her, cutting her off. Another pulled up on her left and braked sharply. When she swung around to go the other way, the van squealed to a stop and blocked the rear, boxing her in.

She dropped her water bottle and scrabbled in her pocket for her keys to use as a weapon—*Go for the eyes*, she remembered Captain Mateja-Jones saying, *and don't hesitate*. Then she saw the key fob and remembered the alarm beacon and tracking device it contained.

Jason pulled up in front of the DeWinters' gate almost a half hour early and buzzed for entry. He could have used his key card, but figured this way, at least the household would know he was here before ringing the doorbell so early.

He'd been awake since six and ready by six fifteen, then had forced himself to sit in his office and do some work while he waited, chafing at the delay. Finally he'd had enough, and had taken off.

"Yes?" His sister's voice sounded through the intercom.

"It's Jason."

Her "Jason, oh, thank God!" response warned him something wasn't right, and he drove the distance from the gate to the main house at a speed the long, curving driveway wasn't intended for.

Mei-li opened the front door before Jason could ring the bell. "She's not here," she said, her face set in lines of worry.

Dirk was right behind his wife, and his expression matched hers. "Hannah says she saw Alana from her bedroom window this morning, heading off the grounds dressed in jogging clothes. But that was almost ninety minutes ago, and she's not back yet."

Jason knew a half-dozen things could have prevented Alana from returning by now, from leg cramps to a hit and run. But those reasons flashed into his mind and were almost immediately discarded. "The beacon," he asked urgently. "Did you activate it?"

"No, not yet. I—"

An alarm suddenly sounded and Jason cursed under his breath, pushing past his sister and her husband, heading for the security room he'd designed when the DeWinters had built this house. "That's the beacon," he threw over his shoulder. "Alana must have set off the transmitter herself."

Three minutes later Jason was in his Jaguar racing down Mount Austin Road, listening to the electronic blips of Alana's portable GPS tracking device getting louder and louder as he gained on whatever vehicle was carrying her.

He couldn't see it yet; he just knew it was somewhere ahead of him, but close. He hit the Bluetooth button on the Jag's steering wheel.

When the disembodied electronic female voice asked him, "By number or by name?" he barked, "By number."

"Number please."

"Five." One was his father's cell phone. Two was his mother's. Three was Mei-li. He'd skipped four when programming his speed dial because four was an unlucky number and no one wanted to be "four." Five was his second-in-command of RMM, Cam Mackenzie.

When Cam answered, he stated, "Someone has Alana. And if my theory is correct, it's the same triad that abducted her before—the Eight Tigers. Only this time I think she was deliberately targeted."

He rounded a bend at a speed that in a regular car would have caused the tires to squeal, but the Jag held the road steady. The electronic beeping was louder now, and in the distance Jason saw a white van. He accelerated until he was almost on the van's tail.

"What makes you think—"

He cut in. "I'm in pursuit now. White van, not new, not too clean." He rattled off the make, model and license plate number. "Probably stolen plates like all the others, but run it just the same."

"Will do. What else?"

"My sister was going to call the police, but she doesn't know about the van. Call Detective Inspector Lam of the Organized Crime and Triad Bureau. Tell him everything."

"Everything?"

Jason smiled to himself at the doubtful note in Cam's voice. "Everything."

Out of the corner of his eye he saw a dark car pulling up alongside him on the right, as if to pass. But they weren't passing. The passenger-side window of the Mercedes was rolled down and the barrel of a semiautomatic rifle was protruding from it.

He cursed and stomped on the brakes, shifting into neutral at the same time so the Jag wouldn't stall out, as a hail of bullets shattered his right and left side windows almost simultaneously.

"Jason! That was gunfire! Are you under attack?" Cam demanded.

But Jason didn't have time to answer. And he didn't have time to thank God he'd slowed just enough so the bullets hadn't passed through him, too, because the Mercedes was swerving into his lane, trying to force him off the road. He cursed again and fought to keep the Jag under control as the larger car made contact with a thump and a sickening shriek of metal on metal.

And as he was pushed farther and farther toward the edge of the cliff, Jason knew with awful certainty this wasn't a fight the Jag was going to win.

Alana came to on the floor in the back of the van. Gagged. Her hands bound cruelly behind her back, just like last time. But this time she wasn't blindfolded, and that terrified her, despite the lingering effects of the chloroform they'd used on her again. Because the men who'd abducted her hadn't been masked, and if they didn't care if she could identify them…that meant they intended to kill her.

She tried to get the terror under control. *At least I hurt them*, she consoled herself, remembering the gashes her keys had made when she'd fought off her attackers. She hadn't managed to gouge out an eye, an idea that sickened her even though she knew it shouldn't. But she'd done some damage to the faces of two of the men before she'd been grabbed from behind and chloroformed.

She could hear harsh male voices from the front of the van, but they were talking in rapid Cantonese and she couldn't understand a word. *I've got to get back to my Cantonese lessons*, she reminded herself firmly, until she remembered…there weren't going to be any more lessons. Not for her.

"Jason! Damn it, Jason, answer me. Are you alive, mate? Tell me you're alive!"

The booming Australian voice pierced the fog surrounding Jason, and he shook his head to clear it. His chest hurt like a son of a bitch where the deployed airbag had protected him from hitting the steering wheel. There was something warm and sticky in his eyes, too, and when he raised a hand to wipe it away, he saw the blood. The words *I'm alive* were automatic.

"Bloody hell, Jason, you scared the crap out of me."

Sudden laughter shook him. "Bloody hell is right," he told Cam. "I'm covered in blood, but I'm alive."

A string of curses filled the air. Then, "Where the hell are you? I'll get an ambulance to you right away."

He blinked and looked around, all at once realizing just how precariously his precious Jaguar was situated, wedged between two trees on the steep slope. If he didn't miss his guess the Jag was a dead loss, but the trees had saved him. He said drily, "I need a tow truck and rescue equipment more than an ambulance. I'm halfway down the bloody mountain."

The electronic beeping growing ever fainter finally impinged on his consciousness, and just like that the fog swirling inside his head was dissipated. *Alana. Abduction. The Eight Tigers.* "Make that call about Alana to Detective Inspector Lam your top priority," he said, his voice crisp and once again in command. "Then worry about me."

"Righto. But how's he going to find her?"

"She's transmitting her location, just like last time. With the right GPS equipment—" Something clicked in his brain. "Macau. They're taking her to Macau." He unbuckled his seat belt, saying, "Belay that order about Detective Lam." Then he punched the remaining safety glass out of the driver's side window with his elbow, preparatory to climbing out. "I need a boat."

Still bound and gagged, Alana feigned unconsciousness when she was transferred like baggage from the van to the cargo hold of a sleek, bright red boat that looked fast. Very fast. She didn't know enough about watercraft to know what this one was. All she knew was that it was bigger than her father's cabin cruiser, but smaller than the yacht Jason had taken her out on.

Jason. She'd tried her best not to think of him. Tried not to remember how he'd rescued her the last time. Part of her couldn't help praying he would somehow rescue her again, but she couldn't count on that. She had to rescue herself if she could, which was why she hadn't let on the effects of the chloroform her captors had used on her had worn off earlier than they'd anticipated. She needed every little edge she could get.

They'd taken her keys away, but not before she'd activated the beacon. And the driver of the van, who was one of the men who'd carried her onto this boat, had pocketed her keys...and her key fob. Which meant even though the transmitter wasn't actually on her, it was close enough for someone to track her. Assuming the beacon's range was great enough to encompass wherever it was they were taking her. So it was still possible Jason might...

If they didn't kill her before he could find her. She'd acknowledged her ultimate fate back in the van when she'd realized she wasn't blindfolded, so she wasn't overcome with fear now. But she also knew they weren't just going to kill her. Otherwise she'd be dead already. So there was a purpose to why she was being transported on a boat. She just didn't know where to, and she didn't know why. But one thing she did know. Whatever it was, it wasn't good... for her.

"Damn it, Jason, would you hold still? You bled like a stuck pig." A bottle of hydrogen peroxide in one hand, cotton swabs in the other, Cam was attempting to clean the wound that was still oozing sluggishly on Jason's forehead.

Jason impatiently waved him off and attempted to rise. "What are you, my nursemaid? I'm fine."

At six-four, Cam had three inches on Jason, and he shoved him back down on the seat. Hard. RMM's MetalCraft Marine high speed interceptor 11M patrol boat, the *Night Wind*, had already departed from the dock ten minutes ago, with Chao at the helm, following the course Jason had laid in based on the GPS coordinates of their moving target. Luke and Logan were setting up the 50-caliber machine guns in the forward and aft gun mounts, and Trevor—the crème de la crème of RMM's sharpshooters—was uncrating sniper rifles from the cache RMM kept stored below decks and methodically loading them.

"If you're too stupid or too stubborn to let me clean that up and put a bandage on it, I'll order Luke and Logan to hold you down, mate. And don't think I won't."

Which made Jason chuckle because, damn it, he knew Cam would do it, too. Besides, they weren't even close to catching up with the boat carrying Alana, which meant there wasn't a damn thing for him to do at the moment except listen to the electronic beeps...and let Cam do his worst. So he gave in with as good grace as he could muster, saying, "A couple of sticking plasters should do it after you mop up the blood. I don't want anything interfering with my vision."

"It'll take more than that, you dipstick. I don't know what you hit if the airbag deployed, but there's a three-inch gash on your forehead from your hairline to your eyebrow. Don't even *think* about using face paint as camouflage the way you usually do, or I'll have to hurt you. Wear a mask instead. That wound will probably need stitches, but for now I'll do the best I can."

The *Night Wind*, designed for intercepting, boarding and seizing high-speed target craft, was already doing forty knots in the relatively calm waters of the South China Sea. Jason had just recently had this boat retrofitted with the latest technology, which, when combined with its speed and versatility, made it the perfect vessel for RMM's covert operations.

They'd skirted north of the Soko Islands and were coming round the southwestern tip of Lantau Island, from which it was a straight shot to Macau, when the electronic beeps began to pick up in frequency and volume.

Jason put his hand on Chao's shoulder and leaned forward to peer through the windshield awash with ocean spray. "Binocs in that compartment right there," Chao said, pointing. Jason pulled out the binoculars and stepped outside the cabin for a better view, quickly focusing on the red boat in the distance.

"Gotta be them," he replied a minute later as he came back inside, forcing his voice to a calmness he was far from feeling. "ETA to intercept?" he asked Cam, who was already punching numbers into a laptop.

"Eight minutes, give or take. Assuming they're already doing best speed and Chao kicks it up a notch." His gaze met Jason's. "It'd be preferable to overtake them in open water."

Meaning, as Jason well knew, it would be best if they were far from any of the islands south of them and there were no other boats in their vicinity. Because their plan was tantamount to piracy. Overtake, intercept, force their target vessel to heave to—at gunpoint if necessary—and board. And at the same time they had to make sure none of the men aboard the other boat tried to use Alana as a hostage...or worse. The fact that they knew damn well she was a prisoner on that boat didn't change the illegality of what they were going to do. "Agreed." He glanced at Chao. "Gun it."

Alana had just maneuvered herself onto her back, despite her bound hands, when she heard what sounded like a burst of machine-gun fire, followed by excited babble in Cantonese overhead. The boat abruptly changed course, throwing her sharply to one side, but its speed didn't slacken. Then the vessel shuddered when something hit it with terrific force, accompanied by another round of gunfire and cries of pain this time.

There was an odd sound she couldn't quite place, sort of a gurgling. Before she could figure out what it was, something cold and wet seeped across the deck on which she lay, and then she knew. Water. Ocean water. *We're sinking!*

Urgent footsteps warned her someone was coming down the ladder into the hold. She quickly closed her eyes to mere slits and readied to defend herself. *One chance*, she thought feverishly, hearing Captain Mateja-Jones in her mind again. *You have one chance. Make it good.* Suddenly a shadowy figure with a gun in one hand was looming over her, his other hand reaching down, and...

Alana's left leg shot up as if it were a piston, kicking the man's gun hand. She couldn't see very well in the hold's dim light, but the grunt he made and the half thud, half splash of the pistol hitting the deck told her she'd managed to disarm him. When he scrabbled in the slowly rising water to recover the weapon, her right leg swung up and over, and her foot connected with his ribs. The man stumbled and fell to his knees. Alana was sure the words issuing from his mouth were curses, but she didn't understand and didn't give a damn anyway. She jerked herself around in what was now a couple of inches of water, levered both knees up, then kicked out with everything she had, making solid contact with the man's midsection and sending him sprawling with a satisfying splash.

Over the harsh sound of the man's continued curses she heard thumps overhead that sounded like boots hitting the deck, and the boat rocked violently. Then what little light there was in the hold was temporarily blocked out when a man disdained the ladder and jumped through the opening, landing with another splash. She readied her now-trembling legs to ward off a new attack, when a deep voice she heard in her dreams said, "Alana?"

Chapter 19

Alana's name uttered in Jason's distinctive British accent, the voice he hadn't been able to disguise from day one, sent a wave of blessed relief through her veins and a rush of tears to her eyes, but the gag kept her from answering. Her would-be attacker scrambled to his feet, and she moaned frantically to let Jason know she was alive and to warn him they weren't alone in the hold.

He didn't seem to need her warning. A series of powerful blows from him, and the man she'd only temporarily incapacitated hit the deck…and didn't stir again.

Jason was at her side instantly, gentle hands raising her up and turning her around. She recognized the whisper of metal against leather, and knew he was drawing his knife from its sheath. "Hold still," he ordered.

Then, just as the first time Jason had rescued her, the gag melted away. "Oh, God. Jason!" Those were the only words she managed before tears of thankfulness closed her throat.

His irreverent "One and the same, *lang loi*" made her choke on laughter as the rope binding her wrists was carefully cut loose. Laughter, because she knew he didn't really mean it that way. Because she knew *him*. Despite the accomplishments that in any other man would have accompanied an ego twice the size of Alaska, despite the quiet confidence and assurance he exuded, Jason was relatively modest and unassuming. He'd only said what he'd said now because he knew her well enough to know she needed something to buck her up, to make her laugh so she didn't start crying.

He sheathed the knife before lifting her effortlessly into his arms and splashing toward the rectangle of light spilling down into the hold from above. "Cam!" he bellowed.

A giant figure appeared in the opening, then strong hands reached down to lift Alana onto the deck. Three seconds later Jason was at her side, and his arms closed around her. Tight. She didn't mind in the least because her arms were doing the same to him, holding him as if she'd never let him go. And now that it was all over, the adrenaline letdown had her silently weeping as if she'd never stop.

He pressed her head against his chest, one hand stroking her hair in soothing fashion. In a distant corner of her brain she recognized there was movement going on around them. But all she could hear was the not-so-steady beat of Jason's heart beneath her ear.

Eventually she cried herself out and raised her head, gasping when she finally got a really good look at him. "Oh, my God!"

Unlike the first time he'd rescued her, he wasn't wearing camouflage face paint. But he *was* wearing a disguising black mask over his eyes. That wasn't what made her gasp, though. That was caused by the white bandage across one side of his forehead, which was secured by a bright red bandanna, giving him a somewhat piratical look. And the bruises already forming on the right side of his face made her exclaim, "You're hurt! What happened?"

"Slight disagreement with a tree. Nothing serious."

The tall man with a shaggy mane of blond hair standing beside them, the man who'd lifted her out of the hold and whose face *was* camouflaged, suddenly snorted. His "Don't listen to him, Sheila" was delivered in one of the broadest Australian accents she'd ever heard. "He's going to need stitches, but the bloody fool insisted on coming to your rescue first." He shook his head in mock disbelief at Jason's supposed stupidity, but his eyes were kind and his voice held rough affection for the man whose arms were still around her.

"Alana, this is Cam," Jason said in a long-suffering voice. "Cam only *thinks* he knows best. Must come from being the oldest of a large family."

Cam winked at her, then grinned. She wiped away the remnants of tears from her eyes with the back of one hand and tried to answer his smile. "Pleased to meet you, Cam. You'll pardon me, I'm sure," she said with the same mock seriousness he'd used, "but I'm awfully glad Jason *didn't* stop to get stitches before rescuing me."

He laughed and clapped Jason on the right shoulder. "She'll do for you, mate." Jason's sudden wince of pain wasn't lost on either of them, and their smiles faded. "Damn it," Cam growled. "Hospital for you."

Jason shook his head. "For Alana, not me. I want her checked out." His gaze turned back to her, a terrible question in his eyes. "They didn't…?"

"No, oh, no!" she reassured him, understanding what he couldn't bring himself to ask. "They didn't."

His profound relief was obvious even beneath the mask. But just as obvious was the assurance that his relief was for *her*, not for him. That his love wouldn't have abated one iota or been altered in any way if she *had* been raped. Her heart swelled with renewed love for this incredible man, and she laid her head against his chest as their arms tightened around each other again. "They didn't even hit me this time," she admitted softly. "Just overpowered me with chloroform."

"I still want a doctor to look you over," he said in decisive tones, his voice rumbling in his chest.

She privately concurred, although not for herself, for the baby. *I want a doctor's reassurance our baby's okay.* But her voice was quietly insistent when she told Jason, "Only if you'll agree to do the same."

Events moved swiftly after that. Another camouflaged man, whom Jason introduced merely as Trevor, came up to them. "This boat's taking on water, Jason…as if you didn't know," he added when his gaze took in their wet clothes. "What do you want to do about the boat…and about them?"

He jerked a thumb over his shoulder, and that was when Alana saw the five men who, with the man still down in the hold, had abducted her that morning. Bloodied, but alive. Tightly bound and gagged, just as she'd been. But alive. Standing guard over them were two blond men in full camouflage, each with a rifle slung over one shoulder.

Her heartbeat stuttered at the instantaneous and terrifying change that came over Jason's face as it morphed from loving concern to implacable anger. And for just a moment she feared…

"No, Jason," she pleaded softly, clutching his forearm, which was like corded steel beneath her fingers. "No."

He glanced down at her, and the frightening expression had vanished. "Did you really think I'd turn them into shark bait, *lang loi*?" he chided mildly. "Much as I might want to for what they planned to do to you?"

He didn't say anything else, but in her mind Alana heard his words from weeks ago. *Not in cold blood... We're not judge, jury and executioner... We want to bring them to justice. Not mete out a death sentence.* And she knew she'd worried for nothing.

"No. Not really," she stammered. "Well, just for a moment... But I know you wouldn't." Then she focused on his last sentence. "How do you know what they planned to do to me?"

Jason's absolute stillness revived her earlier fear. But all he said was, "I know. Let's just leave it at that." He turned back to Trevor, "Let's get them aboard the *Night Wind*. And the one in the hold, too. We'll decide what to do with them on the way back. As for this boat..." He smiled, but it was a smile she'd never seen on Jason's face before. Cold. Ruthless.

Whatever that smile meant, Trevor seemed to get the message. His answering smile matched Jason's. "Consider it done."

Jason and Trevor transferred Alana to the *Night Wind*, and saw her safely ensconced on a seat in the cabin, before she thought of something. "Oh. One of the men who abducted me has my cell phone as well as my keys and beacon key fob. I assume the beacon is how you located me, and I want it back. I was never more grateful for any electronic device than I was when I remembered I had it."

Trevor glanced at Jason, then back at her. "I'll get them, ma'am."

After he left, Alana said with certainty, "He was involved in my first rescue, too. Not the driver of the van that took me home—the other man."

"What makes you say that? We were all—"

Alana mentally added the word he didn't say: *disguised. We were all disguised.* Just as they were all disguised today. She smiled faintly. "I recognize his voice. Same way I recognized yours."

He didn't bother trying to deny it, but he didn't confirm it verbally, either. The flash of admiration in his eyes, though, betrayed him.

A dark-haired man entered the cabin just then, and Jason introduced him by his first name, too. She wasn't upset when she figured out why he wasn't giving her last names... she didn't have a need to know. And what she didn't know she couldn't inadvertently reveal.

"Pleased to meet you, ma'am," Chao said politely before taking the seat at the helm and unlocking the controls.

"Him, too," she mouthed at Jason. "He was the driver."

"You're entirely too perceptive, *lang loi*," he murmured.

"And don't you forget it," she teased. "You'll never be able to lie to me and get away with it."

And just like that, Alana slid a verbal knife between Jason's ribs again, all unaware. The knowledge that he *had* lied to her from day one hurt worse than the airbag that had punched the breath from his lungs earlier.

She must have read something in his set expression because her smile faltered. "I was just teasing, Jason. I know you'd never try to deceive me."

He almost blurted out the truth then and there. "About that," he began, but then Trevor walked in and the moment was lost. "Here you are, ma'am. Cell phone, keys and key fob." He handed Alana's belongings to her. To Jason he said, "All set," as he took a seat across from them, and Jason nodded his understanding.

Cam, Luke and Logan suddenly crowded into the cabin,

and Cam told Chao, "Good to go," before taking a seat on the other side of Alana.

Chao started the engines immediately, and in less than a minute the *Night Wind* was pulling away from the now-listing Eight Tigers boat.

"Which one ran you off the road, Jason?" Cam asked in the manner of a man who was just making conversation. "Could you recognize him?"

Alana turned startled eyes on Jason. "Someone ran you off the road?" Before he could answer, the question cleared from her face. "Of course. That's what you meant when you said you'd had a slight disagreement with a tree."

"Thanks, Cam," Jason said drily, glancing over Alana's head at his friend and mouthing the words *You're toast* at him. He removed his mask, debating what to tell Alana. Then his gaze slid to meet hers. "I was already at the DeWinters' when you set off the beacon. I was on the road a couple of minutes later, and I was right behind the van that had you."

"Oh, Jason." She leaned thankfully against his undamaged shoulder. "I was praying when I was in the back of that van. Praying you'd rescue me again. I knew I shouldn't count on it, but…I couldn't help hoping."

One corner of his mouth flicked upward in a half smile. "If they hadn't run me off the road, they'd never even have gotten you on their boat in the first place."

"One man against six?" There was a doubtful note in her voice.

"Are you questioning my manhood or my resolve?" he teased and was rewarded by a somewhat watery chuckle.

"They ran Jason off the road after they failed to stop him with bullets," Cam volunteered in the voice of one who was merely trying to be helpful.

Alana's hand tightened on his shirt. "They shot at you?"

"Thanks, Cam," he repeated even more drily than before. To Alana he whispered softly in her ear, "They'd have to kill me to stop me, *lang loi*. Guess they figured that out."

"Oh, Jason."

Across the cabin Trevor glanced at his watch and stood, turning around to gaze through the open doorway at the rapidly receding Eight Tigers boat in the distance. No other craft were anywhere in sight. He tugged something from his pocket and Jason tightened his arm around Alana.

"Wait for it," he said quietly.

Alana raised her head from his shoulder. "Wait for what?"

Trevor said matter-of-factly, "Three, two, one, boom," and pressed the detonator button.

An explosion rocked the air, and the Eight Tigers boat disintegrated in a fireball. The ignited fuel in its tanks caused flames to dance atop the surface of the ocean for a few seconds…then they disappeared, one by one. Until all that was left was a black smudge in the distance and a cloud of smoke that quickly dispersed.

"You…you blew up their boat." Shock was evident on Alana's face.

He'd known it wouldn't be easy for her to accept that RMM's tactics were sometimes…problematic. But it was best she know now. It was one thing to *tell* her he and RMM broke the law on occasion. It was another thing for her to witness it firsthand. "Prostitution, drugs and pornography made using trafficked women paid for that boat," he reminded her. "And we had to rescue you, no matter what it took."

"Yes, but…"

"We fired on that boat. Rammed it. Boarded it. Took six men prisoner. That's piracy and kidnapping, any way you look at it." His voice was steady. "We couldn't leave physical evidence behind. It's bad enough there are six men in the hold who could testify against us…although in order to do that they'd have to admit kidnapping you. And they'd have to be able to identify us, which we've made sure they can't do." To make his point, he lifted the mask he'd removed earlier. "So as long as there's no physical evidence…"

"You and RMM are in the clear. I understand."

He searched her eyes for long moments, and she held his gaze. "I think you *do* understand," he said finally. Un- utterably relieved.

She nodded. "That's why I want to join RMM."

He did a double take. "What?"

"You told me that if a woman trained as you train, if she was as dedicated to the cause as you were…you'd let a woman join your ranks."

He stared helplessly. "Yes, but…"

"You said the members only recruit their trusted friends. What I just witnessed is something no one outside of RMM has ever seen. Which means you trust me."

Shock held him silent for a minute until he acknowl- edged Alana was right. He *did* trust her. Not just person- ally, but professionally. Still… "That doesn't mean you're physically up to the challenge, though."

"I've been training for the past six weeks. Ever since I went to Zakhar. Running. Lifting weights. Hand-to-hand combat, too—I asked Juliana, and she assigned the head of her security team to work with me, Captain Mateja-Jones." She smiled in self-deprecation. "I'll never be as good as Angelina. But I'm a lot better prepared than I was when I started out."

His thoughts swirling, all Jason could think of was Alana putting herself at risk the way he did. Gambling with her life. His first reaction—*absolutely not!*—was purely self- ish. Because he couldn't bear the idea of anything happen- ing to her. Because he'd give his own life to keep her safe.

But…did he have the right to make that decision for her?

"You don't have to decide now. I need more training before I'll be ready. I just wanted you to understand how I feel. I'm not asking because I love you and I want to share this with you…although I *do* love you and I *do* want to share this part of your life." She smiled faintly. "I want to join RMM because of what it stands for. You were called to do this work, Jason. It's a moral calling. You can't *not* do whatever you can to protect the innocent. I feel the same way."

Chapter 20

The *Night Wind* docked just long enough to offload Jason and Alana, then it took off again for parts unknown. *Unknown to you, maybe*, she told herself. *I'm sure Jason knows where they're going.*

She'd already figured out the other RMM men couldn't just walk off the boat as if nothing had happened—they had to remove the disguising camouflage face paint before they could be seen in public, for one thing. Not to mention they had to do something with the six men in the hold. And they had to do it in such a way that the prisoners couldn't identify the RMM members.

"Superficial" was all Trevor had replied when Jason had asked about the men's injuries, something she'd wondered about, too. She'd seen blood on at least two of them, so it was good to know it wasn't something serious.

Jason had radioed someone shortly after the other boat had been destroyed, and he'd told her that person would call the DeWinters to let them know she was safe. But as soon as they were in cell tower range, he'd texted his sister and she'd texted Dirk. Then she'd had to laugh when she received his reply.

Aren't you glad now you didn't make him grovel yesterday?

Alana started walking up the dock as soon as they were off the *Night Wind*, but Jason caught her hand. "Hang on a second," he told her. "There's a car waiting for us, but I have something to say first."

When she turned around at his request, however, he didn't say anything for the longest time. Just stared down at her as one emotion after another flitted across his face. Love was there. Matched by a desire that mirrored hers for him. And a yearning that tore at her heart. Finally he said in a tight voice, "I can't let you go. I thought I could. I thought I could let you choose. But I can't. I *can't*."

"Jason…"

"No. Hear me out. There are things I need to tell you. Things I hope will make you understand why I don't want children. But after today I know I can't let you go. Ever. So if not having children is a deal breaker for you—"

"It's not that, Jason," she interrupted. "Honest." *Perfect opening*, she thought, but once again he stopped her…this time with a kiss. Then another. And another. Until they were both so aroused their breathing was ragged.

"Love me," he whispered, pressing his forehead against hers. "You have to love me, because God help me, I love you."

"I do, Jason. Oh, I do." All at once she heard Dirk's words in her mind again. *There's a gaping hole in Jason's psyche, and I don't know if the woman exists who could fill that void. Who could love him enough to heal him.*

And in that instant she knew this wasn't the time to tell him about the baby. First she needed Jason to believe she loved him for *him*. Then…when he felt secure in her love—a week from now, or two or three, or however long it took—then she'd tell him. And she'd explain that it was *because* she loved him she wanted this baby so desperately.

So when he said, "If you love me, then…will you marry me, *lang loi*?" in a voice he couldn't possibly know betrayed just how unsure he was, she merely nodded. Then kissed him with everything she had in her. Wanting to convince him she loved him the way he *needed* to be loved…so she could heal him.

Jason took Alana to a private clinic instead of a public hospital. She was whisked into an examining room almost before she'd finished filling out her paperwork, but not before Jason was taken for his own examination…at her insistence. "I'm not going in unless you agree," she said stubbornly. "X-rays, stitches and whatever else needs doing."

Secretly relieved he didn't argue with her, Alana had watched him vanish through the waiting room door less than half a minute before her own name was called.

She changed into the examining gown common to doctors' offices in the US. But unlike the US, she didn't have long to wait before the doctor appeared, a smiling Chinese woman in her mid- to late-fifties, whose English was as impeccable as her own.

Alana insisted, "I'm fine. I know I'm fine." Then she took a deep breath and confided, "But I'm pregnant. Not quite seven weeks. All I really need to know is if I should worry about the effects of chloroform on my baby."

Confusion played over the doctor's face as she glanced down at the admitting form, on which Alana had deliberately left off any mention of her pregnancy…because Jason had been sitting right next to her, watching her every move as she filled it out.

"I couldn't put it on the form," Alana explained. "He—the baby's father—doesn't know yet, and I…this wasn't the time to tell him. But I have to know if my baby's okay."

"I think so, but let me confirm," the doctor said, sitting down and logging on to the computer in the examination room. The next five minutes were the longest of Alana's life, and she'd never prayed as hard as she was praying then. Finally the doctor swiveled around and said, "I don't think you have anything to worry about. Especially if your exposure was relatively short."

"A minute or two at the most. Just enough to knock me out temporarily."

"Then I wouldn't worry about it." The doctor's smile held understanding. "But let's give you a full exam anyway, all right?"

Alana sighed with relief. "Okay."

When the doctor was done she removed her latex gloves, saying, "A-okay on the baby front. How about you? Morning sickness yet?" When Alana shook her head, the doctor explained, "It usually starts around six weeks, but every woman is different. And some women never experience it at all. You might be one of the lucky ones."

She made a few notations on Alana's chart, and without raising her head asked, "Have you seen an ob-gyn yet?"

"No, I…there hasn't been time. I just found out about a week ago, and…"

"And you're still in a bit of a shock."

"Well…yes."

"Don't wait too long. You'll want to start on prenatal vitamins right away." The doctor jotted down a name and phone number on a pad of paper, then ripped off the page and handed it to her. "Give her a call. She's one of the best ob-gyns in Hong Kong. Her patients swear by her. She's so much in demand I don't think she's accepting new patients at the moment, but mention my name and she'll take you as a favor to me."

Touched, Alana smiled her gratitude. "Thanks."

"So…" the doctor continued, "I assume I shouldn't congratulate Jason on his impending fatherhood just yet? Oh, don't worry," she reassured a suddenly alarmed Alana. "You're my patient. Anything you tell me is confidential, including this."

"You know Jason? Personally, I mean?" She hadn't known she was going to ask the question…until it popped out of her mouth. Then she realized she'd just confirmed he *was* the father, something she hadn't planned on telling anyone else until she told Jason.

"His mother is one of my best friends, so I've known Jason since before he was born."

"Oh."

"I assume that's why he brought you to me, because he knows me and trusts me. He doesn't trust many people. Understandable, of course, under the circumstances."

Under the circumstances? That seemed an odd sort of thing for the doctor to say…unless she knew about Jason and RMM. Alana almost asked her what she meant, then stopped herself. Jason had trusted her with the knowledge of his illegal activities. She wasn't about to let on to someone else that she knew…even if that other person knew about them, too.

The doctor stood and held out her hand to shake Alana's. "For what it's worth, Jason's a wonderful man… and I'm not just saying that because his mother's my friend. So don't be afraid to tell him about the baby. Soon. He might surprise you."

* * *

Much as Jason yearned to take Alana to his condo and make love to her all night long, two things stopped him. First, he needed to rendezvous tonight with Cam and the other RMM men from the rescue this morning, to discuss their plans for bringing down the Eight Tigers once and for all.

Second, and more important, Alana needed time to recover from today. She might insist she was fine, and the doctor might have given her a clean bill of health. But no way was she up to the prolonged bout of lovemaking he'd planned. And he didn't trust himself to be able to stop once he started. Easier not to start at all.

So he took her home to the DeWinters' estate. Where he said hello to his sister and brother-in-law in less than thirty seconds and led Alana out to the gazebo shielded from the main house by a bower of hibiscus bushes and bougainvillea.

He wanted to do it right this time. Formal proposal. Formal betrothal. He wanted to place his ring on her finger and know she belonged to him the way he belonged to her...until the breath left his body. And maybe even beyond that. Because the way his heart was pounding now, even heaven wouldn't be heaven unless Alana was there. Unless he could see her smile and know that all was right in his world.

This time she did more than nod.

"I'd be honored to be your wife," she whispered, holding out her hand so he could slip the ring on her finger. It fit perfectly...a good omen. And he noted without comment the tiniest tremor in her hand. Not as if she was unsure or afraid, but as if this was the fulfillment of her secret hopes and dreams, too, the way it was for him.

One kiss, he promised himself. But one kiss wasn't

enough. One kiss would never be enough. When he finally let Alana go he was hard and aching and wanted nothing more than to take her right there in the gazebo.

She murmured something, but the rushing blood in his veins blocked her words. "What did you say?"

Her fingers tightened on his sleeves. "I said don't ever do this to me again." She laughed shakily. "Don't kiss me as if 'and' is on the agenda in a place where 'and' is impossible."

That made him laugh. "Never again," he promised her. "But I'm not the only one to blame here. You kissed me back."

"I know." A wistful smile touched her lips. "I should have known better. I should have remembered you make me forget everything when you kiss me."

An admission that could only be answered with another mind-blowing kiss. "Enough," he said, finally tearing his lips away from hers. And though he'd told himself he wouldn't ask, the words were out before he could stop them. "Next month? Will you marry me next month? I've waited forever already."

The slow smile she gave him melted the last vestiges of ice encasing his heart. "I'd be honored, *lang jai.*"

"I'll contact your embassy and mine to see what we need to do to make it happen. I have dual citizenship through my parents—British and Chinese—but I was born in the UK and I want this to be legal six ways from Sunday." He touched her cheek. "I'll call you as soon as I know anything." Then he smiled and added, "And before then, too. Because…just because."

They walked hand in hand back to the main house, and when Mei-li and Dirk saw the two of them, Jason and Alana didn't even need to say a word. Mei-li threw her arms around Jason, exclaiming, "I'm so thrilled, I can't even…

There are no… Alana is so perfect for… I was hoping and praying… Oh, Jason!"

Dirk grinned and leaned over to kiss Alana's cheek, murmuring, "This is only the second time since I've known her she's been unable to finish a sentence." He waited a beat. "The first time was right before I proposed…when she knew I was just about to."

Which told Alana Jason's sister was ecstatic over their engagement. A conclusion confirmed when Mei-li embraced her, saying, "I always wanted a sister." She cast a teasing glance at Jason before hugging Alana again. "Brothers are well enough, but a sister is…a *sister*. I'm so glad it's you."

After Jason left and Alana was able to escape to her room, she calculated the time difference and called her cousin. "Guess who's engaged, Jules?" she asked when Juliana answered.

"Hmm," her cousin pretended to ponder. "Let me think." She named a famous prince, one the tabloids had speculated about for years.

When Alana exclaimed, "No, of course not. Guess again!" her laughter pealed.

"Oh, honey, it's you." Deep happiness colored her words. "I'm so thrilled for you. You have no idea how worried I was—I know how much you love him." She paused for a moment. "So I take it he changed his mind about children when you told him about the baby?"

That question burst Alana's bubble, and she had no answer. When she didn't say anything, Juliana's voice sharpened. "You *did* tell him about the baby, didn't you?"

Alana sighed. "Not yet."

"Oh, honey, why not? You *have* to tell him."

"I know. *I know.* It's just… I told him Friday night I

couldn't agree to his 'no children' stance. And…it was terrible, Jules. He broke my heart. But something happened today—I don't want to go into it now, but I promise I'll email you all about it—well anyway, he…he said he can't give me up. That if not having children is a deal breaker for me…he'd agree to it."

"Yes, but there's a huge difference between agreeing to children in theory, and knowing it's a fait accompli."

"I know that. And I *will* tell him…before we get married."

"When's the wedding?"

She drew a deep breath and held it, wincing as she admitted, "He wants it to be next month."

"Next *month*?" Juliana didn't have to say that didn't give Alana much time; she already knew it. "Oh, honey…"

"Please just be happy for me, Jules," she pleaded. "I love him so much—it just *has* to work out."

Her cousin's voice softened. "Of course I'm happy for you. Worried, of course—who wouldn't be?—knowing what I know. But if you love each other, that's half the battle." Then she addressed the other elephant in the room. "Have you told your parents?"

Alana winced again. "Not yet. There's a twelve-hour time difference between here and there, and I…I don't want to wake them." That had nothing to do with why she was dreading telling her parents, and her cousin knew it.

"It makes no difference to me, honey. You know that. Everything you've told me about him says he's a wonderful man. And you love each other. That's precious and rare, and I'm thrilled you found a man who means as much to you as Andre means to me. But it's going to be an issue for your parents. It shouldn't be, but it will. Have you thought about how you're going to tell them about Jason's parentage?"

No, she hadn't thought about it. Because she'd never allowed their insular prejudices to guide her actions...rule her thoughts. And she had no intention of starting now. Just as she had no intention of even *introducing* Jason to them... until they understood she wouldn't tolerate anything they said or did that might hurt him. He was hers to cherish and protect, just as she was his.

"I won't let them hurt Jason." Her voice was low but contained a thread of steel. "Even if it means cutting myself off from them."

There was a moment's silence at the other end. Then Juliana sighed with thankfulness. "I'm so glad you feel that way. You have no idea."

"Why do you say that?"

"Because it's the difference between love and *love*. Selfless love, not selfish. Not that I thought you... I didn't, but... It means you really love him. That the rest of the world can go hang if you have him."

Alana considered this for a moment. Then softly, more to herself than to her cousin, said, "Yes."

Alana was still filled with that same quiet strength of purpose when she called her parents at 9:30 that night. Sunday morning at home, this time of day, her parents would be leisurely getting ready for the 11:00 a.m. church service they attended. Not that her parents were particularly religious. They weren't. Attendance at church was merely a social obligation to them. But it meant she knew exactly where her parents would be and how long they'd have to talk.

When her mother answered the phone, she said, "Mom? It's Alana."

"Hello, darling. Your father and I were just talking about you."

"You were?"

Her mother's tinkling laugh sounded. "Of course. Are

you ready to admit you made a mistake taking that job over there working for that actor? Is that why you're calling?"

Alana gritted her teeth. She hated the way her mother said *that actor*, referring to Dirk. Dirk, who'd willingly sacrificed her services when Juliana needed her. Dirk, who'd paid her full salary the entire time she was gone. Dirk, who'd cared enough about her to warn her that Jason might break her heart, and conversely to advise her how best to deal with him when he called to apologize.

If that was how her mother talked about Dirk, who was white through and through, what would she say about Jason?

"No, Mom. That's not why I'm calling." She drew a deep breath and let it out slowly as a calming technique. "I wanted you and Dad to know I'm engaged."

"Engaged?" Her mother's voice rose in pitch and volume. "As in…engaged to be *married*?"

"Yes." Then she waited for the outburst.

"Who could you possibly have met over there that you'd want to marry? Do you know his family? What does he do for a living? Alan!" This last was said away from the phone as her mother called for Alana's father. Alana knew she wasn't meant to hear, but her mother's voice came through loud and clear. "She's *engaged*, Alan. Your daughter's *engaged*."

It wasn't really funny but she chose to be amused at how whenever she did something one of her parents disapproved of, she suddenly became "*your* daughter," as if the disapproving parent disavowed her.

Her amusement faded away when her father took the phone. "Who is he? How did you meet him? What does he do for a living?" were the machine-gunned questions aimed at her. "Does he know you're one of the Virginia Richardsons? Is he after your money?"

"I don't *have* any money," she reminded him, answering his last question first. "Just that little trust fund from Grandmother Richardson."

"Yes, but when your mother and I die you'll be a rich woman. Are you aware there are men out there who prey on gullible young women? *Rich*, gullible young women?"

"Jason's not like that," she began. "He makes a decent living working for Wing Wah Enterprises here in Hong Kong. He's—"

Her father cut her off, pouncing on the name. "Jason? Jason who? What's his last name?"

"Moore. Jason Moore."

"Moore? We don't know any Moores. What's his background? Who are his family? Where does he come from?"

Alana drew another calming breath. "Jason's father is a baronet, Sir Joshua Moore. Perhaps you've heard of him? He's a famous producer and director." As soon as the words left her mouth, she knew she'd made a mistake. She shouldn't have tried to impress her snobbish father and instead just told him Jason's family background didn't matter. That his *character* was what counted. And when it came to character, Jason had everyone, including her, beat.

"In the movie industry?" Disdain dripped from his voice. "Like your cousin Juliana? Like that actor fellow you work for?"

She bit her tongue to hold back angry, defensive words and said as evenly as she could, "Yes, Dad. Like them."

"Ridiculous," her father snorted. "This is what comes of letting you take a job recommended by your cousin. You would have thought that now she's a queen she'd be more circumspect, but she's just like her mother."

"Don't you dare say anything against Juliana's mother, Dad. Don't you dare!"

"Don't think you can talk to me like that, missy!" her

father roared. "I'm still your father, and you'll treat me with respect!"

"Respect where it's earned, Dad." The words came pouring out of her. "I've had it with the way you and Mom talk about people in that way. And I'll tell you right now, I won't stand for it when it comes to Jason. Understand? Jason's father is British, but his mother's Chinese, and—"

"Eurasian?" The absolute shock in her father's voice infuriated Alana.

"If you say one word against him—one *word*—I'm no longer your daughter. You hear me? Think about that and decide what's more important—me, or your prejudices!" With that she disconnected.

She sobbed once, then laughed a little hysterically as she realized how satisfying it would have been to slam the phone down on her father. But you couldn't do that with a cell phone—you could only disconnect. *There should be a slamming app*, she told herself with a hiccuping laugh. *It'd make a fortune!*

Then she buried her face in her hands, weeping in earnest. *Not* because of her parents. Because she'd just figured out why Jason didn't want children.

Chapter 21

Jason had no sooner hung up the phone Monday morning after arranging to take Alana out to celebrate their engagement when he received a cryptic text from Cam.

The pigeons have gone home to roost as we hoped, he read. Call me?

He unlocked a desk drawer he always kept locked, pulled out a disposable cell phone that couldn't be traced to him, then called Cam's corresponding throwaway. "Tell me some good news," he said when Cam answered.

"Those gizmos your company manufactures came through for us once again."

Jason smiled. He'd designed those electronic devices himself and had overridden the objections of the board of directors for the manufacture of the prototypes. He was close to inking a deal with the FBI in the US, MI5 in the

UK and the Chinese government for use by law enforcement in all three countries. The design was simple. Tiny enough to be installed in a cell phone's battery compartment and drawing its power directly from the battery, it was powerful enough to send a signal that could be tracked from miles away. It also transmitted in real time every keystroke made on the cell phones, including phone numbers called and texts sent.

Jason wasn't worried about the legality of the device's usage by law enforcement the way the board of directors had been—that was up to the jurisdictions intending to use it. All he cared about was how effective it was for RMM.

All six of the men who'd abducted Alana yesterday morning had been released on a relatively remote island, but one with adequate cell towers. *After* the *gizmos*, as Cam called them, had been surreptitiously installed on their cell phones. The minute the *Night Wind* was out of sight, one of the men had sent out a Mayday call. Another RMM boat, disguised as a fishing vessel, had been in the vicinity and had picked up the signals, then tracked the boat the Eight Tigers had dispatched to rescue their men from the remote island. But all info gleaned from that operation had been reported at last night's meeting. Which meant something else must have occurred for Cam to contact him this morning.

"Let's have it."

"I think we've identified one of the upper echelon of the Eight Tigers."

Jason walked in the front door of Wing Wah Enterprises Tuesday morning, briefcase in one hand, cell phone in the other, trying to text with the thumb of one hand.

Sorry I had to cancel last night, lang loi. Can I make it up to you tonight? Six-ish? Dinner, and…?

He smiled to himself as he remembered Alana's playful response when he'd texted her that last sentence before. From there it was a short segue to memories of that night he would cherish until the day he died. Memories he had every intention of adding to tonight.

As he'd put in his text, his plans to take Alana out to dinner and back to his condo last night had come to naught because of an urgent RMM strategy session to deal with what Cam had told him yesterday. She'd understood when he'd called to apologize. *No apology necessary*, she'd insisted so adamantly he'd believed her. *You do what you need to do. We have all the time in the world to celebrate.*

So tonight they'd have their one-day-delayed celebratory dinner, after which he would finally make love to her again as he'd longed to do since their first time. Only this time she wouldn't turn away from him in shame. This time there would be no moonlight goodbyes.

But before he did that, he would confess everything. Who he really was. Why it mattered so much she loved him for the man he was inside, not the public figure the business world knew. Tonight he would once and for all put his past firmly behind him, because none of it would matter…if Alana loved him. Understood him. Believed in him.

And…if she asked him…if she fixed those amethyst eyes on him and asked with the little catch in her voice that only surfaced when something meant the world to her, he'd make love to her without a condom. All. Night. Long.

Jason had just hit Send and was tucking his phone in his pocket when he heard an angry voice resounding through the lobby. He looked up and saw an older man loudly berating the female receptionist.

"Jason Moore. How many times do I have to tell you?

J-A-S-O-N M-O-O-R-E. My daughter said he works here, and I'm not leaving until I see him."

Obviously embarrassed, the receptionist looked left and right. She caught sight of Jason, but loyal employee that she was, she didn't say anything except, "I'm sorry, sir, but I don't have a *Jason* Moore in the employee directory. I have a *J.C.* Moore, but he's an extremely busy man, and unless you have an appointment, I don't think—"

"He'll see me." Three words spoken through gritted teeth.

"If you'll give me your name," she said in a placating tone, "I'll ring upstairs and see if Mr. Moore is available."

"The name's Richardson. Alan Richardson."

Jason had been heading for the executive elevator, but he halted abruptly at the name. *Alan Richardson? Has to be Alana's father.*

"Tell…*Mr.* Moore—" the sarcastic emphasis told his listeners Alan Richardson resented using the honorific "—that I'm here to discuss my daughter."

Jason turned around and walked up to the desk. "I'm Jason Moore, Mr. Richardson," he said mildly, holding out his hand. A hand he quickly withdrew when it became painfully obvious the other man had no intention of shaking it.

"*You're* Moore?" Alana's father seemed incredulous. "*Jason* Moore?"

He went cold all over at the implied insult. "I assure you," he said with an icy smile, "I'm the man you've come to see." He glanced at the receptionist. "Sign Mr. Richardson in under my name, please. What conference room is available?"

The receptionist nervously checked her screen. "Five East is free until nine, sir."

"Fine." He gave her a warm smile, very different from

the one he'd given Alan Richardson. "Block that room off for me, please."

"Yes, sir."

He turned back to the other man and indicated the direction of the elevator. "Shall we?"

Jason had barely ushered Alana's father into the conference room and closed the door behind them before the man's throttled anger spilled over and an accusation was thrown at him. "Alana says she's engaged. To *you*."

Unsure exactly what she'd told her father, Jason merely raised his eyebrows and said, "Yes. Alana has honored me by agreeing to—"

"My daughter…and *you*." The contempt was almost palpable. "Playing on her sympathies, no doubt. Feeding her a pack of lies to get your filthy hands on her money. Taking advantage of a sheltered innocent, that's what you're doing!" Rage mottled the older man's features, and the next words out of his mouth were a slur.

Jason froze. Suddenly he was thirteen years old again, just starting boarding school. Hearing schoolboy taunts from his paternal cousins and their friends that sliced through his soul. The same words Alana's father had just used.

He'd been too shocked back then to react at first, but Sean had waded into them, fists flying, shouting, *You take that back!* Then David had joined Sean, and finally Jason, when the shock wore off. Three boys against a dozen. Black eyes. Bloody noses. Split lips. The Three Musketeers had given as good as they'd gotten, until two of Jason's cousins had run for the headmaster, who'd soon put a stop to the fight. The dozen had pointed their fingers at Sean as the instigator. Sean, the best, most loyal friend a boy—or a man—could ever have. Sean, who could never stand to see injustice done, who always stood up to bullies.

Sean, who was dead now, but who lived on forever as one of the founding principles behind RMM.

The past receded, and Jason focused on the man who'd thrown words at him he hadn't heard in forever. Words he'd sworn no child of his would ever hear in that context… because he would never have children.

Alana's father. Who, if Jason married Alana and agreed to her conditions, would be his children's grandfather. A man who'd just deliberately insulted him with words both of Jason's grandfathers had used toward him when he was barely old enough to understand what they meant.

His parents would have been devastated if they'd known. They adored both their children, and it would have created an irrevocable rift between them and their own fathers, which was why Jason had never told them. He'd never told his sister, either. By the time she'd been old enough to understand, both grandfathers had come to grudgingly accept Jason's existence…but he'd never forgotten. The only ones in Jason's confidence—and he'd sworn them both to secrecy—were Sean and David. Only they'd known the searing pain those words had caused him.

Words that still had the power to wound even after all these years. Words no man should ever hear addressed to him, much less an innocent boy who hadn't chosen to be born. Words against which there were no defenses.

Alana stared in shock at the man who'd just done his damnedest to break her heart…again. Trying to understand what made no sense. None. Not after the way he'd kissed her on Sunday. Not after the text he'd sent her this morning. "You've changed your mind." She blinked. "Just like that, you've changed your mind."

His face was a stranger's face, all emotion wiped clean. "I thought I could go through with it, but I can't. You want children—I can't give them to you. So…" He shrugged.

"You can, but you won't."

"Semantics…but yes. I won't."

"I see." She didn't, but what else was there to say?

She walked a short distance away from Jason and stared out into Victoria Harbour, watching with detached interest as a couple of sailboats colorfully painted like pirate ships from two centuries ago floated past, followed by an ugly, modern container ship. *Only in Hong Kong*, she thought, still in that detached state.

Jason had been silent and withdrawn when he'd picked her up earlier, but she'd just figured he had something RMM-related on his mind, so she hadn't questioned him about it. But when he'd driven them here to the Avenue of Stars, then walked with her to the Bruce Lee statue she knew held special meaning for him and said he needed to talk to her, she'd wondered why he'd chosen such a public place. Now she knew why. He knew her well enough to know she wouldn't cause a public scene.

Only…she wasn't buying it. Something was going on here, something Jason refused to tell her. Some reason she *knew* she could explain away…if only he would confide in her. But he was a man. And men could be stubbornly *male* over the stupidest things, things that made no sense to women.

She turned to face him again. And something in the tense way he held himself betrayed him—whatever the reason he was doing this, it wasn't because he didn't still love her. Desperately. She almost told him in that instant she knew the secret he'd guarded so closely. That she'd figured out why he didn't want children. But the closed expression on his face told her this wasn't the time. Jason wasn't ready to listen.

She waited until a giggling group of teens stopped for selfies at the Bruce Lee statue then moved on. "Is this the moment where I'm supposed to throw your ring at you and vow I never want to see you again?" she asked calmly. "Because if that's what you thought would happen, I'm afraid you're doomed to disappointment."

He made a dismissive gesture. "I don't want the ring. Keep it. I—" He cut off the rest, but she thought she knew what he'd intended to say. *I chose it because it matches your eyes.* Words he'd said to her in an emotion-filled voice that hadn't been quite steady when he'd slid the ring on her finger Sunday.

She almost blurted out, *It's not the ring I'm talking about, you idiot*. But she didn't because there was a shadow in his eyes. Those dark, expressive eyes that haunted her dreams. Eyes that said he was steeling himself to do this, for a reason that made sense only to him.

"I will. I'll keep it. I have no intention of taking it off, now or ever."

"What's that supposed to mean?"

"It means I'm engaged to you."

His face darkened with the first anger he'd ever directed at her. "I told you—"

"I heard what you said. You've changed your mind. I get that. You're breaking our engagement." She nodded. "But that just means you're no longer engaged to me. That doesn't mean I'm not engaged to you. I am. I love you, and I intend to marry you. Maybe not next month." She gulped back tears and forced herself to smile as if she wasn't dying inside, swearing at the same time he'd never know what that light tone cost her. "Maybe not even next year. But someday you'll tell me what this is really all about. And until then…" She raised her left hand and wiggled her fingers so he could see the ring he'd given her. "Until then, I'm engaged to you."

He grasped her shoulders so tightly she suddenly wanted to weep over what that said about him, about how much he still loved her. "Alana…"

She fought for composure, hanging on by a thread. Maybe she'd cry when she got home, but she wasn't going to cry now. "It's okay, Jason. I understand. Honestly, I do." She cupped his cheek in comforting fashion and forced herself to smile again. "Just remember I love you, and I'm not giving up. Ever."

Alana stood in the curving driveway in front of the main house, watching the taillights on Jason's car disappear around the bend. Then she drew one sobbing breath before she reined her emotions in tightly. *You're not going to cry about this*, her brain insisted. But the ache in her chest begged for the emotional release only tears could bring.

"Alana?" Dirk's voice from the doorway had her swinging around. "Mei-li said you were spending the night with Jason." He indicated the overnight case at her feet. "Are you okay?"

She pasted a smile on her face. "No, but I will be."

"Anything I can do?"

The honest concern in Dirk's voice made her fiercely glad she'd taken the job as his executive assistant. He and Mei-li had quickly become friends as well as employers, and she easily understood why Dirk was so dear to Juliana's heart.

She shook her head. "I wish there was, but no, there isn't. Not this time." She drew a deep, calming breath. "I suppose I should tell you before Jason says something to Mei-li. He broke our engagement tonight."

"He *what*? Has he lost his mind?"

She laughed a little at that. "No. He's just…confused."

Dirk stepped outside in the gathering darkness and closed the door behind him. "So what are you going to do?"

"I'm not giving up. I'm not running away, either. I'm not… I'm just…not. Period. I'm not going to do any of the things Jason might expect me to do." Her lips tightened with resolve. "I told him I understood. I don't, of course, but that's neither here nor there, because I know he still loves me. So I told him I'm still engaged to him, even if he isn't engaged to me."

At the flash of admiration in Dirk's eyes, she added softly, "I haven't forgotten what you once told me about him. Maybe my love won't be enough to heal him, but I'm going to do my damnedest. If I fail, it won't be for lack of trying."

Three nights later Alana was again roused in the wee hours of the morning by the ringing of a phone. Heart pounding with sudden fear, she immediately thought of Juliana. *Please God, no, not her baby!* But then she realized it was her cell phone, not the landline, and when she stumbled out of bed to answer it, her mother's voice sounded in her ear.

"Your great-aunt Susan has passed away," Alana's mother announced. "Can your father and I assume you'll fly back for her funeral?"

Alana pushed a tangle of hair out of her face and glanced at the clock on her nightstand. "It's a quarter to three, Mom. This couldn't have waited for a few hours?"

"I would have thought you'd want to know right away," her mother huffed. "If you were home where you belonged instead of halfway around the world—"

"Don't start, Mom. Not now." A tired yawn took her

by surprise, and she rubbed her eyes, trying to focus. "I haven't seen Great-Aunt Susan in..." She tried to recall exactly, but it was too early for her brain to be firing on all cylinders, especially after the jolt of fear a minute ago over Juliana's baby. *College graduation?* she thought. *Was that the last time?* If so, it was more than four years ago. And she'd never been all that close to her anyway.

"Yes or no, Alana? Will you make the funeral or not?"

"I just took off work for six weeks when Juliana needed me," she began. "I don't know if Dirk will let me have more time off, and I—"

"It's not as if you need that job anyway," her mother stubbornly asserted. "If he says no, just tell him you're going anyway."

"I can't do that, Mom!"

"Fine. Your cousin Juliana already told her father she can't make it—her doctors have advised her not to fly in her condition. At least *she* has an excuse." Her tone of voice indicated she thought it was a lame excuse at best, but then she added, "I'll just tell your father and your uncle you're too selfish to consider their feelings."

"Mom!" If her mother hadn't mentioned her uncle Julian, Alana wouldn't have minded missing the funeral. She wasn't close to her father, but her uncle was a different story. "I'll ask Dirk. That's all I can promise. When's the funeral? If Dirk says yes, I'll have to see about booking a flight."

Alana waited until morning to approach Dirk. "I hate to ask," she told him. "Especially after leaving you high and dry for six weeks not that long ago. And if you say no, I'll totally understand."

"Not a problem."

"I wouldn't ask, except...Juliana's dad has been special

to me since I was a little girl, and…you see… I don't want him to think…"

"You don't have to say any more. Family comes first. And funerals…well…they're not really for the dead. They're for the living. I might not have expressed it at the time, but I was always grateful afterward that Juliana was there for me at Bree's funeral."

With that Alana remembered Dirk had buried his first wife in the nightmare glare of publicity that always surrounded him, and quickly changed the subject. "My great-aunt's funeral is on Monday. I checked and there's an early Sunday flight I can take. Since the flight home crosses the International Date Line, that means I arrive home on Sunday. I can fly back the day after the—"

Dirk shook his head, cutting her off. "Don't do that. Don't try to rush back. It's a hellishly long flight, and you'll need time to recuperate before you get back on a plane. Besides…" He shot her an understanding smile. "It'll be good for you to spend some time away from Hong Kong right now. So everywhere you look doesn't remind you of Jason. Why don't you just plan to stay a week or ten days?"

"I'm not going to run a—"

"It's not running away," he threw in. "It's just taking a breather. I admire you for your determination to stick it out, believe me. But it can't be easy." He paused before admitting in a low voice, "Been there, done that."

"Oh, Dirk, I know." She put her hand on his forearm in empathy. Yes, her boss had eventually found love and happiness again with Mei-li, but that didn't erase the memory of his loss and the terrible aftermath.

He patted her hand, acknowledging they understood what each other had suffered, then unwittingly delivered a body blow. "At least you won't have Jason's baby as a constant reminder, the way I had my daughters."

Chapter 22

Jason watched Alana's plane take off from a distance, then put his new Jaguar into gear and drove away from the airport toward RMM's secluded hideaway near Repulse Bay. *It's for the best,* he told himself. *And once she's home, her parents will do their damnedest to keep her there. Permanently. Then you'll never have to see her again.*

Only…out of sight didn't equate to out of mind. He still wanted her. Needed her in the most elemental ways. Still yearned to be the man she loved, even though he'd told himself time and again he shouldn't, because as much as he hated to admit it, Alana's father was right; he'd only ruin her life.

The world had changed since his childhood, but some things would never change. Overt prejudice had become politically incorrect over the years, but covert prejudice was still rampant. There would always be those who looked down on him—and on Alana if she married him—because of something over which he had no control.

The ache would never go away, though. The ache to see her tender, loving smile; to hear her voice saying his name the way she'd said it the night she'd pledged herself to him; to gaze into those incredible amethyst eyes with their long, dark lashes and see the love for him shining from them. Even more, seeing the evidence of her steadfast belief in him. In the man he was.

A voice from the depths of his soul cried out, *Alana!* As if he could call her back. Then he ruthlessly attempted to quash that voice. "It's for the best," he harshly reiterated, shifting gears and slowing for the bridge traffic. "She doesn't need *you* in her life the way you need her."

But the internal argument continued the entire drive, and he was mentally exhausted by the time he arrived.

The High Tiger checked his watch, and forcibly prevented himself from drumming his fingers on the desk in his home office as he waited for the phone call that would deliver the good news. *Patience*, he reminded himself.

He'd carefully planned this assassination. He'd privately sounded out the other six members of the ruling council and they'd reached a consensus: Lin Fang, the man in charge of prostitution, had to go. The High Tiger had then arranged for the man who would be promoted to their ranks as the newest enforcer to be the assassin removing the old one. It would be poetic justice…if the High Tiger believed in justice of any kind.

The phone rang, startling him out of his reverie, and he snatched at the receiver. "Yes?"

"No" was the prompt response, and he was startled. Not just because of the answer, but because the Aussie voice belonged to one of his fellow Tigers on the ruling council and not Bao Zhi, the designated assassin and future enforcer.

The High Tiger was always cognizant his phone could be tapped, but his entire home was swept daily for electronic listening devices, so he didn't hesitate to ask, "What happened?"

"Complete failure. Bao Zhi was shot, and is now in police custody. Lin Fang was spirited away. We don't know who, but it's not the Hong Kong Police…so we can hazard a guess."

The name "RMM" remained unspoken, but both men were thinking it. If RMM had Fang, they could use the attempted assassination to their advantage, convince him no one except the Eight Tigers would have dared to take his life. Would Fang crack? Reveal names he'd sworn to keep secret? The High Tiger wouldn't bet against it, and he was a man who'd bet on the longest of long shots before, had taken gambles most men wouldn't dare—and it had paid off for him.

But this had epic disaster written all over it. Fang was weak. Would he plead to a lesser charge in exchange for turning on his fellow Tigers? Men who'd attempted to kill him?

The High Tiger nodded to himself. *Without a doubt.*

The Eight Tigers had one chance and one chance only to stave off ruin: kidnap the head of RMM and offer to exchange him for Fang to keep Fang from spilling his guts. Which meant the High Tiger had no choice.

"I'll get back to you," he told the caller abruptly, then hung up. He picked up the receiver again and punched in a number he'd never used before. He'd insisted on having a number where this tightly guarded secret source could be reached—insurance, he'd always thought of it. But in the past this source had always contacted him, not the other way around.

When the phone was answered he said, "It's me. I need a name you have always refused to give me. And I need it now."

The man on the receiving end slowly hung up the phone, having promised to give the High Tiger the name he demanded. But only in person. And at another remote location. He unlocked the bottom drawer of his desk and pulled out a revolver. A totally illegal weapon. One his original employer had given him many years ago, when Great Britain was turning Hong Kong over to the Chinese government and nearly all of the city's residents were panicking, not knowing what that meant for the former British colony.

He'd kept the revolver all these years, cleaning it periodically and keeping it loaded, but never firing it. Tonight he would. Because much as he despised the man who'd founded and headed up RMM, as much as he wanted to hurt him personally, he could never reveal that man's name. *That* would be a betrayal of his one-time employer who was dead now, but who still commanded his loyalty. The man who'd left his company…and his fortune…to his grandson, Jason Moore.

Alana collapsed into a wingbacked chair opposite her mother and kicked off the shoes that were pinching her toes, incredibly relieved the funeral was finally over and she could be comfortable again. She'd get up in a minute and go change out of the funereal black her mother had insisted Alana wear…but not until her toes stopped complaining about the too-tight pumps she'd borrowed, which were a half size too small. She'd been forced to wear them at the last minute instead of her own because her mother had exclaimed in horror, "*Not* open-toed shoes, Alana! What are you thinking?"

As if Great-Aunt Susan or *anyone* at the funeral would have cared what shoes Alana wore. But she hadn't had the heart to argue, so she'd dutifully donned the shoes her mother had quickly unearthed from the vast selection in her walk-in closet, and had gone off to pay her last respects.

But she was glad she'd attended the funeral after all. She'd sat in the pew next to her uncle Julian and tried to fill Juliana's place with a man both she and her cousin loved unreservedly.

The funeral had taken more of a physical toll on her than she'd thought it would, however. She'd never experienced morning sickness—apparently she was one of those women who were lucky that way—but she *did* seem to tire more easily these days, something Juliana had warned her to expect.

"That went off well," Alana's mother said with satisfaction, breaking into her daughter's thoughts. "And thank goodness you didn't mention anything about your fiancé!"

She was startled for a moment, then remembered she'd never told her parents about her broken engagement. Dirk and Mei-li—yes, of course. And Juliana, who'd been sworn to secrecy. "Why *thank goodness*, Mom?" she asked now.

"Because we haven't told anyone, you goose, and it would certainly have raised questions about him. Questions your father and I aren't prepared to answer."

Alana debated with herself, wondering if she should say anything, then mentally shrugged her shoulders. "You don't have to worry, Mom. Jason broke our engagement." She counted back. "It'll be a week tomorrow."

"He did? Then that means your father's trip to Hong Kong wasn't wasted." Her mother smiled with gratification at the news. "Why didn't you tell us right away?"

Ice water trickled through her veins, and she said slowly, "When was Dad in Hong Kong?" A suspicion suddenly formed, one so monstrous she didn't want to think it, but… "He never came to see me."

Her mother's mouth formed a surprised O, confirming her suspicion.

The ice dissipated in a flash. Alana sprang to her feet, comprehension and fury combining to make it impossible to stay seated as she confronted her mother. "Dad went to see Jason. Didn't he? *Didn't he?*"

"Don't use that tone of voice with me, Alana. Your father only did what any father would do."

"Oh. My. God," she breathed. "Do you know what he's done? Do you have *any* idea?"

She whirled and ran from the room, forgetting her borrowed shoes in her haste. She checked in the doorway to her father's office, where her dad and Uncle Julian were enjoying a snifter of her father's prized cognac after the funeral.

"I have to talk to you, Dad," she said abruptly.

"You're interrupting, Alana," her father chided. "Your uncle was speaking. Can't it wait, whatever it is?"

She shook her head vehemently. "No, it can't wait."

Uncle Julian put his snifter down on a side table and stood. "Perhaps I should—"

"No," Alana insisted. "Please stay. I want you to hear. I want you to know what—" She choked as emotions welled up in her throat. Not just anger and hurt on her own behalf, but for Jason. Jason, her knight *sans peur et sans reproche*. Jason, who'd been wounded as no child should ever be wounded, but had still managed to grow into a man in whom she had nothing but pride.

"You went to see Jason last week, Dad. Don't try to deny it," she cried when he opened his mouth. "Mom already let it slip. What did you tell him?"

"I only said what any father would say." But his eyes shifted under hers.

"You *liar*."

"Alana!" This from a shocked Uncle Julian.

Tears were forming, but Alana struggled to hold them back. "Look at him, Uncle Julian. He's lying. He went to see the man I love...a man so wonderful, you just can't imagine...and he said something to him." She was sobbing now, tears coursing down her cheeks. "Something that hurt Jason dreadfully and made him break our engagement. And I want to know what he said."

Julian looked at his brother. "Alan? What did you do?" When Alana's father refused to answer at first, her uncle demanded again, "What did you do?"

"I told him when she came to her senses, she'd be ashamed. Of him...and any children they had."

"Alan! You didn't!" Julian exclaimed.

"I have every right to protect my daughter," her father blustered. "Especially from a man like him."

"A man like him?" She swiped the back of her hand against her eyes. "What bothers you most, Dad? That Jason's father works in the movie industry? Or that his mother is Chinese?"

The silence that greeted this accusation was all the confirmation she needed.

She squeezed her eyes shut and covered her mouth with her hands to hold back renewed sobs...for Jason. Who'd done nothing—*nothing!*—to deserve this. When she had herself under control again, she confronted her father. "Do you know what you've done, Dad? Do you know Jason saved my life, not once, but twice? And the first time he didn't even know me, but he risked his life for me. He would have died...gladly...to rescue me." She placed a hand over her abdomen, as if shielding the innocent life she carried against her father's prejudice.

She turned to her uncle, smiling through the tears at the man she'd always wished was her father. "You'd like him, Uncle Julian. You would. He doesn't care what the world thinks of him—he just does what's right. Always. And he loves me. He loves me enough to sacrifice our love… because *he*—" she flung a hand in her father's direction "—told Jason he wasn't worthy of me, when it's actually the other way around."

"You don't know what you're saying, Alana. I offered him a quarter of a million dollars to break things off with you, and…" His eyes turned crafty. "He bargained me up to half a million. He's nothing but a damned fortune hunter!" The triumph on her father's face was painful to see.

"Oh, Dad. You think you know him, but you don't. He didn't do it for the money." She wouldn't put it past her father to lie about this, too, but if it was true, she knew where the money had gone. Not into Jason's pocket…but into the RMM coffers.

"Of course he did it for the money. A man like him—"

"I told you on the phone that if you spoke one word against Jason I was no longer your daughter," she said fiercely. "And I meant it. As of this moment you are de—"

"Don't say it!" her uncle warned sternly. "Don't descend to his level." Then he faced his brother. "All these years, Alan. All these years I've held my tongue. But your daughter's right. You crossed the line. What you did is despicable, and I'm ashamed to admit you're my brother."

He turned back to Alana. "What do you want to do? What can I do to help?"

"I wasn't returning to Hong Kong until next week. But now…oh, Uncle Julian, I *have* to see Jason as soon as possible. I have to explain…"

She gulped and scrubbed the tears from her eyes with the heels of her palms. "And I have to tell him about our baby."

Her uncle ignored her father's startled gasp and patted her cheek. "Of course you do. Tell you what. You go pack. I'll get on the phone with my travel agent and book your flight."

This is the last time, the High Tiger promised himself as he switched trains. *The last time I accede to this man's demands for the utmost secrecy. Once I have the name, I no longer need the information this man provides. Because once I know who the High Dragon of RMM is, once I exchange him for Lin Fang—who is not long for this earth—then I can destroy him. And without him, RMM loses half its strength.* He smiled to himself, ignoring the jostling of the train's other riders. *Oh, yes, once I have the name...*

As always, the High Tiger saw the wizened little man in a business suit seemingly before the other saw him, but he knew that wasn't true. He watched for the trifolded newspaper signal and was relieved to see it. He didn't want to have to do this again.

He took a seat on the bench next to the man on the now-deserted boat dock, demanding as he did so, "His name. Tell me his name."

The man shifted toward him, and suddenly there was a gun in his hand. "I'm afraid I can't do that," he said softly.

And in the instant before the bullets tore into his flesh, the High Tiger realized he should never have agreed to these clandestine meetings in remote locations without his bodyguards. He should never—

Jason cursed into his body microphone. Followed by, "Shots fired! Repeat, shots fired! One man down—not our target. Move in!"

A half-dozen RMM men swarmed onto the dock, suitably disguised, semiautomatic rifles at the ready. The elderly man stood and calmly dropped his gun before anyone could demand he do so. Then stood passively as he was frisked for other weapons and handcuffed to the railing. One man removed his glove and checked for a pulse on the body sprawled on the dock, then silently shook his head. Another man bagged the revolver, careful not to disturb any fingerprints.

By the time Jason arrived from his vantage point on the hill above the dock, there was nothing left to do, except ask why.

"Why?" he asked his executive assistant, a man who'd been with Wing Wah Enterprises since Jason's grandfather's day.

"Why did I kill him?"

"I don't care why you killed him. I want to know what I did to you to make you betray me to him."

A supercilious little smile touched the man's lips. "That was the one thing I refused to do." When Jason shook his head, not following, the man explained, "Hurt you, yes. Leak whatever information I could find about planned RMM raids, yes. But I could not betray the CEO of Wing Wah Enterprises. Undeserving as you were to be *his* grandchild, your grandfather picked you to run his company. If I had told the High Tiger of the Eight Tigers—oh, yes," he continued in that superior way when Jason exchanged meaningful looks with the men on either side of him, "that is who he was. If I'd told him who the High Dragon of RMM was, he would have killed you. And *that* would have been detrimental to the well-being of your grandfather's company."

Jason glanced at Trevor Garrett on his left, asking with

his raised eyebrows if this made any sense to the other man. Trevor shrugged. "I've heard stranger tales."

Jason looked back at his executive assistant. "So it wasn't money."

"Of course not. The stock shares your grandfather left me in his will meant I didn't even have to work…although I did."

"And it wasn't anything I did to you?" he asked, still trying to understand. "I never insulted you? Made you lose face?"

"Of course not. In many ways you were a kinder and more considerate employer than your grandfather was."

"Then why? Why did you want to hurt me? Hurt RMM?"

"Because you didn't deserve to be your grandfather's heir." The elderly man turned his head and spat, then muttered the same insulting words Alan Richardson…and Jason's grandfathers…had used. "You and your sister both."

Jason was suddenly grateful Alana's father had confronted him a week ago. That he'd already faced down the memories from his childhood, helping take away the sting now, so that the reminder almost didn't hurt. Almost.

He breathed sharply, then turned to Trevor. "Call in an anonymous tip to the police. Leave the body where it is, and leave the gun." He measured distances with his eyes, then said, "And leave him cuffed to the railing."

"Jason," Trevor warned in an undertone.

"I know," he told his second cousin, his eyes conveying a message. "When we hear the sirens, we'll go." He turned to his other men. "The rest of you…" He tilted his head back toward land, and one by one the RMM members melted into the night.

Jason and Trevor waited for the police sirens, then headed out. They were halfway up the hill when they heard a single gunshot. Trevor looked back, but Jason never did.

Chapter 23

When Jason's smartphone rang at ten that night, he recognized the ringtone he reserved for his closest friend. "Hello, David."

"So tell me why you left the gun where he could reach it," David asked without preamble. "Because he could blow your cover?"

Jason didn't try to prevaricate. "Would you believe that never occurred to me until afterward?"

"Then why?"

He smiled faintly, even though his friend couldn't see it. "Because he was an old man. Because out of loyalty to my grandfather he *didn't* betray who I was to the Eight Tigers…even though he had ample opportunity. Because it's the kind of thing my grandfather would have done—allow him to save face. So he wouldn't have to stand his trial for murder, wouldn't have to suffer the indignity of jail at his age. Pick one."

"Damn it, Jason, one of these days you'll go too far!"

"That's not what you said when we turned over Lin Fang and his confession. You were ecstatic, and not inclined to look a gift horse in the mouth."

Silence at the other end acknowledged the truth of this, silence that was finally broken when David asked, "How did your executive assistant know anything about RMM anyway? He wasn't a member."

Jason winced. "There were various pieces of electronic equipment I bought from and through the company for RMM's use. All open and aboveboard, but invoiced to me personally. Individually they were innocuous enough. But taken as a whole...a discerning eye could detect a suspicious pattern. And he had access to my electronic calendar from the moment I took over as CEO of Wing Wah Enterprises. I used coded notations, of course, but he must have eventually figured out what they meant."

"How'd you know he was the one betraying you?"

"I didn't. Cam found out." Jason wasn't about to reveal *how*. When Jason had first suspected RMM had a traitor in its midst, he'd discussed his suspicions with Cam. Without Jason's knowledge or consent, Cam had installed illegal wiretaps on the phones of everyone it might have been... including his own brothers.

I'd just as soon you didn't mention it to them, mate, Cam had told Jason afterward. *Not that I really suspected them any more than I suspected anyone else. But it wouldn't have been fair to Patrick, Trevor and Chao if I wiretapped them and not Luke and Logan.*

Damn it, Cam, Jason had protested. *One of these days you'll go too far.* Which, considering that was what David had just said to him, was really rather funny now that he thought about it.

So long as we found out who, Cam had replied with a touch of smugness. *And now that we know who...*

So RMM had set a trap to catch Jason's executive assistant with the man they'd assumed was a member of the Eight Tigers triad. They'd never dreamed it was the High Tiger himself, or that he'd be shot and killed while under surveillance.

Now it was just a matter of mopping up. Something Jason was glad to leave in David's capable hands. Detective Inspector David Lam, and the Organized Crime and Triad Bureau.

Jason and David conversed for a few more minutes, mostly about Lin Fang, who'd sung like a canary once he realized his fellow Tigers had turned on him and had set him up to be assassinated. Even Jason had been astonished at the extensive reach of their criminal enterprise. He'd known about the prostitution—including their abductions of women for their brothels in Macau. And he'd known about the drugs and the pornography. He'd made a mental note while Lin Fang was spilling his guts to follow up on the two women RMM had rescued. But he hadn't been aware of the extortion connection. Money laundering. Kidnapping. And gun running.

Shutting down the Eight Tigers triad would make a serious dent in organized crime in the SAR. Which meant RMM could take a small breather. Great for the other guys, who'd been stretched thin over the past few months. Not so great for him…because he'd have more time than he wanted to think about Alana.

Dirk stood in Jason's office, staring out at the view. "Impressive. No question." Then he turned toward his brother-in-law. "Mei-li would tell me to mind my own business." He smiled faintly. "And you can tell me to go to hell in that snooty British accent of yours. But I've grown fond of Alana, so I'm going to stick my nose in where it doesn't belong."

A muscle jumped in Jason's cheek at Alana's name, but then he steeled himself until his muscles ached because he figured he knew what was coming.

"You were engaged to Alana…and now you're not." Dirk said conversationally. "So…what does that mean? You loved her…and now you don't?"

"I never said that." The words were wrung from him before he turned and stalked to the far side of the room, staring out the other window…at nothing. After a moment he swung around, defiantly confronting his brother-in-law.

Dirk was nodding slowly, as if he was processing Jason's unwilling admission and fitting it in with the facts as he knew them. "I love your sister more than I ever loved any woman in my life," he said softly. "You know that. But that doesn't mean I wouldn't have given anything I had if my first wife—the mother of my children—hadn't died." He paused to let that sink in.

"You're throwing away the best thing that ever happened to you…on purpose. And that pisses me off." A sad little smile touched the corners of Dirk's mouth. "We don't always get second chances in life."

"I don't need a second chance. I know what I'm doing."

"Do you?" Dirk raised one eyebrow in inquiry. "Do you really? I doubt it." Before Jason could respond, he said, "You know, I warned Alana about you." When Jason gave him a questioning frown, he nodded again. "Yeah, way back at the beginning. I told her you're an extremely complicated man with a lot of emotional baggage. Which is nothing but the truth. I also told her I didn't think you'd break her heart deliberately." His voice hardened. "Which turns out to be a damned lie. Alana loves you. Do you know how rare and precious that is? Who the hell do you think you are to play God with her life?"

Jason flinched, but that was the only reaction he allowed himself. "Look, I don't know what Alana told you, but I—"

"Nothing. Not a damned thing except that even though you're no longer engaged to her, she still considers herself engaged to you." Dirk stood there for a minute as if waiting for something. But when Jason said nothing, he made a sound of disgust and strode toward the door. He turned around at the last minute, his hand on the doorknob. "Think about what you're doing, Jason, before it's too late. Think about your reason for breaking off your engagement, whatever it is. Weigh that against a woman who believes in you so completely she refuses to accept it. A woman who could have just about any man she wanted…but she's set her heart on you. Then decide what you're going to do." With that he was gone.

Jason stared at the closed door through which Dirk had left, his thoughts in turmoil. Think about what he was doing? Except for his work with RMM, he'd done nothing *but* think about it since Alan Richardson had shown up a week ago to tell him he wasn't worthy of Alana.

Alana.

Would the ache of missing her never go away? Was he doomed to spend the rest of his life seeing her everywhere he turned? Hearing her voice in his mind? Yearning for the touch of her hand, the smile that lit up her face and tore at his heart?

He didn't just miss her in his bed, though the nights had been endless ever since he'd told her he couldn't marry her after all. So why had he done it? Why the *hell* had he done it?

He'd laughed when Alana's father at first offered him a quarter million US dollars to break off their engagement.

An offer that had soon risen to a half million. *You'd better take it*, the other man had threatened, *because if you marry Alana, I'll make sure you never touch a penny of Richardson money, you hear me? I'll disinherit her if she marries you. Cut her off without a dime. Then where will you be? No better off than you are now!*

He'd laughed again at the meaningless threat, shaking his head in refusal. *I'm no fortune hunter, Mr. Richardson. In fact, I—*

But his laughter had merely fueled the older man's rage, who'd then viciously spat out, *Alana doesn't love you. She couldn't possibly. You're just part of a rebellious phase she's going through, like taking this job here in Hong Kong. She'll come to her senses eventually. And when she does, she'll be ashamed. Not just that she tied herself to a man like you, but of any children you have, too.*

Ashamed. He couldn't bear the thought that Alana might someday be ashamed of having loved him. Married him. Borne his children. He couldn't bear it.

"But she's not like that," he murmured to himself now. "She's not like *him*. She'd never be ashamed." So why had he let those intentionally hurtful words influence his actions? Why had he played right into her father's hands and broken off their engagement?

Profound shock transfixed him when the answer finally dawned. *"You're* ashamed," he whispered. "You. Not her. You."

He shook his head vehemently as if he could banish the insidious little voice inside his head that way, the voice that taunted him with the unpalatable truth. *Don't continue lying to yourself the way you've lied for years. You're ashamed. That's why. You thought your grandfathers' prejudices never touched the man you are, but you were wrong.*

That's why their words had the power to wound you. Because deep down you think they just might have been right.

He wanted to violently refute that assertion…but he couldn't. Suddenly everything fell into place with appalling ease. His vow that no child of his would ever hear himself referred to by those hateful words *wasn't* why he'd broken off his engagement; he'd already overcome that when he'd asked Alana to marry him. No, he'd walked away from her for one reason and one reason only—he'd looked at himself through his grandfathers' eyes and found himself wanting. He'd broken Alana's heart because he'd judged himself unworthy of her…accepting her father's assessment of him. Of *them*.

All at once his brother-in-law's words swept through his mind, and he stabbed the intercom button for his new executive assistant. "Mrs. Liang, I need the corporate jet ready to go no later than eight tomorrow morning."

"Yes, sir" came the prompt reply. "Going where? They'll need to file a flight plan."

He thought for a moment. Where had Alana said her parents lived? Then it came to him. "Richmond, Virginia. That's in the—"

"US. Yes, sir, I know it. I'll buzz you once they have a takeoff time."

"Good. And clear my calendar for the next week, please."

"What about the board of directors' meeting on Friday?"

"Reschedule it." He'd never done that with a board of directors' meeting before, but Alana was more important.

He hung up and immediately began planning his next move. *Should I call her? Text her?* he wondered. *Let her know she was right and I was wrong, and I'm on my way?*

No. Better to take her by surprise. Her reaction when he showed up unexpectedly might be the best indication of just how badly he'd screwed up by ruthlessly discarding the love of a woman who believed in him. Who understood the cause for which he'd worked so tirelessly. Who'd even trained in secret to dedicate her own life to the same cause—not just because of him, but because she *believed* in it the way he did.

He could search the world over and never find another woman like Alana. So perfect for him. And all she asked was that he let her love him and give him children created from their love.

"Stupid," he muttered. "You're supposed to be so damned smart. Then you go and make a colossal blunder like this."

Filled with restless energy, he paced his office, back and forth. Back and forth. Thinking. Planning. Concluding that all he could do now was throw himself on Alana's mercy and beg her forgiveness. Then tell her everything. Everything. Including what he'd just learned about himself. And pray as he'd never prayed before that she still loved him when he was through.

Jason stopped abruptly at the expansive window in his corner office that faced out over Victoria Harbour when something caught his attention. On good visibility days like today, the sun sparkled off the water and the boats plying the harbor, and you could see Tsim Sha Tsui, the southern tip of the Kowloon mainland, from here.

A sudden compulsion made him grab his smartphone from the desk and head for the door. "Call me on my cell when we have a departure time," he told Mrs. Liang, stopping at her desk on his way out.

"Yes, sir. But in case something can be arranged for tonight, where will you be? Close enough to make it to the airport in time?"

"Tsim Sha Tsui for the next hour. Then I'll head home and pack a bag." With that he was gone.

He valet-parked at the Peninsula Hotel as he always did, then walked over to the Avenue of Stars. He didn't know why the urge to visit the Bruce Lee statue there was so strong, just that it was. When he finally reached it, he waited for the tourists to leave, then just stood there. Staring at the statue of a man who'd come to symbolize so much to so many…including him.

Bruce hadn't been pure Chinese, either, he remembered now. Bruce's mother had been Eurasian, just like Jason. And Bruce had married a white woman, back when that had been an unwritten taboo. A Caucasian man having a liaison with a Chinese woman—so common it was hardly worthy of comment. A Caucasian man *marrying* a Chinese woman, on the other hand, as Jason's father had done, was a rare occurrence back then. But a Chinese man and a Caucasian woman? Practically unheard of. And yet… Bruce had done it. He and his wife hadn't hesitated to bring children into the world, either. Children born of their love… just as Jason's parents had done.

That brought him right back to thoughts of Alana and the children she wanted to give him. Could he risk it? Could he *not* risk it when it meant so much to her?

He breathed deeply and once again reached the decision he'd already reached twice before. *But…third time's the charm*, he acknowledged. *This time there'll be no changing my mind again. This time's the real deal.* He swung around, intending to go home and pack for a week's absence, then stopped as if he'd been pole-axed.

Alana stood there, not ten yards away.

He'd dreamed of her, waking and sleeping, and for just a moment he thought she was a figment of his imagination. But when he mouthed her name, she came closer. And closer. Until she touched his cheek and said, "Hello, *lang jai.*" Breaking the spell.

"Where did you come from?" he asked in stupefaction. "I mean…hell, I don't know what I mean. How did you find me?"

"I took a cab from the airport directly to Wing Wah." She laughed a little. "They guard their employees like a hawk—did you know that? But when I asked for you and gave the receptionist my name, she called upstairs and a woman who said she was your executive assistant came down. She's really nice, by the way," she said as an aside. "She told me where you were."

"I didn't tell Mrs. Liang I was coming here," he protested.

"When she said Tsim Sha Tsui, I just *knew* where you'd be. I don't know how I knew, just that I did." She smiled when he just stared down at her, still not quite believing she was here. "Your Mrs. Liang offered to keep my luggage, too, so I could—" She stopped all of a sudden. "I'm chattering, aren't I? I get that way when I'm nervous. And I'm super-nervous right now."

"Why?"

"Why am I nervous?" Her smile faded. "Because I know why you broke our engagement. Because I know my father came to see you…and what he said."

"Alana—"

"I *know*, Jason, so you don't have to pretend. I made him tell me everything." Her eyes were pools of sadness, as if what she'd learned devastated her as much as her father's words had devastated him just over a week ago. She drew a deep breath and added softly, "Then I told him I was no longer his daughter."

Jason's throat tightened, and he couldn't have spoken right then to save his soul. His eyes squeezed shut for endless seconds as *hallelujah!* reverberated in his soul. After all this time he'd finally found the woman who would count the world well lost if she had him. The woman who would sacrifice everything for him…the way his mother had sacrificed for his father. Then all he could think was, *Ten years. Ten years I've waited for this moment. For this woman.* And when his eyes opened again they were damp.

But she wasn't done. "And I know why you think you don't want children. But I knew that even before I went home."

"Alana—"

She cut him off again. "No, let me finish. There could never be anything except pride for me in being your wife. Being a mother to your children. How could you believe my father when he said I'd be ashamed? I'm not my parents, Jason. Please, *please* believe that."

"May I speak now?"

She laughed again, the musical sound he loved, and delicate color flooded her cheeks. "Oh. Of course!"

"I believe you. But you didn't need to tell me. I'd already figured it out, and I was—" He snapped his fingers. "Which reminds me." He whipped out his phone and pressed speed dial. "Mrs. Liang? It's me. Can you cancel the corporate jet? I won't be needing it after all."

He smiled to himself when she said, "I've been expecting your call, sir, ever since Miss Richardson showed up here. I hope I'm forgiven for telling her where you were. I rather thought you might want me to."

"You thought right. Have you already rescheduled Friday's board meeting?"

"Not yet. I was putting together some alternative dates for the board when Miss Richardson appeared. Once she did…"

"I can see you're going to be a gem, Mrs. Liang." He held up one finger to Alana, indicating he'd just be a minute more. "Keep the board meeting where it is on the schedule, but cancel everything for tomorrow. I won't be in the office."

He disconnected and realized from Alana's suddenly stricken expression that something was wrong. Then he cursed himself for a fool. *Corporate jet. Board meeting.* She'd obviously put two and two together.

"You don't just work at Wing Wah Enterprises, do you? You—you're someone high up in the ranks. CEO?"

He cupped her cheek. "I was going to tell you…"

She backed away from his touch and her eyes widened as something else suddenly clicked for her. "You didn't *rent* that boat, did you?"

"Yacht. And no, I didn't."

"You…lied to me?"

He heard the hurt in her voice, saw the pain in her eyes, and winced. "Not exactly."

"Then what…exactly?"

Nothing but the truth would serve. "I wanted to tell you a dozen times. But each time something held me back."

"What?"

"I wanted to be loved…for me," he admitted in a low voice. "Is that so hard to understand?"

Her eyes softened. "*I* loved you for you. Couldn't you tell?"

Her usage of the past tense made his heart clutch. "Loved?"

She shook her head. "Love."

"Then, can you forgive my deception?"

Now it was Alana's turn to close her eyes for a moment. Then she sighed and looked at him again, a yearning expression on her face. "If you can forgive mine."

He frowned. "I don't—"

"I should have told you right away. As soon as I knew," she blurted out. "But I was afraid."

"Afraid? Of me?" His tone rose in incredulity.

She shook her head. "Afraid of what you might try to make me do." Her voice was little more than a whisper. "Because you said you didn't want—"

Then he got it. "Children," he finished for her. Shock held him motionless for a moment. "You're pregnant?"

She nodded solemnly. "I tried to tell you, but I couldn't. You were so adamant! Then, after you rescued me the second time and you said you couldn't let me go, I was going to tell you. I really was. But I didn't want you to think I only cared about having a father for my baby. I wanted you to be secure in my love before I…" Her eyes beseeched him. "Can you understand?"

"You're carrying my child." All at once the image he'd tried so hard to suppress rose in his consciousness. Alana with their baby in her arms. He drew her gently into his embrace, almost as if in a dream. Then his arms tightened unexpectedly as wonder welled up in him. Followed quickly by a joy he'd never in a million years imagined he'd feel at the idea of fatherhood. But then…he'd never in a million years imagined Alana, either. Intense happiness and fierce pride combined to make his voice unsteady when he repeated, "You're carrying my child."

She buried her face against his chest. "I don't love you because of the baby," she whispered. "I want this baby because I love you with all my heart."

Epilogue

Not even two hours later Alana lay naked in Jason's arms. In Jason's bed. In the aftermath of lovemaking so intense she'd wept again from the emotional and physical release. He'd been hesitant at first…worried he'd somehow compromise her pregnancy if he made love to her the way they both wanted. And though she'd quickly assured him she wasn't as delicate as she appeared, she'd been touched by his concern for the baby he hadn't realized he secretly wanted.

They cuddled without words for the longest time. Then she stroked a hand down his cheek…the strong column of his neck…until she touched the braided gold chain he wore. She searched for and found the medallion, fingering the raised dragon on one side, the phoenix on the other. The symbols of RMM.

"My father said he offered you half a million dollars to break off our engagement," she whispered. "But I knew that wasn't why you did it."

"It wasn't."

She rubbed her cheek against his chest and lifted the medallion to her lips. "I thought he was lying when he said you accepted his offer. But even if he wasn't lying, I knew if you took the money it would be for RMM, not for you."

"I considered it," he admitted. "I thought it'd be poetic justice if I took his money and used it in a way that would gall him if he knew the true purpose. But then I realized a man like him…he'd never understand. All he'd see was what he expected to see—a man with no honor."

"You're right." She drew a trembling breath. "But I still want to know why you believed him and not me." She swallowed hard. "The whole flight back to Hong Kong, all I could think of was you thought I was the kind of woman who—" Her voice broke with emotion she couldn't quite contain. "How could you, Jason? Don't you know me at all?"

He tightened his arms around her. "I never thought that," he said in his deepest voice. "Never. It was all me." He went on to explain the revelation he'd had in his office this afternoon. Those deeply buried feelings of shame that had finally seen the light of day. "Left over from my childhood. Completely irrational. But still. There. Once I finally acknowledged them, they lost their power over me."

They were silent for a few minutes. Then Alana snuggled closer and asked, "So…corporate jet? You were coming after me? I didn't need to jump on the first flight back to Hong Kong my uncle could book for me?"

He laughed softly. "Yes. I suddenly realized what an idiot I was being, and I was coming to get you. I was going to beg your forgiveness and throw myself on your mercy. Then confess everything." He kissed the top of her head.

"But I don't think I can ever express what it means to me that you came to me, *lang loi*."

"I think I can imagine. Because knowing you were coming to find me despite everything…" She propped herself up on his chest and stared solemnly down at him. "I'll treasure that knowledge as long as I live."

"So…you forgive me for deceiving you about my real identity. Right?" She nodded, but he said firmly, "I need to hear the words, Alana."

"I forgive you." She smiled the smile that had first captured his heart. "And you forgive me for not telling you about the baby. Right?"

"There's nothing to forgive."

She shook her head. "Just like you, I need the words, Jason."

"If there was anything to forgive, I would forgive you," he compromised.

She laughed at that and murmured, "You are such a *man*."

He rolled her over so suddenly she gasped, then squealed when he found the heart of her desire and caressed her until she melted against his hand. "And aren't you glad I *am* a man?" he demanded. "*Your* man, for better or for worse?"

"Yes," she whispered, love and desire mingling in her expression and in her voice. Then she recited softly, "'For better, for worse. For richer, for poorer. In sickness and in health…'"

"'To love and to cherish,'" he continued, then drew a deep breath. "I will, *lang loi*." A fervent promise. "I'll love you and cherish you, to death…and beyond."

He levered himself up and unclasped the chain he hadn't removed since the day he'd had the dragon and phoenix medallion made right after Sean's funeral. Then stared down at it for a moment, thinking about what it symbolized. Not just for RMM, but in the Chinese philosophy of feng shui. Then he looked at Alana, and he knew his heart was in his eyes when he handed her the medallion.

"I never told you," he said in a low voice as he closed her fingers around his gift. "But the dragon and the phoenix—"

"Symbolize everlasting love and marital happiness," she finished for him with a little smile.

Stunned, he asked, "How did you know?"

"I researched it online. Because I wanted to know everything I could about the man you are. The two cultures that shaped you. Because…no matter what you decided, I wanted my baby to know all about his or her father. To be proud of him. To grow up to be like him someday."

Jason bowed his head for a moment, unexpected emotions threatening his self-control. "I don't know what to say."

Her voice held tenderness and understanding. "Just say *ngoh oi lei* again, *lang jai*."

His head shot up. Even more stunned than before, he could only stare in disbelief. "What?"

"I looked those words up, too." Her smile deepened. "That's what gave me the courage to never give up on you, Jason. Because you said those words to me our very first time, even though you said them in Cantonese because… because you didn't want me to know you were saying 'I love you.' Because you didn't want me to know you loved me even then. The same way I already loved you."

"But you never said you loved me then."

She rolled her eyes at him. "Of course not." She didn't say *you idiot*, but her expression conveyed she was thinking it. "If I had, you would never have touched me that day." Her voice dropped. "And I wanted you to touch me, Jason.

I wanted you to make love to me. Just like I want you to make love to me now."

There could only be one response to that confession, and Jason made it.

Eons later Alana surfaced from a pleasurable dream, only to find it wasn't a dream. Her head was pillowed on Jason's chest, and one of his hands was idly caressing the bare skin of her back, sending little electrical sparks shooting everywhere. Then she suddenly remembered something. She jerked into a sitting position and began frantically scrabbling through the tangle of sheets. "Where is it?"

His voice was early-morning husky. "Where's what?"

"My—here it is!" Her fingers located the dragon and phoenix medallion, and she raised it triumphantly, dangling it from its chain.

He caught it in one hand and gently took it from her, then used both hands to clasp the chain around her neck and settle the medallion in place. The chain was too long and the pendant nestled between her breasts. "You'll need a shorter chain if you're going to wear this…as a member of RMM."

She caught her breath. "You mean it? Really? You'll let me join?"

He smiled the faint smile she loved. "It's not just up to me. I told you once that anyone who's added to the organization is a risk to every one of us. So we put potential recruits to a secret vote of the entire organization. One nay vote and the answer is no, because we have to trust each other. Implicitly. But for what it's worth, you've already got Cam's vote. And Trevor's. Where they lead, the others usually follow."

"What about you?"

He shook his head slowly, suddenly serious. "I try not

to influence anyone, either yea or nay. But since I'll be the one proposing adding you to the organization..." His smile returned, and he drawled with the understatement for which the British were justly famous, "It's a fair bet they'll know how I intend to vote."

"Oh, Jason!" She threw her arms around him, hugging him fiercely.

He kissed the top of her head. "I have to ask. Would you...would you mind waiting until after the baby's born?"

"Of *course* I wouldn't mind," she assured him. "I would never put our baby at risk."

"I'm glad you feel that way," he whispered, his arms tightening around her. "But I'll be honest. The alpha male in me says I'm an idiot for letting you risk your life for RMM the way I do—the British side of me, too, not just the Chinese side. But I can't make that decision for you. It has to be your choice."

A new emotion unfurled its petals inside Alana as intense love for this man overwhelmed her. It would *kill* him if anything happened to her. She knew that as surely as she knew she'd never recover if anything happened to him. But the respect that dictated he let her choose her own path? Priceless.

"'Let us have faith that right makes might,'" she quoted softly. Listening to his heartbeat accelerate to the words that meant the world to him...and to her.

I made the right choice, she thought, pure joy permeating throughout her body. Not just to love Jason and steadfastly believe he would eventually see the light despite all evidence to the contrary, but to believe that heroes still existed in the first place. To believe that good *could* triumph over evil when there were men like Jason to see to it. Men for whom the words *duty*, *honor* and *justice* weren't just words, but a solemn pledge.

"*Ngoh oi lei, lang jai,*" she breathed, entrusting her heart into his safekeeping as she'd entrusted her life to him from the moment they'd met. "*Ngoh oi lei.*"

* * * * *

If you loved this novel,
don't miss these thrilling titles from Amelia Autin:

THE BODYGUARD'S BRIDE-TO-BE
KILLER COUNTDOWN
A FATHER'S DESPERATE RESCUE
LIAM'S WITNESS PROTECTION
ALEC'S ROYAL ASSIGNMENT
KING'S RANSOM
MCKINNON'S ROYAL MISSION
CODY WALKER'S WOMAN

Available now from Harlequin Romantic Suspense!

*Love pulse-spiking romance and
spine-tingling suspense?
Don't miss this exclusive excerpt from
FATAL THREAT
The latest FATAL book from
New York Times bestselling author Marie Force!*

A JOGGER SPOTTED the body floating in the Anacostia River just south of the John Philip Sousa Bridge.

"I hate these kinds of calls," Lieutenant Sam Holland said to her partner, Detective Freddie Cruz, as she battled District traffic on their way to the city's southeastern quadrant. "No one knows if this is a homicide, but they call us in anyway. We get to stand around and sweat our balls off while the ME does her thing."

"I hesitate to point out, Lieutenant, that you don't actually *have* balls to sweat off."

"You know what I mean!"

"Yeah, I do," he said with a sigh. "It's going to be a long, hot, smelly Friday down at the river waiting to find out if we're needed."

"I gotta have a talk with Dispatch about when we're to be called and when we are *not* to be called."

"Let me know how that goes."

"To make this day even better, after work I have to go to a fitting for my freaking bridesmaid dress. I'm too damned old to be a damned bridesmaid."

His snort of laughter only served to further irritate her, which of course made him laugh harder.

"It's not funny!"

"Yeah, it really is." With dark brown hair, an always-tan complexion and the perfect amount of stubble on his jaw, he really was too cute for words, not that she'd *ever* tell him that. Everywhere they went together, women took notice of him. For all he cared. He was madly in love with Elin Svendsen and looking forward to their autumn wedding. Wiping laughter tears from his brown eyes, he said, "I won't make you wear a dress when you're my best-man woman."

"Thank God for that. I need to stop making friends. That was my first mistake."

"Poor Jeannie," he said of their colleague, Detective Jeannie McBride, who was getting married next weekend. "Does she have any idea that she has a hostile bridesmaid in her wedding party?"

"Of course she does. Her sisters left me completely out of the planning of the shower, no doubt at her request. I'll be forever grateful for that small favor." Sam shuddered recalling an afternoon of horrifyingly stupid "shower games," paper plates full of ribbons and bows, and dirty jokes about the wedding night for two people who'd been living together for more than a year. The whole thing had given her hives.

But Jeannie… She'd loved every second of it, and seeing her face lit up with joy had gone a long way toward alleviating Sam's hives. After everything Jeannie had been through to get to her big day, no one was happier for her— or happier to stand up for her—than Sam. Not that she'd ever tell anyone that, either. She had a reputation to maintain, after all.

She'd been in an unusually cranky mood since her husband, Nick, left for Iran two weeks ago for what should've been a five-day trip but had twice been extended. If he didn't get home soon, she wouldn't be responsible for her actions. In addition to worrying about his safety in a country known for being less than friendly toward Americans, she'd also discovered how entirely reliant upon him she'd become over the last year and a half. It was ridiculous, really. She was a strong, independent woman who'd taken care of herself for years before he'd come back into her life. So how had he turned her into a simpering, whimpering, cranky mess simply by leaving her for two damned weeks?

Naturally, the people around her had noticed that she was out of sorts. Their adopted thirteen-year-old son, Scotty, asked every morning before he left for baseball camp when Dad would be home, probably because he was tired of dealing with her by himself. Freddie and the others at work had been giving her a wide berth, and even the reporters who hounded her mercilessly had backed off after she'd bitten their heads off a few too many times.

During infrequent calls from Nick, he'd been rushed and annoyed and equally out of sorts, which didn't do much to help her bad mood. Two more days. Two more long, boring, joyless days and then he'd be home and things could get back to normal.

What did it say about her that she was actually *glad* to have a floater to deal with to keep her brain occupied during the last two days of Nick's trip? *It means you have it bad for your husband, and you've become far too dependent on him if two weeks without him turns you into a cranky cow.* Sam despised her voice of reason almost as much as she despised Nick being so far away from her for so long.

Twenty minutes after receiving the call from Dispatch, Sam and Freddie made it to M Street Southeast, which was lined with emergency vehicles of all sorts—police, fire, EMS, medical examiner.

"Major overkill for a floater," Sam said as they got out of the car she'd parked illegally to join the party on the riverbank. "What the hell is EMS doing here?"

"Probably for the guy who found the body. Word is he was shook up."

Dense humidity hit her at the same time as the funk of the rank-smelling river. "God, it's hotter than the devil's dick today."

"Honestly, Sam. That's disgusting."

"Well, you gotta figure the devil's dick is pretty hot due to the neighborhood he hangs in, right?"

He rolled his eyes and held up the yellow crime-scene tape for her. Patrol had taped off the Anacostia Riverwalk Trail to keep the gawkers away.

The closer they got to the river's edge, the more Sam began to regret the open-toe sandals she'd worn in deference to the oppressive July heat. The squish of Anacostia River mud between her toes was almost as gross as the smell of the river itself. She had her shoulder-length hair up in a clip that left her neck exposed to the merciless sun.

Tactical Response teams had boats on the scene, and from her vantage point on the riverbank, Sam could see the red ponytail belonging to the Chief Medical Examiner, Dr. Lindsey McNamara. She was too far out for Sam to yell to her for an update.

"Let's talk to the guy who called it in," she said to Freddie.

They traipsed back the way they'd come, with Sam trying to ignore the disgusting mud between her toes. Officer Beckett worked the tapeline at the northern end of the area they'd cordoned off. He nodded at them. "Afternoon, Lieutenant. Lovely day to spend by the river."

"Indeed. I would've packed a picnic had I known we were coming. Where's the guy who called it in?"

"Over there with EMS." Beckett pointed to a cluster of people taking advantage of the shade under a huge oak tree. "He was hysterical when he realized the blob was a body."

"Did you get a name?"

Beckett consulted his notebook. "Mike Lonergan. He works at the Navy Yard and runs out here every day at noon." He tore out the page that had Lonergan's full name, address and cell phone number written on it and gave it to Sam.

"Good work, Beckett. Thanks. Keep everyone out of here until we know whether or not this is a crime scene."

"Yes, ma'am. Will do."

"Why would anyone run out here during the hottest part of the day?" Sam asked Freddie as they made their way to where Lonergan was being seen to by the paramedics.

"For something called exercise, I'd imagine."

"When did you become such a smart-ass? You used to be such a nice Christian boy."

"Things began to go south for me when I got assigned to a smart-ass lieutenant who's been a terrible influence on my sweet, young mind."

"Right." Amused by him as always, Sam drew out the single word for effect. "You were easily led." She approached the paramedics who were hovering over Lonergan. "We'd like a word with Mr. Lonergan," she said to the one who seemed to be in charge.

He used a hand motion to tell his team to allow her and Freddie in. The witness wore a tank top, running shorts and high-tech running shoes. Sam put him at midthirties.

"Mr. Lonergan, I'm Lieutenant Holland—"

"I know who you are." His shoulders were wrapped in one of those foil thingies that runners used to keep from dehydrating or overheating or something like that. What did she know about such things? She got most of her exercise having wild sex with her husband. Except for recently, thus her foul mood.

Lonergan's dark blond hair was wet with perspiration. His brown eyes were big and haunted as he looked up at them.

"Can you tell us what you saw?" Ever since she'd taken down a killer at the inaugural parade, she was recognized everywhere she went. She hated that and yearned for the days when no one recognized her. But that ship had sailed the minute her sexy young husband became the nation's vice president late last year. Her blown cover was entirely his fault, and she liked to remind him of that every chance she got.

"I was running on the trail like I do every day, and when I came around that bend there, I saw something in the water." He took a drink from a bottle of water, and Sam took note of the slight tremble in his hand. "At first I thought it was a garbage bag, but when I looked closer, I saw a hand." He shuddered. "That's when I called 911."

"How far out was it?" Sam asked.

"About twenty feet from the bank of the river."

"Was there anything else you could tell us about the body?"

"I think it's a woman."

"Why do you say that?" Freddie asked.

"There was hair." Lonergan took another drink of water. "Once I realized what I was looking at, I could see long hair fanned out around the head." He looked up at them. "Do you think it's that student who went missing?"

Sam made sure her expression gave nothing away. "We'd have no way to know that at this point." The entire Metro PD had been searching for nineteen-year-old Ruby Denton for more than two weeks. She'd come to the District to take summer classes at Capitol University and hadn't been seen since her first night on campus. The story had garnered national attention thanks in large part to the efforts of her family in Kentucky.

"I bet it's her," Lonergan said.

"Do me a favor and keep that thought to yourself for now. No sense upsetting the family before we know anything for certain."

"That's true."

Sam handed him her card. "If you think of anything else, let me know."

"I will." After a pause, he said, "I was out here yesterday, and she wasn't there. I would've noticed if she'd been there."

"That's good to know. Thanks for your help."

"It's sad, you know? For someone to end up like that."

"Yes, it is." She stepped away from him to confer with the paramedic in charge. "Is he okay?"

"Yeah, he's in shock. He'll be fine. You think it's Ruby Denton?"

"I'll tell you the same thing I just told him—we have no way to know until Dr. McNamara gets the body back to the lab. Until then, we'd be speculating, and that sort of thing only makes a hellish situation worse for a family looking for their daughter. Ask your people to keep their mouths shut."

"Yes, ma'am. No one will hear anything from my team."

"Thank you."

"What's going on over there?" Freddie asked, drawing Sam's attention to the tapeline, where Beckett was arguing with a bunch of suits.

"Let's go find out."

They walked back the way they'd come, along the trail to where Beckett held his own against four men in suits with reflective glasses and attitudes that immediately identified them as federal agents.

"What's the problem, gentlemen?" Sam asked.

"There she is," one of them said in a low growl that immediately raised Sam's hackles.

"Let us in," another one said. "Right now."

"I'm not letting you in until you tell me what you want," Beckett said. "This is a potential crime scene—"

"We need to speak to Mrs. Cappuano." The one who seemed to be in charge of the Fed squad took another step forward. "It's urgent."

Sam's heart dropped to her belly and for a brief, horrifying second she feared her legs would give out under her. *Nick...* Why would federal agents have tracked her down at a crime scene in the middle of her workday unless something had happened to him?

Please no.

Sam immediately began bargaining with a higher power she didn't believe in. She'd give up anything, anything in this world except Scotty, if it would keep the man in front of her from saying words that could never be unsaid or unheard.

Only Freddie's arm around her shoulders kept her from buckling in the few seconds it took for Sam to recover herself enough to speak. "What do you want with me?"

"We need you to come with us, ma'am."

"That's not happening until you tell us who you are and what you want," Freddie said.

In unison they flashed four federal badges.

"United States Secret Service," the one in charge said. "We need you to come with us, ma'am."

Sam didn't recognize any of them. Why would she? Nick's detail was in Iran, and Scotty's was with him. "I...I'm working here. I can't..." Bile burned her throat as her lunch threatened to reappear. With her heart beating so hard she could hear the echo of it strumming in her ears, she somehow managed to choke back the nausea. Later she'd be thankful she hadn't puked on the agents' shoes. Right now, however, she couldn't think about anything other than Nick. "Has something happened to my husband?"

Freddie tightened his grip on her shoulder, letting her know his thoughts mirrored hers. That didn't do much to comfort her.

Looking down at her with a stone-faced glare, the agent said, "We're under orders to bring you in. We're not at liberty to discuss the particulars with you at this time."

"What the hell does that mean?" Freddie asked. "You can't just take her. She's not under Secret Service protection, and she's working."

"I'm afraid we *can* take her, and we will, by force if necessary."

"What the fuck?" Beckett spoke for all of them. At some point he'd moved to the other side of her.

Like someone flipped a switch, they moved with military precision, busting through the tapeline, grabbing hold of her arms and quickly extracting her before her stunned colleagues could react. Sam fought them, but she was no match for four huge, muscled, well-dressed men who whisked her away with frightening efficiency.

In the background, she could hear Freddie and Beckett screaming, swearing—at least Beckett was—and giving chase, but they, too, were no match for this group. Before she knew what hit her, she was inside the cool darkness of one in the Secret Service's endless fleet of black SUVs, the doors locking with a sound that echoed like a shotgun blast.

"Move," the agent in charge ordered.

The car lurched forward just as Freddie and Beckett

reached it. Freddie pounded once against the side window with a closed fist before the car pulled out of his reach.

Sam watched the scene unfold around her with a detached feeling of shock and fear. Something awful must've happened. That was the only possible reason for this dramatic scene. She was far too afraid for Nick to work up the fury she'd normally feel at being kidnapped by federal agents. Her hands were shaking, and her entire body was covered in cold chills.

If Nick had been harmed in some way or if he was… *No, no, no, not going there.* If he was hurt, what did it matter if Secret Service agents had grabbed her? What would anything matter?

She bit back the overwhelming fear and forced herself to focus. "Would someone please tell me what's going on here?"

* * * * *

ROMANTIC suspense

After befriending Mandy Wright in a snowstorm, Brody Booth is certain they'll stay "just friends." That is, until a killer forces Brody into a protector role that brings all his worst fears about himself to bear.

Read on for a sneak preview of
SHELTERED BY THE COWBOY
by New York Times *bestselling author* Carla Cassidy,
the next thrilling installment of
THE COWBOYS OF HOLIDAY RANCH.

Most people gave him a wide berth, but not Mandy. He shoved those thoughts away. She was nothing more to him than a woman in trouble, and he just happened to be in a position to help her. It was nothing more than that and nothing less.

He left the bathroom and blinked in surprise. All the lights were off except a nightstand lamp next to Mandy's bed and the glow of two lit candles on the same stand. The room now smelled of apples and cinnamon.

"I hope you don't mind the candles. I always light a couple before I go to sleep."

"I don't mind," he replied. Hell yes, he minded the candles that painted her face in beautiful shadows and light. Hell yes, he minded the candles that made the room feel so much smaller and much more intimate.

He walked over to the sofa and found a bed pillow and a soft, hot pink blanket. He placed his gun on the coffee table, unfolded the blanket and then stretched out.

"All settled?" she asked.

"I'm good," he replied.

She turned off the lamp, leaving only the candlelight radiance to create a small illumination. Too much illumination. From his vantage point he could see her snuggled beneath the covers. He closed his eyes.

"Brody?"

"Yeah?" he answered without opening his eyes.

"Somehow, some way I'll make all this up to you."

Visions instantly exploded in his head, erotic visions of the two of them making love. He jerked his head to halt them. "You don't have to make anything up to me," he said gruffly. "Now let's get some sleep."

"Okay. Good night, Brody."

"Good night," he replied.

Seconds ticked by and then minutes. When he finally opened his eyes again she appeared to be sleeping. Candlelight danced across her features, highlighting her brows, her cheekbones and her lips.

He couldn't be her friend. She was too much of a temptation and he couldn't be friends with a woman he wanted. He didn't want to be friends with anyone.

He'd see her through this threat, and then he had to walk away from her and never look back.

Don't miss
SHELTERED BY THE COWBOY by Carla Cassidy,
available September 2017 wherever
Harlequin® Romantic Suspense books
and ebooks are sold.

www.Harlequin.com

HRSEXP0817